"*The Laying on of Hands* is a nostalgic literary journey that wraps around a reader's heart. It warms the soul, feeds the spirit and reaffirms the power of love."

—NORMA L. JARRETT, AUTHOR OF *SUNDAY BRUNCH*

"*The Laying on of Hands* is a rich and absorbing story as warm and lush as the South where it is set. In this remarkable book, Brenda Rhodes Miller has given us engaging characters who touch deeply and transform us, much as the miracles they perform, showing us in the process the amazing healing power of love."

—CHRISTOPHER BENSON, AUTHOR OF *SPECIAL INTEREST* AND COAUTHOR OF *DEATH OF INNOCENCE: THE STORY OF THE HATE CRIME THAT CHANGED AMERICA*

The Laying on of Hands

A Novel

Brenda Rhodes Miller

HARLEM MOON
BROADWAY BOOKS
NEW YORK

Published by Harlem Moon, an imprint of Broadway Books, a division of
Random House, Inc.

PRINTED IN THE UNITED STATES OF AMERICA

Visit our website at www.harlemmoon.com

First edition published 2004

Book design by Caroline Cunningham

Library of Congress Cataloging-in-Publication Data
Miller, Brenda Rhodes.
    The laying on of hands/ Brenda Rhodes Miller.—1st ed.
        p. cm.
        1. Aged women—Fiction. 2. Women healers—Fiction. 3. African
American women—Fiction. 4. African American Methodists—
Fiction. 5. Racially mixed people—Fiction. 6. Women—Mississippi—
Fiction. 7. Women—Alabama—Fiction. 8. Mississippi—Fiction.
9. Alabama—Fiction. 10. Creoles—Fiction. I. Title.

    PS3613.I5327L39 2004
    813'.6—dc21
2003049901
ISBN 0-7679-1556-9

10 9 8 7 6 5 4 3 2 1

With abiding love and gratitude,

I humbly dedicate this book to my parents,

Mr. and Mrs. Charles T. Rhodes (nee Carolyn Lolita Bolden).

Their 46 years of marriage gave me ample reason to believe

that passion can rule one's life.

Go ye all into the world, and preach the good news to every living thing. Those that believeth and are baptized shall be saved; but those that believeth not shall be damned. And these signs shall follow they that believe: In my name shall you cast out devils; you shall speak with new tongues; you shall take up serpents; and if you drink any deadly thing it shall not harm you; you shall lay hands on the sick, and they shall recover.

—MARK 16: 15-18

Acknowledgments

Like an old-fashioned quilt pieced by hand from colorful scraps of fabric, *The Laying on of Hands* includes bits of stories from family and friends stitched together by my imagination. Entirely a work of fiction, the resulting patchwork quilt covers Miss Muchie's life.

Special thanks go to Della Russell, Bessie Samples and Joyce Ladner for sharing their Mississippi recollections with me and to Wiley Bolden, Gary Cooper, Dora Finley, Melanie Shelwood and Lolita Cusic who were priceless sources of story ideas. My late grandmother, Lottie Twyner Rhodes, inspired the character that bears her nickname of Muchie.

The best children in the world are Lauren, Jay and Ben Cooper who deserve a huge debt of gratitude for their patience in reading multiple versions of the novel while contributing helpful perspectives. Thanks to the Rev. Courtenay L. Miller who caused me to reconsider the meaning of love and forgiveness.

I am grateful to Sally Arteseros for her guidance, and to my hardworking and inspired agent, Olivia Blumer, who loved Miss Muchie from the very beginning.

Janet Hill, my editor, is a woman wise beyond her years and helped me make the pattern of Miss Muchie's life clear and vivid. By believing in Miss Muchie, Janet has given me a priceless gift . . . the joy of sharing a story with you.

The

Laying on of

Hands

Chapter One

1987

The last sixty-odd years of my life I've lived in and around Mobile, Alabama. It straddles a river and a bay, sitting like a gangly boy smack-dab at the end of the G M & O Railroad line that first brought me here.

I came to Mobile straight off a farm deep in Wayne County, Mississippi. When I was a girl, night riders plagued the state. Their faces were hidden but their evil was plain, at least to colored people, who bore the brunt of it.

The harm they caused made my papa and others like him angry. It chipped away at their dignity by abridging their rights as Americans.

People endured years of insults, but they found ways to fight back.

"If I owned Mississippi, Alabama and hell, I'd rent out the other two and live in hell," Papa often said, and every time he'd spit. Papa was a great one for spitting when he was agitated or when he was glad. Sometimes he'd spit through his teeth just for the fun of it. Mother finally broke him from spitting in the house. But let him get outdoors and he'd spit up a storm.

Buccatunna, Mississippi, was the nearest town to our farm. It was little more than a single dusty street behind the train tracks. About all Buccatunna had going for it was two churches, a one-room schoolhouse and a blacksmith who worked under a shed without any walls.

Times he wasn't sweating over his anvil, the blacksmith ran the trading post and took care of the mail. Then he called himself the postmaster.

The train came through once a week, mostly on account of the mail. They delivered mail by throwing a sack out the window. When the postmaster had outgoing mail, he put the sack on a long hook that jutted out from an upright beam. That way the rail man could grab it when the train slowed down.

Once in a while the train actually stopped in Buccatunna. Not to say there were very many visitors coming through. It was usually people leaving, who wasted no time getting on the train.

I'm 80 years old now and a lot has changed from when I was a girl. For one thing, Mississippi has given up some of its wicked ways toward colored people. For another, Buccatunna now boasts a K-Mart, a few gas stations and a public library.

Papa has spit his last and our family farm has long since shrunk to just a few acres surrounding the old home place.

But when I was a girl, that farm, my family, the Methodist Episcopal church and school made up my whole world.

The Tyler family came by its land when the government granted each colored person forty acres, trying to make up for slavery. All the Tylers held on to their land and farmed it wisely. Unlike some, they never ruined the land by planting the same crop year after year.

My papa and his mother, Tyler Mama, were healers. Since the first Tyler set foot in Mississippi, there have been healers in the family.

Though there were other healers in Wayne County, Papa and Tyler Mama were at the top of the heap.

They were the closest folks got to a doctor in our neck of the woods. Anybody who sought their help got it and not one dime would they take for their troubles.

When there was an injured man who needed seeing to, my papa dropped everything. Sick men seemed to rest easier under Papa's care regardless of their troubles.

Papa could work wonders with livestock too. He raised cattle himself and he had a gentle way about him that settled even the most skittish creatures whether they stood on two legs or four.

Seemed like just about every woman in Wayne County sent her man to fetch Tyler Mama one time or the other, usually in the middle of the night. She had a sharp tongue that could make anyone quake in his boots, especially the hapless man who came for her at the wrong time, be it too soon or too late.

"You thoughtless, no account, son of a buck. Didn't I tell you to come for me straightaway when she first began to feel an ache in her back?"

Tyler Mama would go up one side and down the other until the poor man was too nervous to speak. But her tongue-lashings did not stop the flow of men asking Tyler Mama to help their wives.

They knew she was a wise woman learned in the cycles of the moon. For longer than most folks could remember Tyler Mama had aided women bearing babies. She never lost a mother or a baby in all her years of going about the county.

It was whispered that Tyler Mama knew how to help the ones

ready to put an end to their childbearing days too. I never doubted that to be true.

Farm folks couldn't survive without healthy animals to do the plowing and hauling. Even dogs had to work. Farmers measured their wealth in milch cows and pigs, chickens and goats. Papa and Tyler Mama tended to them too.

Good-hearted as she was, Tyler Mama often complained there was no rest for the weary when it came to healing.

Despite her grumbling, she spent any free time she had tending nearly half an acre of herbs and flowers. Her shelves were lined with scores of neatly labeled compounds made by her own hand using her plants.

"To treat the ills that flesh is heir to," she'd explain.

She made a special draught to clear the lungs, and she had remedies for just about every kind of stomach ailment there was.

Papa said Tyler Mama could brew up tisanes that would let even a guilty man sleep soundly through the night before his execution. Folks all over Wayne County swore by her skill.

Men being the way they are, they drew the line at letting even an elderly woman like Tyler Mama tend to their bodies.

Many's the man who hobbled, limped or was carried to our door seeking Papa's attention. Some came walking on two good legs but broken inside.

No matter, my papa knew just what to do. He even had a secret remedy that cured men unable to do their husbandly duties anymore.

"I don't see why in the world you help them get more babies when they can't feed the ones they've got," Tyler Mama said. "All you're doing is making more work for me."

"Poor men don't have much joy in life, Mama, leastways they can have love. Don't begrudge them that."

She'd give an exasperated snort at Papa's remark. Sometimes, she'd stand on her tippy toes to pull Papa's ears.

He could easily lift Tyler Mama like a rolled-up rug. Sometimes he'd do just that, which tickled her though she pretended to be angry.

Growing up around two such powerful healers, you'd think I might have seen my gift for what it was early in life and welcomed it. Especially since healing seemed to run in our family like being left-handed, which I am.

But I ignored that fact and all the other signs staring me right in the face. I wanted no part of being a healer. It seemed like nothing but a world of trouble to me.

People in need coming at all hours of the day or night to get Papa or Tyler Mama was bad enough.

But then the ones who'd been healed would show up at the most inconvenient times to say thank you.

Whether it was to bring a bushel of sweet corn, a mess of fresh fish or jars of homemade jam, the thankful ones came trudging up to our gate whenever they took a notion.

The only decent thing to do was invite them to sit for a spell in the shade of our porch. Folks lived so far apart, whenever visitors came it ranked as a special occasion.

Mother felt duty bound to offer them a glass of cold tea in the summertime or hot cider if the weather was chilly. Most times I was the one Mother called on to prepare the refreshments.

Unexpected guests thought nothing of staying half the day. Hospitality required Mother to stretch whatever meal she was preparing to feed extra mouths when it came time to eat.

It never failed that our worrisome visitors ate like the butcher's dog, gobbling up everything in sight. Most times I'd be wolf cub hungry myself.

Only fear that some celestial hand—or Tyler—might slap the taste right out of my mouth kept me silent. Otherwise I would have raised the hymn, "Bread of Heaven, Bread of Heaven, feed me 'til I want no more," to shame our guests into eating less.

Instead, I made do by filling my plate with an extra helping of rice so our company could dine sufficiently.

To my way of thinking, being a healer was more trouble than it was worth. All it meant was a lot of extra work and worry *and* giving up your sleep and your supper whether you felt like it or not. I never could see the sense in that.

Especially since a lot of folks were of two minds about healers. People who would only trust Tyler Mama and Papa to care for them weren't the problem. Poor, misguided souls who tried to pick and choose among the other healers were the ones who caused trouble.

Papa based his healing in faith and the knowledge that most sickness came from the way people lived and worked and what they ate. Before he did a single thing, he listened to what the men who came to him had to say about what had happened to them and how they felt. Papa made notes in his little tablet to keep a record.

But he never took any credit for his gift.

"Healing doesn't come from me. It works through me plain and simple. After I've done all I know to do, I lay hands on the sick, bow my head and pray the gift will take over and do the rest. God does it, not me."

Bogus healers blamed illness on spells and curses. They relied on superstition, offering messy charms and foolishness like walking around the graveyard holding a lighted candle as remedies. Men who went to them were lucky if they lived to regret their mistake.

When sick men realized the false healers could not help them, they turned to Papa, but the damage was done. They came angry and suspicious, more hurt and frightened than they'd been in the first place.

Honest healers and jackleg healers in the same county caused a lot of confusion. It was enough to make people distrust all healers.

I was certain that healing was not for me.

Chapter Two

1919

Early one summer morning, right before I turned thirteen, Tyler Mama handed me a big willow basket and her shears.

"Come carry these for me while I work in the garden today, Charlotte." She marched out of the house without a backward glance.

Tyler Mama didn't let anyone touch her gardening things, and I was surprised she wanted me to help her but I was thrilled at the same time.

My grandmother was a round, high-yellow woman who looked like she'd been cut out of butter. She was small in stature, but she had a way about her. It made her seem like she was six feet tall. I could practically eat soup from the top of her head, but I still looked up to her.

I truly believed my grandmother had hung the moon. I loved the ground she walked on and the air she breathed. Matching my longer stride to her tiny steps, I happily followed her to the garden.

"With all the rain we've had, the weeds will soon overtake the plants," Tyler Mama said, pointing to clumps of greenery that looked like plants to my untrained eye.

She tied her sunbonnet under her chin and a scarf around her neck. I stood watching her with a big grin on my face.

"Make haste, Charlotte. These weeds won't pull themselves."

I got on my knees and started pulling what I hoped to God were weeds.

Tyler Mama worked me hard in the hot Mississippi sun that day. But I didn't care if she ran my legs off, I was glad she let me be with her.

Not that I was her pet. More than once she rapped my knuckles with a stick when she saw my hand hovering over one of her plants that I mistook for a weed.

"Pay attention to what you're doing, Charlotte. Don't go tearing out my good herbs with your carelessness. Can't you see the difference between them and the weeds?"

At first I couldn't, but my sore knuckles helped me develop a more discerning eye.

The next day, Tyler Mama let me help her again. For the rest of the summer, every time Tyler Mama had gardening to do she handed me her basket and shears and off we went.

In the cool of the evening, she allowed me inside the little cottage where she dried her herbs and made her medicines.

I stood in the middle of the room amazed at the array of herbs hanging in neat bunches from rods that crisscrossed each corner. There was a brick fireplace at one end and a long wooden table under the glazed windows at the other end. A shelf lined with neatly labeled bottles covered one wall. It caught my eye and I walked toward it.

"Don't stand there gawking, Charlotte," she said, with her hands on her hips. I looked around for something to do, but the room seemed in perfect order.

"Everything looks very tidy, Tyler Mama," I replied.

"Of course it is. I can't stand squalor," she announced and handed me a broom.

"Tyler Mama, you have a whole lot of herbs in here. When they're dried up most of them look alike. How do you know which is which?"

"It takes time, Charlotte. You must try and remember how they smell when they're fresh. Dried herbs smell the same, sometimes a bit stronger."

Tyler Mama could talk for hours if I held my peace and listened quietly. I kept waiting for her to repeat herself, but she never did. Not one single time.

She knew all manner of interesting things and delighted in surprising me with new facts. I figured if there was anything she didn't know, it simply wasn't worth knowing.

My grandmother was the oldest person in our family, and her head was full of family history. But the way she told it made it seem like a story. I knew she was getting ready to tell me about yet another relative when she put both her hands on her cheeks and took a deep breath.

"You've never met . . ." is how every family tale began. And did those relatives of ours ever have some strange and unusual names, almost as interesting as their stories.

Uncle Weedie, New Dell, Moo, Mr. Yay Baby, Miss Duck, Mee-Aw, Uncle Ammie, Nanny Med, Sister Kick, Dot-Dot, Nan, Letie-Pie, Aunt Lova and dozens more came to life when Tyler Mama talked about them.

Seems like just about everybody in our family had the name they were christened with and then the name folks called them. Papa carried on the tradition by giving his children special names of their own.

Ever since I was knee high to a duck, he'd called me Muchie, because according to him, I had so *much* sweetness in me. I was his *muchie* sweet little girl.

I figure I'm lucky he picked Muchie to call me over Sweetie. Going around with a name like Sweetie would have been hard for me to live up to.

Although everyone else called me Muchie, Tyler Mama insisted on calling me Charlotte because it was her name too.

Tyler Mama loved to sing, especially church songs. If she didn't know the words to every song in the Methodist hymnal, she sure had me fooled.

She'd start out the morning with, "This is my Father's world. And to my listening ears, all nature sings and round me rings the music of the spheres."

Hearing her sing, "Sweet hour of prayer, sweet hour of prayer, that calls me from a world of care," signaled that the day's work was done.

And poetry! Lord God Almighty, Tyler Mama could quote big hunks of the Bible and long passages of Shakespeare and every other kind of poetry I didn't know then and barely know now.

But she never could stand to have a whole lot of nattering going on while she was telling a story or quoting somebody famous or singing her favorite songs. Tyler Mama demanded to be the star of her show.

God help the ninny who tried to steal her thunder. Maybe that's why she preferred an audience of one.

In a big family like ours that was a rare luxury. Tyler Mama often got vexed with all the talking delegates in our house. She'd shut her mouth tight as a new pair of shoes, snatch out her Bible and take to praying for all she was worth.

A lot of people thought Tyler Mama an especially devout woman, what with her breaking into silent prayer in the middle of family gatherings and all. I knew when she started praying like that she was simply irked beyond speech.

As we puttered about the garden tending her medicinal herbs and the flowers she loved so well, Tyler Mama taught me many things.

"You see this herb here, Charlotte?" She pointed to a greenish-gray plant festooned with little purple flowers. "Some call it shepherd's purse. A good-sized mouthful will slow down bleeding after a woman has a baby. Purple archangel works the same."

"What makes a woman bleed, Tyler Mama?"

"It is part of being a woman, child. That's a subject for another day."

"Does it taste nasty, Tyler Mama?" I asked.

"Indeed it does. That's why I keep it steeped in honey. You're a smart girl for asking, Charlotte."

I beamed at her compliment, before she pulled me up short.

"Don't stand there grinning like a Cheshire cat, girl. Fetch me some of that red raspberry yonder, now."

Pulling a long face, I did as I was told.

"None of your sulking now, Charlotte, it's not becoming."

"Yes ma'am, Tyler Mama."

"Smiling will give you a better class of wrinkles than frowning. You'll see when you get to be my age."

As she talked, Tyler Mama gently folded the red raspberry leaves into a scrap of fabric before settling the package in her basket.

"Charlotte, see if you can reach over behind the yarrow and snip me off a big piece of yellow dock."

"Tyler Mama, what's yellow dock for?"

"It helps a nursing mother keep up her strength. Builds up her blood."

"You sure do talk about blood a lot."

Tyler Mama shot me a look that might have frozen *my* blood had the sun not been so blasted hot.

"Can I cut some of your pretty flowers for Mother?"

"Since you've got those big old shears in your hand, I imagine you *can*. But what do you suppose a polite person would say?"

"*May* I please cut some flowers for Mother, Tyler Mama?"

"Certainly, Charlotte. You'd be surprised how much a bouquet of sweet-smelling flowers can lift a woman's spirits. Remember that."

Rather than be a big hen's ass and ask Tyler Mama why I should remember something so obvious, I held my tongue.

Tyler Mama tolerated my questions, but she clearly preferred to work in solitude. After all, she'd been going out alone for more than thirty years to deliver babies in Wayne County.

Not once in all those years had she displayed the slightest interest in sharing her vast knowledge of female matters with anyone.

That is, until the day she declared to my papa that I was to become their assistant and follow in their footsteps.

Chapter Three

1920

Tyler Mama and Papa both had a lot of good in them. That generally balanced out the bad part, which was that they had the hottest tempers in Mississippi. And both were stubborn as rocks.

The day Tyler Mama announced her plan to train me to be a healer all the good and bad in Papa flared up like a barn fire. But Tyler Mama didn't back down. She didn't even blink.

It was no secret that when Papa and Tyler Mama locked horns, it made sense to run for cover. They were like biblical monsters scorching the earth beneath our feet and darkening the air above our heads over who would be the boss.

Even my own mother, who stood guard with Papa when it was rumored that cross-burners were roaming the county, refused to get in the middle of any fuss between her husband and her mother-in-law.

Mother took a leaf from Tyler Mama's book. She retreated to the kitchen where she shut her mouth, closed her eyes and took to praying as hard as she could while Papa and Tyler Mama argued in the parlor.

I stood behind the parlor door listening to Tyler Mama and peeping through a crack in the wood.

"Charlotte is a smart girl with a good head on her shoulders. She has plenty of sense even young as she is. Let her learn what we know. Then she can carry on when I'm gone and you too. This child is strong and able."

"No, no," my papa objected. "Muchie is too young for such business as ours now, Mama. It's too hard and she's too tender-hearted. Let her get tough first."

"Charlotte knows how to work hard. Shame on you if you let your foolishness stand in the child's way."

Tyler Mama stood up to give her some height over Papa.

"Her way? Seems like to me it's your way, Mama. Let the child be a child as long as she can. No harm in waiting a while longer."

Tyler Mama glared at him until he turned away.

"I'm getting old and so are you. Now is the time for Charlotte to learn from us. Why wait until I've forgot more than I remember? Now is the time to teach her, while she's still steady."

It wasn't like Papa to sit still when he was in the midst of a disagreement, but Tyler Mama could be something of a bully. She pinned him in his chair with her stern gaze. Papa started cracking his knuckles, but he didn't look away again.

"Muchie is just a baby, Mama. Better we should wait until the girl is closer to her own womanhood. Sickness is an ugly thing. No need to fill a young girl's life with it. No need at all."

"Childbearing is not sickness, son. Young girl or old woman both can ease a laboring woman in her suffering. If you don't want Charlotte to help you, then please God, why can't she help me?"

So that's what Tyler Mama had up her sleeve. From the very

beginning she'd wanted me for herself. She never intended for me to work with my papa tending sick animals and hurt men. I wondered if Papa had seen through her little ruse.

And that's when I joined my mother praying. Only I prayed that neither Tyler Mama nor Papa would get their way this time.

"Please God, don't let her make me a healer. I am *not* going to be a healer, even if it means I can spend time all the time in the world with Tyler Mama. Keep me away from the trouble and worry and responsibility of healing. I don't want to tend to women. Please God, please make her see I want no part of healing. Protect me from Tyler Mama's will."

Over and over I asked God to give me an escape from following Tyler Mama's path.

As she and Papa continued to argue, Tyler Mama gave me my first glimpse of how fearsome mother love can be. She used it to wear my papa out.

Holding her hand to her bosom, she threw her head back and heaved a huge sigh. "Son, when you came into this world, you were just a little scrap of blue flesh. My womb was gushing blood, and I feared the worst for both of us. But before I fainted dead away, I grabbed you up and held you to my mouth. With my next-to-last breath I sucked your airways clear."

"Mama, please. Can't we talk about Muchie now and not you? What does my birth have to do with her? Don't you dare try and make me feel guilty."

Tyler Mama went on as if Papa had not even spoken to her. "It was me who saved you from death, by the grace of God. Though I was close to death myself, I saved you. When I breathed my own life into you, son, I never thought I'd live to see the day that you would be so selfish."

Tyler Mama collapsed in her chair and covered her face with

her hands. With each sharp intake of breath, she shook her head from side to side as if crying.

Papa spit on the floor. Then he peered around the room with a guilty look on his face.

"Is it selfish to protect my child? She's just a little girl, Mama. Don't rob her of her childhood. You go ahead and call me selfish all you want. But that won't change how I feel."

"How can one healer deny another the chance to use her God-given gift?"

"Are you talking about yourself again, Mama?"

"Don't you dare be flip with me, son. You know as well as I do that Charlotte has the gift. Waiting is not the answer. Charlotte has healing hands. Just like you and me. I feel it as sure as I feel love for you."

That startled me so much I stopped praying to stare open-mouthed at Tyler Mama. Did she really think I had healing hands or was she using that to make Papa give in?

"Be careful what you say, Mama. It will be hard for Muchie to have healing hands. Why force such knowledge on a child?"

Their debate raged on throughout the evening. Each of them dredged up new ways of saying the selfsame thing. Everyone in the house was sick to death of tiptoeing around in silence while Papa and Tyler Mama argued.

Except for me. Each time they resumed their battle, I hoped to satisfy my growing curiosity about the healing gift Tyler Mama said I had.

Tyler Mama held fast to her position that I had healing hands. Finally Papa admitted he too had noticed the signs.

Neither one of them said what the signs were. What had Tyler Mama and Papa seen in me that I could not see?

I wanted nothing to do with healing. But according to them, I had little choice in the matter. How could that be?

But that night there was no stopping their screaming and shouting disagreement. Once or twice, Tyler Mama even threw things against the wall. Papa spit each time she did.

Yet even in the heat of the violent verbal battle, neither one ever sank to the level of trading physical blows. It was a time when men hit women and parents struck children without giving it a second thought. Most families thought it was normal behavior. Though it was a fact that my papa would fight any man alive if he had to, in our family, words were the only weapon ever used.

Tyler Mama and Papa tried to outdo each other over two long days and nights, hurling words as sharp as straight razors. I wondered how they would be able to look each other in the eye again. If anyone said such hurtful things to me, I doubted I could find any forgiveness in my heart.

Finally they called a truce of sorts.

"I can't fight you anymore, Mama. I don't believe Muchie is ready yet, but I won't stand in your way. Just don't take her along too fast. Be careful, Mama, you know what being a healer means. Please, be careful with Muchie."

I was on my own then. I would have to convince Tyler Mama that healing was not for me. Gift or no gift.

But what she'd said about me having healing hands stuck with me. I held my hands out in front of me and turned them palm up and palm down. I held each hand up to the light, examining them closely for any sign of what Tyler Mama saw.

I balled my hands into fists and then stretched my fingers wide. But my hands told me nothing. All I saw were two rough brown hands with broken nails. The same hands I'd always had. Only now, according to Tyler Mama, they were healing hands.

Chapter Four

1921

Once she had my papa's grudging permission, Tyler Mama spent the next year wearing down my resistance to being a healer.

"Don't ever turn your back on learning, Charlotte. When you learn something, no one can take it away from you."

"But I don't ever want to get up in the middle of the night like you do. It's too hard to be a healer."

We were in her herb cottage, and I walked over to the window to hide my face from Tyler Mama. I didn't want her to see how confused I was. I tied the end of one braid into a knot, pulled it loose and tied it again.

"God gave you the gift he wanted you to have. And your gift will make room for itself, child, Proverbs 18:16 says so."

"But what good is a gift if you don't want it?"

Turning to look at Tyler Mama, I saw that she was smiling. "All you can do is thank God for giving it to you. Do you think I wanted my gift when I was your age? No, no. I wanted nothing more than to get married and have a family. But God had other plans for me. He gave me the husband and children I wanted, but he also gave me the healing gift he wanted me to have."

I was no match for Tyler Mama. She had too many wiles. Knowing how much I loved her, she wooed me with hours and hours of her undivided attention.

She gave me many glimpses into the secrets surrounding female matters, which made me feel grown-up and wise.

In time, Tyler Mama won me over. I threw myself into learning all she would teach me about being a healer.

The herb cottage was my classroom, and Tyler Mama gave me lessons about birthing and being a midwife in the confines of its stout brick walls. No one dared disturb us when we were in the herb cottage, and only school could lure me away from it.

"I keep two birthing bags stocked at all times, Charlotte. One ready to use and one waiting in reserve."

She made a neat row of all the items needed for the bags.

"Put one block of soap in each bag. No telling if folks will always have soap in their homes. Always clean your hands before you touch a laboring woman."

"Why do you have all these rags?"

"I use them to wipe the woman's face, to sop up any blood or fluid and to dry the baby once it's born. It's better to carry everything you need than to depend on what you might find in another woman's home."

Tyler Mama pointed to small balls of twine, starched sheets and her homemade herbal unguents.

"The twine is for tying the cord. The grease will help the mother get her baby out without tearing. I like to have sheets because some country folks lay right on the ticking, and I don't know whether it's clean or not."

In the secure side pockets of each bag, she tucked small bottles of opium tincture. "If a woman is really suffering and frightened, a few drops in water will settle her down," she said.

Tyler Mama sent me to fetch wood for a fire. When the fire was burning strongly, she poured freshwater into a cast-iron pot and set it over the heat. "Let the water get good and hot, Charlotte. You'll need to boil those scissors and my little knives a full fifteen minutes."

Tyler Mama covered her dress with a big white apron and tied a kerchief over her hair as the water began to boil.

"Ever since a laboring woman grabbed me by my hair and wouldn't let go, I've tied up my head when I'm attending a birth. You should too."

"Yes, ma'am, I shall."

"And while those things are boiling, heat the flatiron to smooth out this brown paper for me, Charlotte."

"What must I do with the paper, Tyler Mama?"

"You're to wrap my instruments in the paper so they stay nice and clean. Careful now, that's metal you're fooling with. Hot enough to burn you. When you lift them out, use this wooden spoon."

I was clumsy at first and dropped her tools on the floor. She made me start all over again until I could clean, boil and wrap them without a hitch.

"Put three belly binders in each bag, Charlotte. After a woman has a baby, she needs help holding herself together. That's why these are wide and made of sturdy cotton. I wrap them around a new mother and pin them tight."

"That must be uncomfortable, Tyler Mama."

"Only if the binder is too tight, Charlotte. You'll want to ask," she said.

Tyler Mama gave me clean white diapers, two big safety pins and two little handmade gowns for each new baby.

"I think the bags are ready now, Tyler Mama," I said with pride.

She shook her head and pointed to a stack of herbs on the table.

"Not yet, Charlotte. Wrap the dried red raspberry in calico and the yellow dock in muslin."

"Why's that, Tyler Mama?"

"I don't want to fumble around looking for what I need when the time comes. It makes it easier on me if each herb is wrapped in its own covering."

"Tyler Mama, what are these two little vials of water? There's not enough water in here to splash a fly."

"It's holy water from the Catholic church over in Jackson. I always keep some in my bag, just in case."

"Just in case what, Tyler Mama?"

"You never know, Charlotte. I've been blessed not to lose a baby yet," she said. Tyler Mama clasped her hands and closed her eyes in prayer. "Thank God for that."

"Is the water for the baby? Even a little baby needs more water than this."

"No, child. That's not what it's for. It's to baptize if a baby is ever on the brink of death. I wouldn't want to deny a child its place in heaven."

"But you're not Catholic, you're Methodist Episcopal just like me."

"Indeed I am and proud of it. But Methodists don't give out holy water and the Catholics do. It's just my insurance, Charlotte. Nothing more."

Tyler Mama used the flat surface of the table to draw pictures of the changes a woman's body goes through in a normal labor. And she explained the steps of labor time and again.

"Labor starts out slow, Charlotte. If you keep a woman calm

she can fall asleep in between her pains. I know that sounds strange, but it's true. Some women need to walk around when they're laboring. Others would rather sit in a chair. Don't let them get in the bed until the very end because it will slow down the birth."

She described what to expect if there were problems.

"You'll want to hold her belly top and bottom. Gently as you can but firmly so you can feel the size and shape of her baby. In time, you'll be able to judge the length of labor by the way the pains feel under your hands."

Finally, she explained the secret of the birthing room bouquet.

"Fresh flowers help a woman focus her mind as she struggles to give birth. Beauty always eases pain. When you leave her, the flowers will brighten the room and remind her there is kindness in the world."

Soon enough, I was tumbling out of bed to accompany Tyler Mama in her travels around the county, watching and learning. She was good about leaving me to my sleep on school nights, but for some mysterious reason, it seemed most women began their labors on the weekends.

Despite Tyler Mama's careful instruction, the first time I actually helped her at a birthing, I was unprepared for the sheer power of it all.

"What makes a woman want to have a baby, Tyler Mama? Nothing in the world could make me want to go through that. It was terrible."

I kept shaking my head and blinking my eyes, trying to erase the images of what I'd seen.

"Terrible? What makes you say that, child?"

"Look at how she suffered all those hours. Grunting and sweating like something wild. It was enough to scare me silly, Tyler Mama."

"But did you see the look on her face when I put that beautiful baby in her arms? Did you see how happy she was and how pleased her husband was when he looked at his wife and baby? It is love, my dear child. Love is what makes people want a baby."

"If he loved her so much, why make her suffer like that?"

"She forgot her pains before we were out of the house good, Charlotte. The baby made her forget. And her husband will never even know what she's suffered. That's the way it is."

"Still and all, Tyler Mama, I can't imagine loving someone enough to go through all that pain, no matter how sweet the new baby might be."

"When you're a woman grown, you'll understand, Charlotte. Love makes everything seem possible."

"You must promise you'll be with me, Tyler Mama. Promise if I lose my everlasting mind one day and actually *have* a baby, promise you'll be with me to help me and give me courage."

"Much as I love you, my darling Charlotte, I can't promise you I'll be here to see you safely married and a mother. That's up to God."

"Well, if God expects any children out of me, he ought to make sure you live a real long time so you can help me!"

"Shame on you, Charlotte. You're not in charge of God's timetable. Let's pray he'll forgive you for being so willful."

Tyler Mama took my hands in hers and stood praying for me so long I thought I'd fall over in a heap.

Chapter Five

❧❀❧

1924

Tyler Mama had me follow her about the county off and on for three years, toting her birthing bag and assisting her in the homes of laboring women.

"Watch everything I do and listen with care, Charlotte. That's the best way for you to learn. There's many ways to help a woman give birth. If she's frightened we must build up her courage. Every living thing in pain responds to kindness," she said.

Whenever Tyler Mama talked about birthing, she pitched her voice low and spoke in the same soothing rhythm she used to calm women in labor.

In time, she let me take on more of her work. I often went out alone to tend a woman through labor. Tyler Mama always arrived in time for the birth though.

I was nervous about my ability to deliver a baby safely. True to the promise she'd made my papa, Tyler Mama took me along slowly. She declined to make me face my fears until I was ready.

Despite that, she gave me the honor of putting the new babies' names in their family Bibles.

"Tyler Mama, how many babies have you delivered over the years?" I asked her, knowing full well she had a little book listing every birth by date, time and family name.

"I don't think of it as me delivering the baby, Charlotte. What I do is *help* the mother birth her baby. The hard work is all theirs. God uses me to bring mother and baby through birthing without harm," Tyler Mama said.

After every birth she made a point of thanking God for his delivering mercies and saving graces.

"Always remember this, Charlotte. Without God, we can do nothing."

One Thursday evening when it was pouring rain, Enoch Wills came from his farm in Chicora, Mississippi, way on the other side of the Chickasawhay River to fetch Tyler Mama.

"The last time I visited that woman I told her not to stir a step from her bed or those twins would come early. Some folks just won't listen."

It was always a pleasure to watch Tyler Mama get ready. She didn't waste any time, but she was particular about her appearance. Dragging a comb through her hair, she quickly twisted it into a fat braid. Even though it was raining buckets, Tyler Mama still dusted her face with powder before stepping into a pair of sturdy boots.

"Run fetch my birthing bag, Charlotte."

"Let me come with you, Tyler Mama. I've never seen twins born. Does it take twice as long as a regular birth?"

"There'll be other times for you to help me with twins. This isn't the first set ever born nor will it be the last, though I imagine that's what the Wills think."

"But you might need me," I insisted.

"Stay and get your rest, Charlotte. There's school tomorrow."

"That's all right, Tyler Mama, I can miss one day. I don't like you going out into this storm all by yourself."

"Mind what I say, girl. I'm grateful for your willingness to help, but I want you to study your lesson now. I expect I'll be back before you get home from school tomorrow."

Tyler Mama checked the contents of her birthing bag and slung it over her shoulder. She tucked her skirts beneath a heavy waxed coat.

I hoped it would keep her dry riding in Enoch's rickety wagon. As he always did, Papa tied a horse behind the wagon for Tyler Mama to ride home.

I ran behind her as she went to the door. Tyler Mama lifted her cheek for me to kiss. She gave me a hug, and I smelled the faint scent of lavender in her hair.

Then she braved the Noah's ark heavy rain with Enoch Wills. They had a long ride ahead of them. I prayed the river was still passable when they got to it.

Tyler Mama was old as white thread and black pepper, but it had never crossed her mind to refuse Enoch. I was grateful to her for allowing me to stay home, but I felt bad that she'd gone without me.

After she went out into the night, I snuggled deep into her bed. The cozy space she'd left behind was warm and still held her smell. I soon fell sound asleep.

Way late in the night, when our entire household was sleeping deeply, a young man named Son Bubba Dean came charging up to our house on his big roan horse.

"Mrs. Tyler! Mrs. Tyler! Come quick. Theola needs you!" Son Bubba shouted as he banged on our front door.

By then, the steady rain had turned into a real storm. Lightning and thunder made the night look like the Fourth of July.

Papa met Son Bubba at the door and reluctantly announced, "Mama has gone over to Chicora with Enoch Wills."

"Lord God, Arthur. My Theola needs Mrs. Tyler. That baby is coming."

"She's not here, Son Bubba, she's over helping Enoch Wills's wife."

Son Bubba was wild eyed. His hair was all matted and his nightshirt was stuffed into his overalls. He looked like a walking scarecrow. But mainly he looked ready to fight Papa about Tyler Mama being gone. To keep the peace I stepped into the light.

"I'm here, Son Bubba," I said, dressed and ready to go with a birthing bag slung over my shoulder.

"Mama has trained Muchie well, Son Bubba. Theola will be fine with Muchie."

With a curt nod of thanks to Papa, Son Bubba hauled me up behind him on the horse. He galloped hell-for-leather in the driving rain to his house.

When we got to the gate, his wife was screaming so loud I could hear her over the crashing thunder. The sound and the cold rain made me shiver.

I jumped down from the horse and ran into the Dean cabin, tossing aside my dripping coat and headscarf. What I saw there made me want to run right back out again. I was scared to stay and scared to go. But I couldn't leave a woman who needed my help. God would never forgive me, not to mention Tyler Mama.

Son Bubba's wife was clearly crazed from her pains. She was alone in the cabin with no mother or sister to comfort her. Everything was in disarray.

Ever since Son Bubba had left her she must have been thrashing about on the bed. Now she was nearly worn out from her labor.

"Theola, I brought Muchie to help you," Son Bubba told her.

Poor Theola turned into a living terror. Soon as she saw him she took to screaming and cursing at Son Bubba, her voice hoarse and rough.

Why had Tyler Mama had to go clear over to Chicora? Why wasn't she here when I needed her? I prayed for Tyler Mama to appear and take over, but I knew she was too far away for that. There was no one to help me, and I hardly knew where to start.

Son Bubba was nearly in tears. He was doing none of us any good standing in the door, twisting his hat and letting the rain blow into the room.

"Go fetch plenty wood for the fire, Son Bubba. Freshwater too. Give me some time alone with Theola," I told him.

"All right Muchie, I'll do that."

Pushing him out, I slammed the door and rushed back to tend to Theola.

My voice was shaking badly, and I could barely get my words out. Beads of sweat popped out on my neck. Suddenly I remembered Tyler Mama's advice and tied a clean rag around my head. For some reason that made me feel a little better.

"I'm here now, honey. You don't have to worry. I'll take care of everything. Just rest easy now," I told her, pitching my voice low like Tyler Mama would.

The cabin vibrated with frantic energy that set my teeth on edge.

"Let's get you out of those clothes and into a nice clean gown. That will make you feel better."

Gently but swiftly, I peeled off Theola's soiled clothing and settled her into the one sturdy chair in her cabin. I pulled up a three-legged stool to hold my bag.

"You keep watching me, Theola. Everything is going to be all right. You don't have to worry about a thing. Are you thirsty? Here, Theola, take a sip of water now."

She gulped the water and slumped exhausted in the chair. I placed her hands on the arms, holding them there as I spoke to her. "Theola, you grip the arms of this chair, honey. When your pain comes, squeeze just as hard as you can. Real hard. Can you do that for me?"

She nodded. Kneeling next to her chair, I wiped her face and smoothed her hair, talking to her all the while.

I put my hands on her belly and felt it for the shape of her baby. I felt again. The baby lay sideways. Breech meant trouble. No baby was likely to get born safely in that position.

If any part of the baby's body felt air before its head came out, instinct would make the baby try to breathe. Then it would suffocate on the fluids inside Theola.

My legs got wobbly, and the only thing I wanted to do was sit down next to Theola and cry.

But there was no time for that. I took a deep breath and tried to push my fear away. I knew what I had to do. Get that baby's head pointing toward the birth canal. Somehow, I had to help Theola's baby turn. Otherwise they might both die.

Running to the washbasin I scrubbed my hands clean, going over in my mind what I'd seen when Tyler Mama turned a breech baby.

Watching and doing were two different things though. The realization opened the door to new fears. I pulled open the neck of my dress, desperate for air in the stuffy cabin. Sweat soaked my back and made me shiver. My hands were shaking so hard I clenched them in prayer to keep myself steady.

"Help me, God. Please help me," I prayed, sweating like a field hand.

I laid my hands on Theola's heaving belly again.

"Listen to me, Theola. Listen real good now. We have to turn your baby. I need you to help me, Theola."

Her eyelids fluttered as she looked at me. Pain and fear clouded her eyes, but she was doing her best to pay attention to what I was saying.

"I won't let anything bad happen to you. Promise you'll trust me, Theola?"

"Yes, Muchie. I shall."

"Trust me, Theola, trust me like you've never trusted anybody in your life. Please. Just trust me."

I was singing to her, "Trust me, trust me, trust me."

My hands knew the shape of her baby, and I began to guide it. Praying without words, I sang to Theola. My whole body was a prayer as I slowly, ever so slowly, felt her baby turn.

All Theola heard was the sound of my voice singing low and steady.

Her contractions were coming closer together. I was scared and dared not miss that moment of stillness between each pain. It was the only time I had to turn her baby.

I felt Theola's belly bunch up with a pain and then it was over. Again I guided her baby in its turning.

Another pain. Stillness. I moved her baby. Turn her baby and wait. Again and again and again the pattern repeated.

Sweat poured off Theola. The bottom of my dress was sticking to my legs. I could feel my hair coming loose from the rag, but I couldn't stop.

It seemed to take forever. Somewhere in that endless time of singing, "Trust me. Trust me. Trust me," and the slow turning and the silent prayers I got lost.

I couldn't see or hear. I couldn't even think. I felt like I was fainting but the fainting went on and on. I was lost in the fainting, lost to myself. Lost somewhere I'd never been before.

All I could do was feel. And what I felt was life. Theola's own life, tired and afraid, yet still strong and protective of the new life inside her.

I was so dizzy I would have fallen to the floor had my hands not been locked on her belly. I was one with Theola, one with her baby, one with God and his healing mercies.

"Muchie, I have to push. I have to push now."

The sound of Theola's voice broke through the endless silence that held me. For a heartbeat I had no idea where I was or what to do. I looked at my hands, at Theola.

Then I understood. It was Theola's time.

"Wait, Theola. Wait. Hold on now. Don't push yet. Just hold on."

My hands told me her baby's head was finally pointing in the right direction. When I pulled up Theola's gown to examine her I could see her baby's head was crowning. It was almost ready to be born.

"Wait, Theola. Let me help you get your baby out." I smeared Tyler Mama's herbal salve on Theola's vagina to ease the baby's passage. "You've been so strong, Theola. So brave. It's time now, honey. It's time. Wait for the next pain and then you can push. Here it comes, Theola. Now PUSH!"

Her labor was over in an instant. And the baby who came slipping into my hands was a fine boy, sturdy as a tiny tree and perfect in every way. He let out a cry that suffused his brown face with rosy color.

"Look, Theola! You did it! Look at this big, strapping baby boy you've got."

I was elated and wanted to dance about the room with her crying baby in my arms, celebrating his birth and the end of his mother's pain. Instead I carefully looked him over from head to toe. Seeing nothing amiss, I wiped him dry and wrapped him snugly in one of the sheets from my birthing bag.

"Take your boy, Theola. Sounds to me like he's hungry," I said before handing him to his mother.

She immediately put the baby to her breast and began nursing him, which made the afterbirth come out. I wrapped it in paper to bury at the end of their land.

Before I did another thing, I bowed my head and thanked Divine Providence for delivering us all. With new energy I tidied up the cabin and packed my things away in the birthing bag. To be sure Theola had nourishing food, I put on a pot of soup using what little I could find in her larder.

Son Bubba rushed in with his armload of wood and a bucket of water.

"Congratulations, Son Bubba. You've got yourself a fine son," I said. "I need to write his name in your Bible to give you a record of his birth."

"We don't have us a Bible, Muchie."

"Well, I tell you what, I need to write down the baby's birth somewhere. Do you have another book I can use?"

"Give her my storybook, Son Bubba. That will do, won't it, Muchie?"

"That will do just fine."

"What's that you're writing, Muchie?"

Son Bubba looked at the words as if he didn't know what they meant. It took me by surprise. Then I understood why he asked. Only half of this young couple knew how to read. I said a silent prayer for them before answering.

"What do you and Theola want to name this fine baby of yours?"

"If he'd been a girl, I would want to name him after you,

Muchie," Theola said shyly. I bent to kiss her cheek, flattered to hear such a thing.

"Let's name him Charles for your daddy and Robert for mine," Son Bubba suggested to Theola.

"That's mighty sweet of you, Son Bubba," Theola said. She looked like she was about to cry. I was feeling more than a little weepy myself.

"Charles Robert Dean it is then. I'll write his name and date of birth on this blank page in your storybook, Theola."

I gave Theola another kiss, shook Son Bubba's hand and took my leave of the new family, praying God to bless them all.

Chapter Six

1924

My shoulders ached from hours of hunching over Theola. Everything I had on felt sticky with sweat and my eyes ran water, gritty from lack of sleep. The rain had stopped, but the road was muddy and I stumbled over broken branches littering the path.

Exhausted, I trudged toward home trying to figure out what had happened to me in the Dean cabin.

Theola and the baby were fine. That much was certain. But I wasn't so sure about me. Ever since I'd gotten lost in Theola's labor I'd felt funny.

It was like waking up after falling asleep in the middle of the day. In the half-light, it was hard to judge the time. Not knowing whether it was morning or evening gave me the same sort of strange feeling I had now.

Tyler Mama would understand. She would explain everything to me. After thirty years of birthing experience surely she'd know what it meant to feel like this. I summoned up my last bit of strength and ran through the gate, eager to unburden myself to Tyler Mama.

Instead of midday farm bustle, only the lowing of cows needing to be milked greeted me.

"Papa? Mother?" I called out to my parents. No one answered.

Bursting into our empty kitchen, my fear multiplied.

"What's wrong? Is somebody sick?" I shouted.

Fear turned into terror when I realized that shadows lining the hallway were actually relatives huddled together and not saying a word.

"Muchie, it's Mama."

I stopped dead in my tracks when I heard my papa's voice.

"She's been asking for you ever since they brought her home."

Shaking my head and crying, "No, no, no!" I grabbed my papa's hand. He led me to where Tyler Mama lay.

She looked very pale beneath our bright patchwork quilt. I'd never seen her look so small and old and tired.

"Tyler Mama, Tyler Mama. It's me. I'm here, dearest. It's me, Charlotte. Can you hear me, my darling?"

I knelt beside her, speaking softly, stroking her hand and kissing her cheek.

Her blue-tinged eyelids, thin as butterfly wings, fluttered at the sound of my voice. I held her plump shoulders in my hands, willing my youth and strength into her little body. Willing her to be herself again.

She stirred under my hands. Opening her gray eyes she looked at me. The faintest glimmer of a smile touched her lips as she whispered, "Charlotte. Use your gift."

Tyler Mama sighed and closed her eyes.

"Tyler Mama, please talk to me. Don't you dare go away and leave me. I have things I must ask you. I need you. I love you,

Tyler Mama. I love you so much. Please Tyler Mama, please be well."

"Muchie, there's nothing we can do," Papa said.

"No, Papa. NO! That can't be true. Help me, Papa. Hold on to her, Papa. We can't let her go."

Papa looked like he was about to cry, but I had no time to comfort him. I placed his hands on Tyler Mama's chest and put my own hands on her shoulders again.

Turning my head, I barked at the others who now filled the room, "You keep praying. Pray just as hard as you can and don't you dare stop until I tell you."

Papa stared at me as if he didn't know who I was. But he obediently began to move his lips in prayer, his big, callused hands resting gently on his mother's bosom.

"Tyler Mama, Tyler Mama, please live. Please, Tyler Mama, I love you so much, please live. Help her, God. Please help her."

But she never opened her eyes again. Tyler Mama seemed to sink deep into the featherbed until she barely lifted the covers. Though Papa and I laid hands on her, though the whole family prayed, she slipped away.

Forever.

I sat on Tyler Mama's bed and held her hand, unable to move. Smoothing her thick gray hair away from her face, I kissed her cheek again. It was already growing cool.

I heard a strangled sob and looked across the bed. My papa sat with his head thrown back and his mouth wide open. His eyes were squeezed shut and tears rolled down his cheeks onto the front of his work shirt. He looked like a brokenhearted little boy.

Papa fell to his knees and nestled his head on Tyler Mama's shoulder. His crying made the bed shake. I ran and put my arms around Papa.

"I'll take care of Tyler Mama. Don't you worry yourself one bit, Papa," I crooned, feeling him tremble in my arms.

He didn't look up. I doubt he even heard me. I stood beside him until Mother came to take his hand and help him from the room.

Once Papa was out of earshot, everyone started talking at the same time. I wanted nothing more than to be left alone with Tyler Mama, but I was forced to hear her sad story over and over again.

"She was coming back from helping that Wills woman way on the other side of the river. Lightning struck a tree and her horse reared."

"It must have been her heart. By the time she got home, she was weak as tea. She could hardly speak."

"Tyler Mama came stumbling into the house clutching her breast and gasping for breath. Papa did everything he could to help her, but it wasn't enough. Her heart just gave out."

"Must've been the shock from when her horse went crazy in the storm. She held on long enough to get home. Her face was white as a linen sheet and her lips were blue."

After the fourth recitation of my grandmother's ordeal, I held up my hand and shouted, "Enough! For the love of God, she's gone now. It doesn't matter what happened. Tyler Mama is gone."

Even though I was the youngest person in the family, for some reason they all listened to me that day. The chattering stopped and we held hands, making a circle of sorrow around the bed where Tyler Mama's body lay.

One of my uncles prayed for her soul and our loss. With a parting touch or a word of love to Tyler Mama, he and the rest of the men soon filed from the room.

The women remained to set about the business of preparing

our loved one for her final journey. No one had to be told what to do. Tradition and custom dictated our every action, whether large or small.

"I'll cover the mirrors," volunteered an aunty, crying as she went about the house carefully draping each looking glass with fabric. Vanity disappeared in the face of death.

Cousin Helen tearfully opened every window and door.

"Tyler Mama's spirit can go free now," she announced when she was done.

With sad tenderness, we washed Tyler Mama in clean rainwater using her homemade lavender soap and drying her with towels that she had embroidered.

"She never sewed herself a shroud," one of the aunties commented.

"Tyler Mama said it was a waste of fabric to do that. She wanted to be buried in her good clothes," another one recalled.

They laid out her navy blue dress, her white crochet collar and her lace shawl. Tyler Mama was soon dressed in her Sunday best.

I brushed the tangles from her soft, sweet-smelling hair. It was crinkled like Spanish moss, and I had a time trying to braid it into the smooth coronet she favored for special occasions.

One of my aunties put pearl ear bobs in Tyler Mama's ears. A cousin pinned Tyler Mama's cameo brooch at the throat of her dress.

Another aunty smoothed cream over Tyler Mama's weathered arms and work-worn hands.

With infinite care, we crossed Tyler Mama's arms over her bosom.

But she still didn't look like herself.

"Where is Tyler Mama's box of Coty face powder?"

"Here it is, Muchie," said Cousin Helen.

"Use this salve to give her lips some color," another cousin offered.

"There, now Tyler Mama looks more like herself," I said.

"Oh, God. Oh, God, she's dead," Cousin Helen began to wail.

Soon every woman present was crying. The men in the family comforted us as best they could when they came to carry Tyler Mama into the parlor.

Cousin Helen pulled the curtains shut making the room dark. My aunties lit four candles, setting one at Tyler Mama's head, one at her feet and one on each side making a cross of light around her.

The family stood together to say the Lord's Prayer. But I couldn't pray. I couldn't even think. All I could do was sit looking at poor little Tyler Mama. How could she of all people actually be dead?

During the rest of that long day and half the night, friends and family came from all over Wayne County to pay their respects to Tyler Mama.

Some brought food, others flowers. Many came just to say thank you one last time to Tyler Mama. Everyone sat with her for a while, to pray and reminisce.

Tyler Mama's body was never left alone during its last few hours on earth among the living.

The next morning, my papa himself gently settled his mother's body into a plain pine coffin that lay on a bed of flowers in the back of our wagon. The little box looked very rough to me. Pathetic and somehow not worthy of my dear grandmother.

"Come on, Helen, help me get more flowers," I said to my cousin.

We ran to Tyler Mama's garden and cut every single thing that was in bloom. Our arms full of sweet-smelling flowers, we carefully arranged them on top of the coffin.

The whole family walked in two long lines behind the wagon. All the way to the cemetery the muddy road sucked at our shoes and slowed our steps.

"It's a shame there's not a Methodist Episcopal minister to say words over Tyler Mama," one of my aunties complained as she followed the wagon.

"No matter, we'll make do with the Holiness preacher," someone replied.

Dropping clumps of damp earth and flowers into Tyler Mama's grave, each of us whispered wrenching words of farewell.

Tyler Mama's family stood watching and weeping as men with shovels filled her grave and patted down the rich Mississippi soil.

The next day, Papa and his brothers walked to the cemetery together. They went to make sure no harm had come to their mother in the night.

Chapter Seven

1925

By spring, the black Mississippi dirt heaped over Tyler Mama had softened into a gentle green mound. But the passing months had done nothing to ease my heart-raw grieving.

I knew she was gone, but I just couldn't make sense of her being dead. My soul and my body ached with missing her. The hurt went deep down into the bottom of my heart. Losing Tyler Mama made me angry with God. It got so I could hardly pray.

One evening months after her death, my papa and I went to the cemetery to plant flowers over Tyler Mama.

"Mama loved her flowers, Muchie. I think she'd appreciate having some here with her," he said as we unwrapped wet rags from the roots of the plants we'd brought.

Papa had a rambling rose, a lavender bush and a rosemary bush, all transplanted from Tyler Mama's garden to her grave.

Turning the earth for the plants, I said, "Papa, you were right when you told Tyler Mama it was too soon for me to learn about healing. I'm not ready to be a midwife."

"What makes you say that, Muchie?"

"I'm not brave and sure of myself like Tyler Mama was. I should have gone in her place that night. Instead, I let her ride clear across the county in a thunderstorm. She'd still be here with us if I'd been brave, Papa."

"Oh, child, listen to you. Don't you think I've reproached myself with the same thought? But you know neither one of us could stop her once her mind was set. Besides, even if you'd spared her going with Enoch, what do you think she would have done when Son Bubba came?"

Papa wouldn't meet my eyes. He kept his head down, as if planting required his undivided attention.

"I hadn't thought of that, Papa. I suspect she would have gone with Son Bubba or anybody else who needed her. That's how she was."

"She was mighty proud of you, Muchie. Said you were a natural born healer."

He stopped his planting to stare me full in the face. Now it was me who couldn't meet his eyes. I busied myself pulling out the wild strawberry vines growing over Tyler Mama.

"No, Papa, I don't think so. I'm just plain scared without Tyler Mama. Something bad could happen at a birth and then what would I do? I don't know enough and now I can't even ask her. I think it would be better for me to stop, Papa."

"But Tyler Mama wanted you to use your gift. Don't you remember? It was just about the last thing she ever said."

Papa knew how to hit me where it hurt. I couldn't even pretend I was working anymore. I sat back on my heels and hung my head in shame, determined not to cry.

"I know, Papa, that's all I've been thinking about. Every night I try to say my prayers . . ."

"Try? What do you mean try, Muchie?"

"It's hard to pray when God doesn't listen."

"Muchie, don't ever doubt it. God hears your prayers. But that's not the same as giving you the answer you want. What do you ask for when you pray, child?"

"I beg God to show me how I can do what Tyler Mama wanted. But I'm scared, Papa. What if I hurt somebody? What if . . . oh, Papa, I just can't do it anymore."

"Half the work of healing is believing in your gift, Muchie. Believing God will use you as he sees fit. When you believe with all your heart, folks will feel your faith and trust you. But if you doubt yourself, you're in trouble. Because you'll be doubting what God's doing with you. Then you may as well give up."

"Papa, if we both have a healing gift, why didn't it help Tyler Mama?"

"Muchie, do you mean why didn't the gift keep her from dying?"

I nodded my head, too choked up for words.

"It would be a lie for me to tell you I understand God's will in these things, Muchie. Maybe we did help Tyler Mama. By laying loving hands on her and praying as she passed from this life to the next. Maybe we gave her just the help she needed."

Papa and I finished our planting. He wiped his hands on a bandana handkerchief and collected our tools. Then he wiped his eyes.

"It looks real nice, Papa," I said looking down. "By the time these plants take root, Tyler Mama will have herself a real nice garden again. She'd like that."

I rested my head on Tyler Mama's wooden headstone. It held the warmth of the sun and I stroked it, remembering how warm and soft her cheek had been. Months of rain and wind had rendered the wood's surface nearly smooth, and I didn't even feel the long splinter caught in the fat part of my palm until Papa took my hand.

Papa eased the splinter out with his fingernails and rubbed a sprig of rosemary on my hand before kissing the hurt place.

"Father, I stretch my hands to Thee. No other help I know. If Thou withdraw thyself from me, Ah! Whither shall I go? Thank you, dear heavenly Father for this child, please heal her broken heart and give her strength. Thank you for my mother. I'm grateful for the many years we had her in our midst. Please allow her loving wisdom to guide and protect us, let her keep watch over us from heaven. Help me, Father, to accept your will and grow in understanding. I pray in the blessed name of Jesus. Amen."

My heart and my hand felt better after Papa's prayer.

. . .

"Look here, there's a letter for me at the trading post. It's from the Methodist Episcopal church headquarters," Papa announced after supper.

He used a table knife to slice open the envelope. A great big smile spread over Papa's face as he read his letter. He looked happy enough to spit if Mother hadn't been in the room. Instead, he slapped his leg with the letter and jumped up to twirl Mother around the table.

"Arthur, what's got into you? What does that letter say?" Mother asked, beaming to see him in such good humor.

"It's about time they decided to do more for Mississippi than hold tent meetings," Papa said as he and Mother stood catching their breath.

"Let me see that." Mother read the letter and laughed out loud.

"It says here they're sending us four missionaries. They want us to prepare for a married couple and two maiden ladies. We're to have a new school and a church of our own. With a full-time minister."

"When are they coming? I read it so fast I clean missed the date," Papa said, taking the letter back from Mother to read it with more care.

"Says they're coming by train from Chicago. My God from Zion, they sure aren't giving us much time to get ready. Looks like they're scheduled to arrive in Buccatunna the day after to-morrow."

Mother immediately went into action, assigning tasks to every member of her household.

"If we're to have beds for them, some of the children will have to sleep in the barn. You girls go change the bed linen. I'll start cleaning the parlor. Boys, clear a space in the barn and get fresh straw to make pallets."

In years past, the white Methodist Episcopal missionaries made their annual trek through colored Mississippi every August. The most they did other than tent meetings was unsuccessfully try and sign up farm boys to go away and study for the ministry.

Our first and third Sunday church had been meeting in the Holiness Church building for as long as I could remember. We couldn't even start our services until the Holiness people finished theirs. Though there were plenty Methodist Episcopal folks in Wayne County, we'd never had a minister of our own. We made do with whichever circuit-riding preacher happened to be in the area. Or we'd call on the Holiness preacher like we did for Tyler Mama.

The visit from the missionaries promised to change everything.

When the house was cleaned to Mother's satisfaction, she turned her attention to preparing enough food to feed her large family and four special guests.

"Get me a ham from the smokehouse," she ordered my brothers.

"Helen, I need you and Muchie to chase down a couple of fat young pullets."

Chickens don't have good sense. Lay out a little feed and they come running, never even seeing the canvas dropping until it's too late.

"Muchie, you chop the heads off," Helen said after she wrung their necks. "That part makes me feel bad."

"I don't see why, the necks are already broken, they can't feel a thing. But all right, I'll do it. You be sure we've got sufficient water boiling to get these feathers loose."

Helen filled an iron pot with water and started a fire beneath it. I dispatched the chickens' heads and hung them upside down to drain out the blood.

"Getting chickens ready for frying is more than a notion," Helen complained.

"The part I hate is plucking, feathers in my nose make me sneeze something awful," I said, dipping one bird in hot water.

Helen and I were sweating like field hands by the time the chickens were mostly bare of feathers.

"Mother will fuss if there's a single pinfeather left on these birds," I reminded Helen, who wrinkled up her nose at the prospect awaiting us.

"I never can manage to singe off the feathers without burning my fingers, Muchie. Won't you do it for me?"

I put a clean stick through the chickens and turned each one over an open flame until their skin was smooth and shining.

"There, these birds are ready for the skillet."

We took the chickens to Mother who was hard at work in the kitchen.

"I wonder if two birds are enough," Mother mused as she began chopping the whole chickens into individual pieces.

Helen and I looked at each other and grimaced. Rather than wait for Mother to send us after more chicken, we volunteered to pick fresh vegetables from the garden.

"I hope these missionaries are worth all this trouble," I declared as we gathered beans and greens and tomatoes to fill our baskets.

"Me too, Muchie," Helen agreed.

Chapter Eight

1925

Regardless of our complaints about the work they caused, my whole family was excited about meeting the missionaries. Mother put fresh flowers in every room and made everyone get all dressed up like it was Sunday. I braided blue ribbons in my hair to match my one good dress.

"Mind your manners, now. This may be the first time they've been around a colored family; you must be a credit to the race today," Papa said.

We stood on the porch waiting to greet the missionaries. Their wagon rolled into our yard at a nice clip. The dust from its wheels made the chickens scatter and cluck in alarm. Our yard dogs yapped at the wagon until a sharp word from Papa sent them scuttling under the house.

"Will you look at that," Papa exclaimed. "They've got two colored fellas with them. One of them is just about the blackest man

I've ever seen in my life." Papa spit on the ground before Mother could stop him.

"Hush, Arthur, don't talk like that in front of the children." Mother shushed Papa as the four white missionaries and their mysterious companions alighted from the wagon.

"Welcome to the Tyler home," Papa said, extending his hand.

The white man, obviously not from Mississippi, gripped Papa's hand in both of his, going up and down like Papa's hand was a pump handle.

We gawked in amazement at that and the funny way the white man talked.

"How do you do? I am Reverend Edwin Leete. Allow me to present my wife, Mamie Leete, and her sister, Miss Cornelia Washburn."

The two women nodded and smiled. "And this is my sister, Miss Annie Laurie Leete."

"Being missionaries seems to run in your family," Papa commented with a smile. Everyone chuckled at his gentle joke.

"We do find it makes travel easier, Mr. Tyler. But wait, you have yet to meet the gentlemen in our party. This is Reverend John Harper, who will be your new minister and school principal. And this is Mr. Edward Preston, who has agreed to help organize your new school as well as teach the upper grades."

Papa shook both men's hands. He winked at them. That drew a smile from their heretofore serious faces.

"Come on in out of the sun and have a glass of cool tea," Papa said.

The four white missionaries and their two colored companions clattered into our house. That left me standing on the porch in a daze.

I'd never seen such a handsome man in all my life. The tall young man introduced as Edward Preston took my breath away.

Whipcord lean, he looked strong with broad shoulders stretching the fabric of his dark suit. He had long legs that ended in nicely polished leather boots. The crisp white collar of his shirt made a striking contrast to his face, which was dark as black plums.

Edward Preston walked with his head up and his back straight, like a gentleman, or maybe royalty. Everything about him pleased me right down to the ground. And he was going to be my teacher.

The sight of him made my heart beat like a thunderstorm. It left me flustered and confused. I couldn't believe everyone else in my family had calmly walked into the house. Just like nothing had happened. Were they all blind? Hadn't they seen the most beautiful man in the world get out of that wagon?

Mother came out to the porch. "Muchie, come in here and help me. With all this company, I need every hand today."

"Yes, ma'am, here I come," I answered, suddenly realizing that the man named Edward Preston was actually inside our house.

I began to put food on the table, straining my ears to hear Edward Preston's voice from the parlor. But how would I know which voice his was? That would have to wait until we ate.

"With two ministers in the house, I imagine our food will be thoroughly blessed this day," Papa joked when he came into the kitchen.

"Oh, Papa, you've always done a fine job of blessing the table," I replied.

"Those are two exceptional young colored men in there. Both educated. Well-spoken too. Shame that teacher is so dark though," Papa remarked as he filched a bit of ham from the platter.

"Why Papa, I've never heard you say a thing like that before."

"Never had any reason to, Muchie," he admitted, returning to our guests.

I looked at Mother with a question in my eyes.

She put her finger to her lips and shook her head to keep me silent. I didn't know what to think about that.

The table practically sagged with food when we sat down. Baked ham and fried chicken, fresh corn, field pies and okra, tender dandelion greens, mashed potatoes and candied yams, slabs of ripe tomatoes, corn bread, Mother's special carrot and apple salad with pecans and, of course, rice.

The banquet displayed Mother's skill. Papa beamed with pride at his guests and his family.

Surveying the abundance of good food on our table, I wondered if anyone would have room for the pound cake and peach cobbler cooling on the sideboard.

Reverend Leete handled the blessing issue nicely. He asked Papa's permission to invite each person at the table to recite a favorite scripture. It took a long time, but I didn't care. I wanted to hear Edward Preston's voice.

"In honor of this sumptuous table and of God's abiding love for us, his children, I offer a verse from the Song of Solomon," he said.

Edward Preston spoke in a rumbling baritone that was softened by the hint of an accent I didn't recognize. I heard him speak and knew I wouldn't rest until I heard that voice whispering in my ear.

I wanted to touch him, to be close to him. It was a totally new and unexpected sensation that left me even more flustered than I'd been when I first saw him.

If he had given me the slightest encouragement I would have taken his hand and walked away from my family without a backward glance. I was ready to follow him to the very ends of the earth that day.

I fear it was all over my face, because he looked at me strangely and then looked at the ceiling. He shared a distant smile with everyone at the table and listened attentively to the remaining scriptures.

"Mr. Preston, Reverend Leete tells me that you were in the Great War."

"Yes, I was, sir. I fought under the French flag."

Noticing Papa's puzzled look, Reverend Leete chimed in, "I actually met Mr. Preston in France, Mr. Tyler. He joined the French army before our side made up its mind to get into the fight. Quite a few Americans did so. I hope you won't hold it against us?"

"Not at all, shows gumption," Papa said, helping himself to more vegetables.

"If I understand correctly, most colored soldiers in the U.S. Army were relegated to labor battalions?" Papa asked as he passed the corn bread.

"Many were assigned to service units, sir. Despite that, they managed to get some serious fighting done too."

"As did Teddy, the French gave him a medal for it," bragged Reverend Leete, turning to Edward Preston.

"I apologize for the lapse, Mr. Tyler. I mean no disrespect," Reverend Leete said, shaking his head. "We've known each other a long time and we've gotten used to calling each other by our nicknames. It feels more natural somehow to call Mr. Preston Teddy. My nickname is Win."

"I've never known a minister to go by anything other than Reverend, but if that's what you prefer, I'm certainly happy to accommodate you, Win," Papa said.

Teddy. His name was Teddy. It was the most perfect name in the world.

"Muchie, will you get us more butter?" I jumped right up to do as she asked. In the kitchen I leaned against the table and whispered his name.

Teddy. Teddy. Teddy. Saying it seemed as natural as breathing.

For the rest of our supper, the only time I heard a word anyone said was when Teddy spoke. He regaled Papa with stories of his service in France and made Mother blush each time he complimented another part of the meal.

The sound of his voice sent jolts of excitement through me. Teddy. Teddy was to be my teacher.

How would I ever manage to survive until school started?

Chapter Nine

❦

1925

"I am gratified by your presence," Reverend Leete announced at a meeting to tell folks about the new school. He adjusted his eyeglasses and held out both his hands.

"As you well know, Mississippi is primarily rural, like your own community. There are few schools in farm areas, and those few are missions of one denomination or the other. I think it is safe to say the state has taken no responsibility for educating colored children."

A rumble of agreement swept the crowd.

"I have good news for you from the Methodist Episcopal Church. We have pledged to build 20 new schools for colored children across Mississippi. Yours will be one of the first, and like the others, it will contain 12 grades."

Cheers and handshakes greeted Reverend Leete's announcement. He held up his hand for silence.

"It will be bound by the rules governing education in

Mississippi, but it will not be limited by those rules. Mississippi provides public schools only for white children. They tend to have an abbreviated school year opening after harvest is done and closing when it is time to plant. However, *your* school will be private and fully supported by the church. Every colored child in the county is welcome regardless of denomination. The purpose of our meeting today is for us to make some important decisions together."

The room erupted in sound. Everyone started talking at one time. Again, Reverend Leete motioned for quiet.

"I am pleased to report Miss Elliott will continue her fine work. She will be teaching children in the primer grades, and there will be two other teachers for the middle grades. Reverend Harper and Mr. Preston shall teach the older children."

This time there was no stopping the questions. Reverend Leete wrote them all down in his little notebook.

"Can our children get nine months of schooling? Just like children up North?" one man asked Reverend Leete.

"They need more schooling to get ahead. Farming is fine for me, but I want better for my children," another said.

"Will the new school teach girls too?"

"Some of us farm for shares. I need my children to help lest we get thrown off the land. How will I get my crop in?" queried the only barefoot man in church.

Men who owned the land they worked hooted him down. They stomped their heavy boots on the wooden floor and jibed, "Red Rooster, Red Rooster, too lazy to crow the break of day."

Reverend Leete turned to Papa for help.

"There's ways around every obstacle. But we'll never get anywhere by depriving our children of education," Papa answered. "If we work together, we can clear every field that needs clearing and then some."

Men and women quickly chimed in with their suggestions. Before long, they came up with a solution that pleased most folks there. Even the barefoot man seemed content.

It was settled like this. Children would do farm work before school and in the evenings. Saturdays too. Five days a week, nine months a year, there would be classes in a brand-new building.

Anyone who needed help with his crop had only to ask.

Folks advised Reverend Leete to set aside work on a church for the time being.

"Instead of putting up two buildings, why not have an auditorium in the school? Let the children use it for their programs. It can do double duty as a sanctuary on Sundays."

The idea made sense, and before long young and old pitched in to build the new school.

And the Methodist Episcopal Church paid for every board and nail. It donated desks and chalkboards, atlasses, tablets, globes and books. The church even paid the teachers' salaries—it was determined that the new school succeed.

"This is a solid structure we're building." Men slapped each other on the back congratulating each other as a long, white clapboard building quickly took shape.

The front door opened into a wide center hall with classrooms on either side. At the end of the hall sat the auditorium. Women sewed curtains for a stage that the men built to take the place of a pulpit.

"The children won't burn up when it's hot like they did in the old school. Look at these screened windows," folks said, raising and lowering the windows to demonstrate how breezes could flow into each room.

Each classroom was outfitted with its own potbellied stove to keep us from freezing in the winter. There was even a big sunny room for the primer grades.

"We'd like to stay here to teach if you'll have us," Miss Leete and Miss Washburn volunteered.

The two maiden lady missionaries stayed more than a year until colored teachers could be hired to teach grades five through eight.

Reverend Harper and Teddy promised to help the older children catch up so we'd be prepared for the high school curriculum they planned to teach. We had a lot of work waiting for us.

When school started, nearly seventy children were enrolled. Like the others, I walked miles to get to school on time.

"What do you think of the new teacher, Muchie?" a girl asked meeting me on the path to school one morning after school had been in session a few weeks.

"Which one?" I parried, stalling for time.

"The good-looking, dark-skinned one, of course. Reverend Harper is nice enough, but he can't hold a candle to Mr. Preston. Don't you think he's handsome, Muchie?"

"Can't say as I've noticed."

She looked at me like I was crazy. All the girls confessed to having crushes on the new teacher. He quickly became their favorite topic of conversation. But I wasn't ready to tell anybody how I felt. I didn't even want to share the fact I knew his special name. It was enough to be able to say it to myself before I fell asleep at night.

The school was the best thing that had ever happened for colored people in Wayne County. We were proud of our new school and our new schoolmasters.

People just couldn't get over their good fortune in having two college-educated colored men to teach their children. What really snatched the rag off the bush was when they found out Teddy could speak perfect French *and* he'd won a French medal for valor in the Great War.

The only thing that ever seemed to bother anyone was Teddy's dark skin.

Many of the colored families in our part of Mississippi were just a generation away from slavery. Still, they were real peculiar when it came to skin color.

Black was what none of them wanted to be. Brown was a little better, but life just seemed easier the more cream you had in your coffee.

Even schoolchildren taunted each other with spiteful rhymes about color. "Black you must live in a shack. Brown you can work in a town. Yellow you'll marry a rich fellow."

"If you're black, get back. If you're brown, stick around. If you're light, you're all right."

I'd heard such nonsense all my life, but never paid much attention to it. Being in the "all right" category meant I'd never taken to heart hateful words about color.

But now, it hit me different. They were talking about Teddy. My Teddy. It wasn't fair. Even if it did make some twisted sense in race-sick Mississippi, it was still wrong and wicked.

Despite their color-struck notions, the good families in the county fell all over themselves extending hospitality to the new teacher.

Teddy and Reverend Harper must have been the most popular men in Wayne County. Every week they were invited to Sunday supper at one home or the other.

"Mr. Preston is coming to our house this Sunday," a different girl boasted during recess each week.

Like my friends, I giggled to hear the news. We made a game of getting ourselves invited too. Whenever Teddy was the guest of honor, there were always two or three girls from school in attendance. If I could get to the favored house walking, I was one of them.

Being a good guest meant bringing a gift to my hostess. Sometimes it was a rice pudding. Rich in thick custard and topped with a sprinkling of freshly grated nutmeg. Or I might come with a bunch of sweet-smelling flowers in hand.

Time and again I made it my business to be where Teddy was. He was such a gentleman he didn't even look my way. I sat with my friends, delighted to be near him.

When he came alone to our house the very first time, he brought my mother a tin of hard candy and my father a Cuban cigar. After dinner, he and my father walked out together to smoke as men did then.

Papa had a lot to say after Teddy left. "That teacher of yours is a deep thinker, good head on his shoulders."

"Do you like him, Papa?"

"Sure I do, I like any man with sense enough to thank your mother for cooking a fine meal."

"He has good manners then, Papa?"

"Indeed he does. And I enjoy his conversation. He knows how to make a man laugh. I still say it's a shame that he's as black as he is though," Papa repeated.

"What a mean thing to say, Papa."

"Muchie, a smart young man like that will be held back because of his color. That's a fact, though he's a fine, well-spoken gentleman otherwise."

If Papa had suspected my feelings for Teddy, there would have been hell to pay. Far as Papa was concerned, I was still just a child with no business thinking about boys, let alone a man.

I had sense enough to keep how I felt about Teddy to myself. No matter. My attachment to him grew faster than a kudzu vine.

Every morning I raced to school to learn my lessons and memorize the shape of Teddy's hands. I sat daydreaming about the curve of his mouth until a sharp word from his lips brought me back to reality.

He was a formal teacher, calling all his students Mr. This or Miss That. Each time he addressed me as "Miss Tyler," I yearned to hear him call me "Muchie."

I was desperate for a scrap of evidence that he felt something for me. I searched every glance that passed between us. I weighed every word he spoke to me.

As time passed, I became convinced that I had fallen in love with Teddy. It was the first time I'd ever loved anyone outside of my family, and I didn't know quite what to make of the feeling.

I had the hardest time not blurting out that I loved him. Fear of looking like a fool made me hold my tongue.

I tried to get his attention by pretending to be stupid. Teddy had no patience with slow students. He threatened to send me back to the primer grades with Miss Elliott if I didn't apply myself to my studies.

Immediately, I mended my ways. I had to be near him, no matter what.

Failing at being a dunderhead, I decided to dazzle him with my brilliance. He praised me when I did well in school. But it was the same praise he offered to every good student.

One day, near the end of his first year as our teacher, I could bear it no longer. I gathered up my courage to speak to him after the other students were gone.

I walked right straight to his desk and leaned toward him, "Mr. Preston, what would you do if you found out one of your students loved you?"

I whispered the question, standing red faced and feeling foolish as soon as the words were out of my mouth.

He appeared taken off guard by my question and would not

meet my gaze. I was determined to stay until he gave me an answer.

"How old are you, Miss Tyler?"

It was not the response I expected and surely not the one I hoped for. But I told him my age with some pride, "I'm nearly seventeen, Mr. Preston. My birthday is in October."

"And how old is this hypothetical student of yours?"

"She's the same age, Mr. Preston."

"I see. And how do you know this, Miss Tyler?"

"Because it is me, I mean it is I who love you, Mr. Preston. I love you, Teddy, and I've loved you from the first moment I saw you, and I can't live another minute without knowing if you love me too."

There, I'd done it, I'd spoken the nickname I'd heard Reverend Leete use. I'd said what had been growing in my heart for months. Teddy stood up and walked over to the windows.

"Miss Tyler, you flatter me. I am not worthy of your love, dear child. You are much too young and innocent to know what you are saying."

"Stop it, don't talk to me that way. I am *not* a child. Girls my age get married all the time. I know exactly what I'm saying. I love you, Teddy. I love you with all my heart."

"And what would your father say about this love you profess?"

"My father?"

"People talk, Muchie. I've heard how your father feels about color. He won't take kindly to his daughter being with a man as dark as I am."

"I don't care about any of that silliness. All I care about is you. Do you care about me even a little?"

"Everyone calls you Muchie, don't they? May I?"

"Oh, yes, Teddy, yes. Please say my name. Call me Muchie."

"Well, Muchie, I am 10 years older than you are. I've been a soldier overseas. I've seen a lot more of this world than you have. People can't change who they are. You're a nicely brought-up girl, and your family has plans for you. They want you to get an education. I'm your teacher. That's all I can ever be to you."

"No, I won't let you say that. You are way more than my teacher. Teddy. You're the man I love. I'll never love anyone else but you. All I need to know is do you love me? Can you love me? You've got to tell me, Teddy, please tell me if you feel anything for me."

I clasped my hands and held them over my mouth, begging Teddy with my eyes.

He stood up and walked away. When he turned he stretched out his hands as if to touch me. Instead, he balled his hands into fists.

"Muchie, I grew up in north Louisiana. We lived so far back up in the country all we had for entertainment was waving to the train when it went by on Saturday night."

"Well, that's all right, Teddy, I'm used to living in the country. I'd be happy to live anywhere as long as it was with you."

"Hush, Muchie, let me finish. My daddy was a well-set-up man, what folks call a man of means, and he supported two families. Lots of men did back then. Some still do, even here in Mississippi, quiet as it's kept. My daddy was a fair-skinned man who married the girl his people picked out for him."

"Your father married your mother, so did mine. I don't understand why you're telling me this."

"It wasn't my mother he married, Muchie. My daddy took a lawfully wedded wife to satisfy his parents, but he'd already given his heart to someone else. He loved my mother, Emma Preston. Daddy moved her off the Creek reservation where her people lived to satisfy himself. He kept her as his shadow wife."

"I don't know what that means, Teddy."

"My mother never got a gold ring or marriage papers. Daddy never stood up before God and the world to claim her. He bought her some land and built her a sturdy house. When I was born, he took care of me, same as his legal wife's children. It was all supposed to be a big secret, but everybody knew."

"But why, why, if he loved her so, why did he marry someone else?" I couldn't believe anyone would do such a thing. I shook my head, refusing to accept the idea.

"Sometimes love doesn't have a thing to do with marriage, Muchie. Maybe it was because my mother didn't have property or the right connections. But, I truly believe it was because she was too dark for his family to accept."

"That's stupid *and* horrible."

"And it's probably exactly the way your father feels about me."

"No, he's not like that. He respects you, Teddy. He thinks you're a wonderful man. Papa is always saying how refined you are and how smart you are and . . ."

My voice faded. I remembered that Papa's compliments in Teddy's presence always ended with his comment later about it being a shame Teddy was so black.

It made me cry to think my dear papa could say such an ignorant thing. I reached out to Teddy, needing comfort as I struggled to defend Papa in my own mind.

He held up his hands, keeping me in my place.

"I can make Papa understand, Teddy. He's a healer. He knows what it's like to be different. Papa always says fear is what makes people judge each other. He's told me time and again how wrong that is."

Shaking his head, Teddy gave me a sad smile. It made me cry even harder.

"That day I came to your house with the missionaries, when I first saw you, Muchie. You had blue ribbons in your hair. You looked beautiful. Happy. Young. Full of hope. It was a joy to see you flitting about in your little apron. But there was something in your eyes that day, Muchie. Something I had no right to see. Child that you were, child that you are. Do you know what I'm talking about, Muchie?"

"I do, although I had no idea you saw me looking at you. I wanted to bite your cheek, Teddy. You were like a sweet, ripe plum, and I wanted to taste you on my lips."

"You are bold, Muchie. I have to give you that." He chuckled.

"Teddy, I never felt like that before I saw you. It was like the whole world changed for me. All I wanted was to be with you."

"I felt it too. You kept popping up wherever I went last summer, and I'd see that look in your eye and it made me question my sanity. But I will not let you ruin your life."

"Teddy, don't you see that without you I can have no life? You are the reason I wake up every morning. You are my life. If you love me, I can live my life. Please Teddy, please. Say you love me."

"Muchie, this whole year I've watched you eagerly grab at learning. At life. I love your courage and your kindness, your beauty, your sweet innocence. God help me, I love you."

I rushed into Teddy's arms, and we held each other close for a moment.

His face was stern, and tears sparkled in his soft brown eyes when he pulled away from me.

"You must listen to me, Muchie. I promised Win I'd stay here for three years. It will take at least that long to get the school on a solid footing. I'm your teacher, and it would be wrong for us to sneak around to be together, much as I've come to love you."

"I can wait, Teddy. I can wait as long as I must."

"When you graduate, I'll speak to your father. That is, if your feelings haven't changed by then."

"The only way they'll ever change is for me to love you all the more, Teddy."

"Until then, we must go on as before. As if there is nothing between us. Can you make me that promise, Muchie?"

"If you want me to promise I'll fly to the moon in my night shift or never speak again until God sends heavenly Glory, you know I'll say yes, Teddy. Yes, yes, yes. Of course, I'll do as you say."

I sealed my promise with our first kiss. Pressing my pursed lips hard against his, I kissed him full on the mouth.

I nearly collapsed from the sheer pleasure of kissing him. The rough brush of his moustache made his lips feel all the softer.

He held my face in his hands for a moment, kissing me back. Then he slid his hands down the curve of my throat to grip my shoulders. His lips parted slightly and I followed his lead. I was dizzy feeling his tongue touch mine. He kissed me until I could barely think.

"Go home, Muchie, go home now," Teddy ordered with a choking sound in his voice, pushing me toward the door.

More than anything on earth, I wanted to kiss Teddy again. Instead I blew him a kiss and ran from the classroom.

All the way home, I relived our kiss, laughing out loud because Teddy loved me. It wasn't until I got to our front gate that I remembered my promise.

Squaring my shoulders, I composed myself. At supper my face revealed nothing.

Chapter Ten

1925

I'd never had a secret before. Teddy and I were the only ones who knew we were in love. It didn't change the way we acted, but it certainly changed the way I felt.

Walking to school each morning, all I thought about was being with Teddy. Finally, I believed what Tyler Mama had said about love. It *did* make everything seem possible.

Counting the mosquito hawks that buzzed along the path, I decided that an even number meant love could change Papa's mind.

If I saw two of the insects mating in flight, it meant Papa wouldn't let his feelings about the color of Teddy's skin stand in the way of my happiness. Hadn't he let me put aside healing when he saw it had broken my heart?

The mosquito hawks gave me a different answer every day, but all I could do anyway was bide my time.

The year was drawing to an end, and I couldn't bear the

thought of three long months without Teddy. I spent every moment I could at school because he was there.

When the whole building throbbed with youthful energy, during recess Teddy organized relay races in an open field behind the school.

"Each team has four runners. I want two younger children and two older ones per team. To make the races fair," he said, assigning the teams.

"You girls collect some sticks. We'll use some for batons and the big ones to stake out the lanes with twine. Miss Elliott, will you act as judge?"

I didn't much like the way Miss Elliott dimpled and blushed when Teddy spoke to her. But I knew better than to let my jealousy show.

The teams lined up, and Teddy waved his handkerchief to start the race. Children clutched their sticks and ran hard, trying to be the winning team. On the last leg of the race, a little boy fell and knocked himself in the head with his stick. His arm was pinned at an awkward angle beneath him. That put an end to the day's racing.

"You boys go fetch Reverend Harper. And get the first-aid kit," Teddy ordered. "Keep the other children outside, Miss Elliott."

He carried the groggy boy into a classroom. I followed him when Miss Elliott wasn't looking.

"Is he hurt bad, Mr. Preston?" I asked.

The little boy looked pitiful stretched out on the floor. I felt sorry for him.

"It appears his arm is broken. See that knob? I think it's bone pressing against the skin. And he's got a gash on the side of his head too. Reverend Harper will need to send for a doctor."

"Let me see."

I knelt beside the little boy and peered at his head and arm. I gently ran my hands over him. He whimpered beneath my touch.

"That's all right. No one's going to hurt you. Just rest easy," I said.

I stroked his forehead and laid my hand on the place where his skin was turning blue. The boy's fear and pain throbbed through my hands strong enough to make me gasp and close my eyes.

I felt myself falling, falling, into a place where there was no sound and no light. There was only a frightened little boy falling with me, lost in the quiet darkness.

The sound of pounding feet and shouting voices broke our fall.

"Here's the first-aid kit, Mr. Preston."

"Reverend Harper is on his way down the hall right now."

I opened my eyes. The little boy was sitting up enjoying being the center of attention.

"Well, son, it looks like you're no worse for the wear," Reverend Harper boomed, checking the boy's arm and head. "Those silly children had me thinking you were half dead in here."

"Sorry for disturbing your lunch, Harper. Seems like it was a false alarm," Teddy announced, slightly puzzled.

"No harm done. Now you children take this young fellow with you and get back to your recess."

I stood to follow Reverend Harper and the others from the room.

"Miss Tyler? Are you all right?"

"Yes, I'm fine. I felt funny a few minutes ago, but I'm fine now."

When we were the only ones left, Teddy asked me, "What happened just now, Muchie? What did you do to that boy?"

"I don't know what you mean. He was scared and hurt and I tried to . . . I don't know what happened. It was like I was falling and then the next thing I knew, well you saw, didn't you?"

"What I saw doesn't match with what I know. That boy's arm was definitely broken, and I expect he had a concussion too. But he walked out of here fit as a fiddle."

"Maybe you were mistaken about his arm?"

"I've seen enough combat injuries to recognize a simple fracture. That boy's arm was broken and now it's not. I knew your father was a healer, but I didn't know you were one too, Muchie."

"I'm not, not anymore, Teddy. My grandmother trained me to be a midwife. When she died, I gave it up. She said I had the healing gift, but it didn't save her. I think she was mistaken about me."

"You're something else, Muchie. If what I saw you do today isn't healing, I don't know what to call it. Go get yourself some fresh air. You look like you need it."

Instead of allowing relay races at recess again, Reverend Harper decided to teach us to play baseball. He assigned boys and girls to each team, drilling us on how to throw, hit and catch.

Some of the girls were too timid to take their turn at bat. I loved the thrill of feeling my bat connect with the ball and watching it sail over the field as I dashed around the bases. Once, I slid home in a flurry of dust and petticoats, knocking the catcher down in the process.

That time, I was safe.

At the end of the year, Teddy gave his students work to do over summer vacation. He handed each of us two books to read.

"I expect excellent book reports from you. Write down my address and mail your reports to me as you complete them. The first week of the new school year I'll let you know how you did," he said.

Privately, Teddy gave me my instructions. "Don't write to me more often than your schoolmates do, Muchie. It might cause talk. I'll think of you constantly and I'll miss you every day," he said with a smile that was almost as good as a kiss.

"We'll be together soon, won't we, Teddy?"

"Before you know it, I promise."

Since I couldn't send Teddy letters telling him everything that was in my heart, I kept a diary pouring out my love and plans for our life together.

I drew little illustrations in the margins. The pictures enlivened my stories about putting up preserves with Mother, and Reverend Harper holding Sunday school under the trees. To protect my diary from prying eyes, I only wrote in it at night and kept it hidden far back beneath my mattress.

True to my word, I said nothing about our love to anyone.

Reverend Harper visited many parents of children in the upper school throughout the summer. He came to our house three or four times.

"Your daughter is one of our best students," he told Mother and Papa as they sat on the porch sipping cool tea.

"Thank you, I appreciate hearing that. Muchie always did have a good head on her shoulders," Papa commented with pride.

"I think she's smart enough for college. How do you feel about that idea?"

"Well, Reverend Harper, that depends. I can't see as how a person with college would be happy living on a farm. I'd hate to lose Muchie."

"I understand your concern, Mr. Tyler. But you've said yourself you want more for your children than being farmers or farmers' wives. Muchie could be a teacher or a nurse or work in an office somewhere."

"That would take her clean out of Mississippi now, wouldn't it, Reverend Harper?"

"It might, but maybe she'd come back and teach in one of the church schools. That is a possibility, especially if she goes to a church college."

After each of Reverend Harper's visits, Papa and Mother stayed on the porch talking late into the evening.

Papa found me in Tyler Mama's herb cottage one morning in the middle of my weekly cleaning. I was sweeping the floor when I noticed him standing in the door with his arms folded across his chest. Wiping my hands on my apron I put my broom aside.

"Come on in, Papa, and have a seat. I can use a minute of rest myself."

"Muchie, our preacher seems to think you have what it takes to go to college. Your mother and I have been giving the idea some thought."

"I'd love to be able to go to college, Papa. If you can spare me, that is. Learning makes me real happy."

"I know it does, child. But college is a serious matter. Takes money and time. I imagine we'll manage with the money. Don't know how I feel about you being gone from home for months on end."

"It would be hard for me too, Papa."

"Let's keep thinking about it a while longer then, Muchie."

Papa stood up and walked around the little cottage. He touched the empty shelves and smiled when he found one little bottle that had rolled to the back. It bore a label covered with Tyler Mama's graceful handwriting. Papa wrapped the bottle in his handkerchief and put it in the bib of his overalls.

"You ever give any thought to healing anymore, Muchie? Using your gift like your grandmother said?"

"I wish I could tell you yes, Papa. But I just don't have the heart for healing. Not anymore."

He nodded his head, took another look around the room and walked out the door.

Chapter Eleven

1926

Summer in Mississippi drags on with each day hotter than the one before. I'd had just about enough of farm work, and the first day of school couldn't come fast enough for me. It rained one day, and I took that opportunity to fuss with my hair.

"How does my hair look, Mother?" I asked, primping in front of the mirror.

I had combed my hair three different ways already. I wanted to find the perfect style to wear when school opened. With only two weeks to get ready for seeing Teddy again, I didn't want to waste any free time.

"It looks fine, Muchie. Here, let me brush the back for you. Any reason you're doing your hair in fancy ways today?"

"Just getting ready for the first day of my final year in school is all."

"I guess that's reason enough. You'll be a high school graduate at the end of this year. That's really something, Muchie."

"What do you and Papa think about what Reverend Harper said? About me going to college if I do well this year?"

"We have thought about it long and hard."

"And what do you think? Oh, don't tease me, Mother. Please tell me what you and Papa decided."

"Your papa thinks once you leave the farm, you'll never come back. I think that's true, but it doesn't worry me the way it worries him."

"You'll let me go then, Mother? Isn't it exciting? But I don't know if I want to go and leave behind everyone at home."

"Is it home, or one special person you don't want to leave?"

My face flushed red. There was no sense denying a thing.

"Why, Muchie, I do believe you have a crush on some boy around here. Be careful, that's all. Your papa won't stand for any foolishness."

I wanted to tell Mother it wasn't just some boy. It was Teddy I didn't want to leave. Teddy. And it wasn't a crush but true love. The only drawback I could see to college was leaving Teddy. I was certain I could not survive a whole year without him.

"Yes, ma'am," was all I said to my mother.

The first semester passed like a dream with Teddy and Reverend Harper giving me extra work to prepare me for college. When I did math problems at the chalkboard Teddy stood behind me to check my work. It felt like there was a magnet drawing me to him. I wanted to fall backwards into his embrace.

It took nearly everything I had in me to keep from flinging my arms around him before I left for home each afternoon. Holding back my feelings left me tense and irritable with everyone except Teddy.

But I kept my promise. And he kept his.

In June the first class in our new upper school held graduation exercises. The next day, Papa threw a big fish fry to celebrate. He invited Teddy and Reverend Harper and Miss Elliott and half of Wayne County.

The boys set up long tables all over our yard that were soon covered with what looked like an acre of food. Women prepared great platters of ripe red tomatoes and sweet yellow onions sliced thick and sprinkled with vinegar and a bit of sugar.

Sitting under the trees, mothers supervised little children who shucked mountains of early corn to boil. The corn was so tender and sweet that children kept sneaking bites of it when no one was looking.

One table was home to corn bread muffins, pans of spoon bread and big trays of puffy, butter-topped yeast rolls. Jars of preserves and pickles, tubs of hand-churned butter, bowls of honeycomb, pitchers of lemonade and sweet tea filled another table.

My maiden lady aunties were the dessert brigade, and their arsenal included nearly every sweet known to southeast Mississippi. There was fudge candy, peanut butter cookies, spiced sweet pecans, plain pound cake, lemon pound cake and chocolate pound cake.

They'd baked devil's food cake with white icing and yellow cake with chocolate frosting. People brought fruit cobblers and puddings to add to the bounty. Several of the men organized the older children to hand crank tubs of homemade ice cream.

Mother outdid herself with gigantic bowls of yellow potato salad that she nestled into even bigger bowls full of ice. Her special recipe included freshly made mayonnaise and coarse mustard mixed with sweet pickles chopped fine and cubes of green onion, celery and bell peppers. Hard-boiled eggs cut in quarters graced the top of the bowls.

At first, the men stood around talking to Papa while he fried enough fish to fill half the Chickasawhay River. Every now and then, several men stepped behind the trees to sneak a swig of gully run whisky.

Some of the men played horseshoes. Others set up checkers and dominoes, challenging the older boys to try and beat them. They started sack races that soon ended in disaster. Corn liquor sipped in the Mississippi sun had grown men falling down shrieking like loons before they got to the finish line.

A few bold young couples walked around together. But there were always people watching to make sure they didn't go too far.

With pride, I saw Teddy making his rounds. He spoke to all the children. Then he complimented the women, making them blush. Teddy joked with the men until they shouted with laughter. It delighted me to see him use his charm to such good effect.

Reverend Harper blessed the food with uncharacteristic brevity, pleading hunger.

Soon plates were piled high with fried fish and everything else. People got down to the business at hand.

We ate ourselves silly that day, laughing and talking as we enjoyed the unseasonably mild weather. Now and then, a gentle breeze blew across the yard.

Even the ants and flies and yellow jackets that usually plague a fish fry were on good behavior.

My cousins had brought their guitars, fiddles and mouth harps to the party. When they began to play I dragged Papa from his seat and pulled Mother into the open space beneath the trees. We danced to the old songs. Entire families lumbered to their feet to join us.

Some people danced in couples, with little girls standing on their daddy's feet and little boys clutching their mothers about the waist. Others danced in threes like Mother, Papa and me, swinging each other in time with the music.

There were even a few old souls dancing alone, content to en-joy the familiar music with a partner only they could see.

"May I have this dance, Miss Tyler?" Teddy asked when the musicians moved smoothly into modern tunes.

"You most certainly may, Mr. Preston," I said. No need for busybodies to know we were on a first-name basis.

"This is the first time I've held you in my arms in public, Muchie," he said softly, leading me as smoothly as if we'd danced a hundred times together.

"It feels wonderful to me, Teddy," I whispered. "Your hand on my back is making me breathless."

I forgot my promise. All that mattered was the jolt that went through me when his thigh brushed against mine on each turn.

Teddy was a good dancer and sure of himself. He guided me skillfully around the roots of the big trees, never missing a step. I leaned back in his arms and smiled up at him.

"I've never been happier in my whole life than I am right this minute, Teddy."

"I plan to speak to your father today, Muchie. Unless you want me to wait?"

"Of course not, Teddy. The sooner you ask him, the sooner we can be together. Do you want me to go with you when you talk to him?"

"No, that wouldn't do. As long as I know you're still willing, your father and I can settle the rest between us."

When I noticed there were fewer people dancing, to avoid be-ing conspicuous, I curtsied to Teddy and went to help Mother.

Out of the corner of my eye, I could see Papa and Teddy strolling together. Both were smoking cigars as they walked to-ward the fields.

After the better part of an hour, Papa came back alone. He

tossed his cigar to the ground, stomping it to shreds beneath his boots. Then he spit and stormed over to my mother.

Red-faced, Papa pulled Mother aside and talked to her, nodding several times in my direction.

I made myself scarce, trying to see if I could spot Teddy in the crowd. He was nowhere to be found.

Chapter Twelve

1926

All our guests were gone, the dishes washed and the yard restored to order. Keeping myself busy I'd managed to avoid Papa ever since I saw him storming at Mother during the fish fry. I was walking to the house after feeding the chickens when Mother called me. She and Papa were sitting in shadow on the porch.

"Come sit with us, Muchie, we need to have ourselves a little talk," Mother said. Her voice was as cold as a well digger's knuckles, and there was no way for me to escape.

"Muchie, I need you to know we're not very happy right now." Papa spit on the ground and patted a space on the swing next to him.

There was nothing for me to say. I sat in the corner of the swing leaving plenty of room between Papa and me and began tying the ends of my braids into knots.

"Mr. Preston asked me if you were spoken for." Papa spit again.

"Yes, Papa."

"He wants to call on you with the intention of marriage plainly on his mind."

"Yes, Papa."

"Stop fiddling with your hair, Muchie, before you make it fall out," Mother said.

"I don't know what made him suggest such an outrageous idea. It put me in a damn awkward position, Muchie. He's a fine man and a fine teacher. But there's no way in hell I'll let him call on you."

"He's an educated man, Papa. You said yourself he has good manners. Please let him come around. Then you can get to know him better. It would mean the world to me."

"Are you saying this man matters to you, Muchie?" Papa forgot himself and spit right on the porch floor. It made Mother suck her teeth. She reached over and swatted Papa's knee with her handkerchief.

"He does indeed, Papa. He means the world to me. I would be honored to have him for my husband. Someday."

Papa glared at me and got up from the swing to pace the porch. I could hear him cracking his knuckles as he walked back and forth.

"Mr. Preston is very dark, Muchie, and he wouldn't make you a proper husband. You must always think of your children," Mother emphasized, as if Teddy's skin color would disable any children we might have.

"That's not fair, Mother. What difference does Teddy's color make? Of all the wonderful things he is, all you can talk about is color. It's not fair."

"You apologize to your mother this minute, Muchie."

Papa paused his pacing to shake his finger in my face. I pulled far back into the swing and it creaked on its hinges. He was heating up for a Tyler shouting match.

Mother dabbed at her eyes with the hanky she was clutching in her blue-veined hand. Her voice quavered when she spoke, "It may not be fair, Muchie, but color matters here in Mississippi."

"But it doesn't matter to me," I said as images of Teddy filled my head.

Teddy was black as Mississippi soil. He was cast-iron skillet black, the color little girls sang about when they skipped rope. "The blacker the berry, the sweeter the juice. Jump, jump, jump 'til it turns you loose."

"Get this straight, Muchie. We will not allow you to have anything to do with him," Papa stated.

"Papa, I swear I'll never marry anyone if I can't marry Teddy."

"Then I fear you'll be an old maid, Muchie. What a pity," Papa spoke to me through clenched teeth.

"It isn't right, Papa, that you should hate Teddy because he's dark."

"You've got no place telling me what's right and wrong, Muchie. You're a child. You know nothing of this world. I don't hate that man, far from it. What I hate is the idea of you marrying him."

"I will marry him, Papa, or I'll surely die."

"You'll marry who I say and when I say. If you speak another word, you'll die when I say. Get out of my sight, Muchie. Go now, before you make me forget I am a peaceful man."

I ran to Tyler Mama's herb cottage to escape Papa's anger. I sat crying with my head on the table and I didn't know Mother had followed me until she spoke.

"Muchie, your papa is a good man. He only wants what's best for you," Mother said, rubbing her hand in small circles on my shoulder.

"But I love Teddy, I love him, Mother."

"Shhh, don't talk about it anymore, Muchie. Go on and cry, you'll feel better after you cry."

Mother kissed the top of my head and pressed her handkerchief into my hand before she left.

It wasn't fair. Why couldn't she and Papa see that color was no reason for denying love? I wrote to Teddy on a piece of paper I found in Tyler Mama's cupboard telling him I was his for the taking regardless of what Papa said.

Then I realized I had no way to give him the note. I folded it into a tiny square and tucked it in the bosom of my dress.

Cousin Helen proved to be an unexpected ally. "Muchie, if you want, I think I can get a message to Mr. Preston for you. It's wrong of them to keep you apart," she whispered when we were alone in the kitchen several days after the fish fry.

"Would you really do that for me, Helen? You might get in trouble."

"Don't worry, I'll be careful. Do you and Mr. Preston love each other?"

"We do, Helen. More than life itself."

Grateful for one sympathetic soul, I told Helen about Teddy. She had a romantic disposition and wanted to hear every detail. I showed her the note I'd written to Teddy.

"You give it to me, Muchie. I'll be your go-between if I can."

Days passed as I did the tedious mending that was now my lot. Papa barely spoke to me. Mother spoke only to chide me for bringing discord into our family.

"Shame on you, Muchie. Your papa is very upset about the way you're acting," Mother snapped when she handed me yet another basket of clothes needing repair.

"The least you can do is look pleasant while you're working," she said. "When you finish the mending, you can get started on the washing. Hard work will do you good."

Papa had built a stone platform about waist high in a corner of the yard near the well. The washtubs sat on the platform eliminating much of the bending and stooping that made washing clothes hard on the back.

As I scrubbed a mountain of dirty socks and underclothes against the washboard, I busied my mind composing passionate letters to Teddy.

Late at night with my hands raw from the hot water and strong soap I scribbled as best I could on paper torn from my old school tablets, hoping Helen would be able to smuggle my letters to Teddy.

There was no way I could see Teddy because I wasn't allowed out of the house without an adult chaperone. Dear cousin Helen was my only salvation.

"No one will ever suspect me, Muchie. They think I'm too scared of my own shadow to do anything brave. But I'll help you any way I can. You can count on me."

"Be careful, Helen. If Papa ever gets wind of what you're doing, you'll be stuck doing mending and laundry along with me."

"This is the only adventure I'm likely to have, Muchie. It's exciting for me."

In every letter he wrote, Teddy repeated his determination to persuade my parents to let us marry. He told me not to give up hope. There had to be a way.

It made me feel bad to deceive my parents and make Helen sneak around. It wasn't fair. I wanted to love Teddy out loud, claim him as mine for the world to see. But Papa and Mother left me no alternative. I wrote Teddy every night and, as often as she dared, Helen played Cupid for us.

"Why don't you elope with him, Muchie? Go somewhere far away and get married. By the time your papa finds you he won't be able to do a thing about it," Helen suggested.

"I couldn't do a thing like that, Helen. Papa would never forgive me."

"He'll never change his mind either," she said.

"Helen, I'm surprised at you. Teddy thinks he can convince Papa and I believe him."

"Maybe so, Muchie. But I doubt it," Helen said sadly.

"Soon as Papa cools off from being mad he'll stop making me miserable. I bet he will change his mind because he loves me."

In case I was wrong, I gave Teddy a surefire way to get around Papa's stubbornness. If I was with child, Papa would certainly let us marry.

Teddy was too much of a gentleman even to respond.

Chapter Thirteen

1926

"Muchie, you must stop moping around the house looking like a sick calf. I've had just about enough of your pouting," Papa announced one morning as I sat on the porch mending sheets.

Since Papa refused to listen whenever I tried to talk to him about Teddy, I conveyed my sorrow and disappointment by putting away my colorful hair ribbons and looking as pitiful as I could. Every day my head was covered with a dark rag and I wore the same faded dress and a dingy old apron to do my work.

"I'm not pouting, Papa. I'm pining away. I may die of a broken heart."

"I'd sooner see you dead and buried in your grave than married to that man," he replied angrily.

"Do you really mean that, Papa?" Tears welled up in my eyes. I tilted my head to one side and looked at Papa. He turned away to spit over the porch rail.

"I wish I did, Muchie, but I love you too much. What makes

you so blasted willful though? You're too young to be this stubborn." Papa shook his head and sat on the porch steps. He looked across the yard into the fields, cracking his knuckles and frowning.

"Papa, please don't be mad with me."

"You've acted a fool long enough, Muchie. I won't let you make me lose my religion. What you need is a change of scenery."

"Oh, Papa. You'll send me to college?" I dropped my mending to run sit beside Papa. I hugged him tight, happy for the first time in weeks. He rested his cheek on the top of my head for an instant.

"No, Muchie, I'm thinking you should go to your godparents for a spell. Work in the mill. That ought to put some sense in your head."

"Papa, please don't do that. Let me go to college instead, like Reverend Harper said. I promise I'll come back. Reverend Harper said I could teach here once I graduate college."

"Too late for that now, Muchie. What's to keep you from getting away at college and then running off with that man? Your godparents will keep you on a short leash. That's what you need to curb your willful spirit."

My pleading and crying failed to move Papa. I was sent away to live with my godparents clear across the state of Mississippi near Vicksburg.

"Muchie, we know you and your folks had a falling out, but don't think we're mad with you because of it," Nan Nan told me the day I arrived.

"We're happy you're here. It will be like finally having a daughter," Parran explained as he introduced me to their six sons.

Nan Nan was a perfect lady, but she ran her home to accommodate its bluff and noisy male character. They lived in a wide two-story house with running water *and* a front and back parlor.

Their dining room was big as a barn, and ten could sit around the kitchen table to eat, which they seemed to do for hours at a time.

Meals were enormous like the house itself and as heavy as the furniture.

"Do you cook like this every morning?" I asked when faced with a breakfast that included eggs, ham, biscuits, grits, fried potatoes, corn beef hash, slabs of bacon, baked apples, buttermilk, coffee and corn bread muffins.

"In the winter, there is a bit more food." Nan Nan laughed. "Boys must eat to keep up their strength, you know."

"Let me help you with the cooking sometimes, Nan Nan. I'm a fair hand in the kitchen if I do say so myself," I offered after a supper even more massive than breakfast had been.

"That's a fine idea, Muchie. The way to a man's heart is through his stomach," she said mysteriously.

"And I've had plenty practice at mending too, Nan Nan."

"There's work for you to do here at the house helping me, Muchie, but your papa is determined for you to work at the mill," Nan Nan said.

"You'll be in the office, Muchie. Keeping time sheets for the workers and preparing their pay envelopes. There's other record keeping for you to do as well. You'll have your hands full up there, but I won't let any harm come to you," Parran assured me.

"What's it like at the sawmill, Parran?"

"It can get pretty rough and tumble, but the workers are good men by and large. I understand you graduated high school. Smart girl like you must enjoy studying. Is that right?"

"Yes, sir. I love to learn new things. Reverend Harper back home said I should go to college. Maybe Papa will let me one day."

"College you say? That would be something. You know much about history?"

"We studied world history and ancient history and one semester of Mississippi history too."

"I declare, that's a lot of studying. Well, I'm going to tell you the history of the sawmill. You know anything about that?"

"No, sir."

"Used to be only slaves worked timber. Then freedom came and everything changed. In all the confusion after the war some free men of color were lucky enough to get hold of a lumber camp."

"How'd they manage that? Colored people in Wayne County have a hard time holding on to their farmland."

"I imagine there was some trickery involved. Money changing hands, records disappearing, things like that," Parran chuckled as he explained.

"The men went looking to hire the former slaves. They knew how to work timber and all of them were out of a job. Let them bring their families with them and earn an honest wage for an honest day's work. The lumber camp threw in housing and meals and schooling for the children."

"They'd be crazy not to take a deal like that."

"Just about every man who'd slaved at the camp came back to get his start as a free man. Some moved on. But a good number stayed and their sons stayed and now their grandsons are working timber for me."

"It must be a real good place to work, Parran. You like it there, don't you?"

"Well now, Muchie, I'll let you in on a little secret. Remember those free men of color I told you about? Well, my father was one of them. The sawmill belonged to him and he left it to me. I let folks think I'm just a hired hand to keep the night riders off me. It's my insurance policy you might say. Should anyone ever ask you, just say some rich white men down in New Orleans own the mill."

"Yes, sir, I will."

Being the only girl in a houseful of boys was something of a shock. My godbrothers ranged in age from 15 to 25, and even the younger ones were big, strapping fellows with loud voices and hearty, backslapping ways.

They fell all over themselves vying for my attention. It tickled me to see them slick down their hair and spruce themselves up for meals.

"Looks like you've made quite an impression on my boys, Muchie," Nan Nan offered. "I hope something nice comes of it."

"I appreciate their kindness just as I appreciate yours and Parran's," I said politely as I kneaded bread dough on cool marble.

Nan Nan had a fascinating contraption installed beneath a cabinet right above the counter where I was working. It was a flour canister with its own sifter.

"Too much flour will make the bread heavy, Muchie."

"I'm sorry, Nan Nan. I just can't get enough of turning the little crank and watching the flour fall down."

"I tell you what, Muchie. You can make a few pies when you finish the bread since you like playing with my flour bin," she laughed.

"I wish I could help you instead of going to the mill with Parran," I said.

"Your papa made his wishes plain, Muchie. I've enjoyed these few days with you. I imagine over the course of a year, there'll be other times we can cook together."

"A year? Papa wants me to stay a year?"

I gave the bread dough a vicious slap and pushed it aside. What I really wanted to do was throw it on the floor and stomp it the way Papa had done his cigar. I was mad enough to spit myself.

Instead I rubbed the flour from my hands and sat down at the kitchen table. Nan Nan stopped what she was doing to join me.

"He wants you to stay long enough to get used to us. You'll like living here, Muchie, once you get over being upset with your papa."

"It's not fair. Papa acts like it's me at fault, but it's really him. He treats me like I turned into a hoochie-coochie dancer with the traveling circus. Nan Nan, did he tell you why he's mad with me?"

"All he said was you were willful and disobedient and he needed our help. Your papa didn't have to say anything else."

"The reason he's raising so much sand is he doesn't want me to marry a good, decent, hardworking, college-educated man who loves me. Does that sound willful and disobedient to you?"

"Is that all there is to the story, Muchie?"

"All that matters. Except I love him too."

"Why is your papa dead set against it then?" Nan Nan put her hand under my chin to look me right in the eye. "Why, Muchie?"

"Papa says Teddy's dark skin will hold him back. That's why Papa won't let us marry."

"Try to look at this from your papa's side. Plenty folks in Mississippi and other parts of the country have been trying to breed the black out for generations. It may not be fair, but it *is* true. Family is all we have to see us through good times and bad, Muchie. Don't tear yours apart over something you can't change."

Chapter Fourteen

❦

1926

Parran proved to be a methodical teacher. He showed me how to travel to the sawmill by wagon, on foot and on horseback, alerting me to every bend and potential danger in the road.

"I doubt you'll ever need to be by yourself, Muchie, either coming or going. But it's best to be prepared. Pretty girl like you can't be too careful," Parran told me.

He gave me a pistol and assigned my godbrothers to drill me on loading and unloading until I could do it with my eyes closed.

"Have you ever fired a weapon, Muchie?"

Parran set up half a dozen tin cans on stumps. He nailed sheets of white paper to posts at several levels. Then he handed me the gun.

"No, sir. Papa kept all the guns locked up at home. There was no cause for me to touch them."

"Let's have a little target practice then. You don't have to be a crack shot, only steady. If anybody ever bothers you, be it man or animal, just aim at its middle. Whatever you hit will slow down anything that means you harm. Then get away as fast as you can."

My first day at the mill, I knew its history, how to shoot and how to get there but very little else. Parran soon remedied that. He spent one whole week going over how to match up the time sheets to the pay envelopes.

"Men don't take kindly to mistakes in their pay. There's different rates for different work and you must note both the hours and the rate on every pay envelope," he warned. "I'm the one who gives them their money, and I don't want any problems."

Once I got the hang of payroll, he taught me to keep track of what he bought and what he sold. "You write nice, neat ciphers, Muchie," Parran told me. "Time you see what those numbers really mean."

Rough-talking men rode downriver on their logs. Some came from as far away as Canada. Parran met them as soon as they came ashore to begin bargaining.

I stood some distance away and watched. It was a sight to see, Parran examining the logs and gesturing approval or rejection. The loggers storming away only to return within minutes and sell Parran their timber.

Parran was a hard taskmaster, but he was fair as the day was long. He bought logs as low as he decently could. Then he drove his men hard five-and-a-half days a week turning out miles of board and plywood for sale all over the state.

From the scraps the workers produced tons of wood chips and sawdust that Parran sold to paper mills in Alabama. His mill even extracted gum turpentine that fetched a good price from the paint companies.

"Parran, you think there's anything else you can make out of trees?"

"If there is, I haven't found it yet. But when I do, I'll try my best to sell it and turn a profit," he said, wiping his face on his sleeve.

"This isn't bad at all, Parran. Papa made working in the sawmill sound like one step from hell. But I like working here with you," I admitted.

"Make no mistake. A logging camp is a dangerous place. Anytime you put men and machinery together, accidents can happen. Muchie, I'm depending on you to keep the office stocked with emergency supplies."

Tyler Mama's training stood me in good stead. Parran was deadly serious about being prepared. "Use this crate, Muchie. Keep clean lint, wooden splints, cloth bandages and a bottle of whiskey in it. Nan Nan says you're handy. Will you stitch together some slings? I'll knock out a few makeshift crutches to keep on hand."

"Are broken limbs very commonplace at the mill?"

"If a month passes without at least one broken arm or leg I consider us lucky."

I soon discovered there was no sense packing away the grain alcohol and liniment. Just about every day two or three men needed simple first aid.

From the loggers on their felled trees to the cutters who moved the logs through the blades, there were always injuries. Even the men who loaded products for transport got their share of splinters and bumped heads.

I was busy from kin to can't keeping Parran's accounts and tending to his men. Sometimes an entire day passed without me having one single thought of Teddy. But I made up for it at night, when I cried myself to sleep missing him.

Months went by and no matter how many pleading letters I wrote to Papa, he wouldn't relent. He remained firm in his determination to keep Teddy and me apart, even if it meant I could never go home. No amount of reported tears would ever sway my stubborn papa, especially when he couldn't actually see them for himself.

Moss Germaine was a hard-drinking man. Parran warned him time and again not to come to work hungover. My godfather threatened to fire Moss the next time he was drunk on the job.

One day Moss came screaming from the cutting shed to the office where I was balancing the accounts. In his left hand, he was holding two fingers from his right hand.

I hollered for help and sat Moss down to tend to him. I could smell the whiskey on his breath. I pushed his two severed fingers back onto the stubs on his right hand and held them there.

Moss would bleed to death if I let go of his hand. I kept holding his mutilated hand tightly in both my own hands trying to stop the bleeding. All that hot blood pouring out and his screaming with pain made me weak. I felt dizzy. My hands couldn't let go of Moss.

I could barely see Moss through a haze. It was like he was far away. I could feel his fear. Being a cripple. Losing his job. Family starving. All of it, the liquor on his breath, last night's music in his head, made me feel like I was fainting. But I kept his hand in my hands.

I heard a door crash open and then Parran shouting.

"My God, which one of you is bleeding? Muchie, Moss, somebody tell me what happened here."

Moss wasn't screaming anymore. Although his blood covered us both, his fingers were again attached to his hand.

He was too drunk to tell a straight story and I could have been drunk myself for all the sense I made when I tried to tell Parran about the accident.

"He came running in here like a bat out of hell. Moss was screaming and bleeding with his fingers cut off, Parran. I promise you they were."

I gulped water from the dipper Parran held out for me. Taking the dipper from him I filled it again to splash cool water on my face. The water made streaks in the blood that was caking on my hands and the cuffs of my dress. I felt bile rise in my throat and hurried to the door for some fresh air.

"You go on home, Moss, and sleep it off. I'll deal with you tomorrow," Parran ordered. Moss tipped his hat to me before stumbling past me out of the office.

"Parran, listen to me, please. I took his cut-off fingers, stuck them back on his hand and held them there. I was scared he'd bleed to death if I didn't do something."

"I can't say as I know what actually happened to Moss, but I can see you had yourself a real bad scare, Muchie. Best I get you home now. Your Nan Nan will see after you," Parran said.

He rummaged in my first-aid crate and offered me a sip from a bottle of whisky. It smelled like Moss Germaine's breath but I took some anyway. The harsh liquor burned my throat going down. I twisted up my face and took another sip before Parran retrieved the bottle and replaced it in the crate.

"Parran, I'm telling you what happened, but I just don't understand how it can be. If you don't believe me, go ask the men in the cutting shed. They'll tell you what they saw. Same as what I saw."

I kept trying to get in Parran's face, but he refused to look me in the eye.

"God is my witness. Moss Germaine came running in here with his fingers cut off and now his hand is whole. How can that be, Parran? How can that be?"

"Hush now, child. You've had a bad scare. Don't trouble yourself thinking about it anymore now. Just come along and let me get you home to your Nan Nan."

I started crying then.

Soon as we rode up to the house, my Nan Nan ran out, shouting questions at seeing us come home early. Her shouts turned into sobs when she saw me covered with blood.

"Oh, God, who hurt you, Muchie?"

Parran quickly jumped from the wagon and whispered in her ear. She stopped crying to stare silently at me. They gently helped me from the wagon like I might break apart instead of simply being covered with Moss Germaine's blood.

"Oh, baby girl, let's get you washed up and into some clean clothes. Nan Nan will fix you a big cup of strong coffee with plenty cream and sugar to make it good."

As she spoke to me in her soothing voice, it reminded me of the way Tyler Mama used to talk to laboring women. Tyler Mama the healer, who said I shared her gift.

"Nan Nan, do you think? What I mean is, could it be the gift, you know, the healing gift?"

Before I could get out another word, Nan Nan started pulling bloody clothes over my head. She wiped my face and hands clean and wrapped me in a soft quilt when I started shaking.

I found the courage to ask her again while sitting at the kitchen table to drink the steaming cup of hot milk and coffee she placed in front of me.

"Did Parran tell you what happened up at the mill?"

"He did, child. You've had a rough time today, haven't you?"

"That doesn't matter, Nan Nan. I don't even know exactly what happened. I got lost in it. When I was holding Moss Germaine's fingers together something felt like it was drawing the life out of me. Do you think I might be a healer like my papa is? Like Tyler Mama was? Do you, Nan Nan?"

"Muchie, there are more things under the sun that we can't explain than there are flies in the chicken yard. Now, drink your coffee."

After his accident, Moss gave up whisky. He became a model worker. Everyone said that was a miracle, but they treated me differently now. Almost as if they were afraid of me.

My work at the sawmill kept me busy, and I tried to put everything about Moss Germaine out of my mind because it troubled me to think about it.

But it wouldn't go away. I kept remembering how I'd gotten lost in Moss Germaine's wounds and then they vanished.

I'd been lost in Theola's labor and then her breech baby turned. And that little boy at school, the one Teddy swore had a broken arm. Lost again and then his arm was fine.

Why did healing come when I was lost in someone's hurt and pain?

None of it made any sense. I wasn't a healer. That ended for me when Tyler Mama died. But she told me to use my gift and Papa always said I had healing hands.

What did they mean?

Nightly, I prayed for understanding. I asked God to unravel my confusion about the times I'd been lost. I begged God for a way to honor Tyler Mama's wish. I prayed for Papa to let me go home and marry Teddy.

I fell asleep praying and my dreams were a jumble of images that were familiar yet frightening. Worries about healing, about love, about color and home filled my sleep.

Sweet visions of Teddy stretched into nightmares in which I fell and fell into thick walls of blood that blocked my path home. Moss Germaine shook his fingers in my face while Papa and Mother laughed. Light skin became dark.

The dream continued and our farm turned into the new

school where Teddy danced with Miss Elliott. Tyler Mama barred me from the herb cottage holding the little boy with the broken arm on her lap. Theola's baby spoke to me in Tyler Mama's voice saying, "Use your gift."

I woke up exhausted every morning, but none the wiser for my struggles.

Chapter Fifteen

1927

"Muchie, I'm worried about you. You're looking poorly. Doesn't my cooking agree with you, dear?" Nan Nan asked with a smile.

I enjoyed fixing breakfast with her every morning before I went to the mill. It was my only female companionship for the day. Working around a bunch of men got lonely.

"It's not that, Nan Nan."

"Why don't you tell me what it is then? I can see your heart is heavy. You're too young to carry sadness around with you."

"I haven't been sleeping well lately, Nan Nan. Ever since Moss Germaine got hurt, I've been having bad dreams."

"Here, eat a piece of bread before you tell me about your dreams. That way, the bad ones won't come true," she said, handing me a biscuit slathered with fig preserves.

"There's no one particular dream exactly. It's everything all mixed up together. Papa is in my dreams, and he's always mean to me. And Teddy and Mother and Tyler Mama, all of them start out being themselves and then they act different."

"I've heard you cry out in your sleep, Muchie," Nan Nan said.

"You have?"

"Yes, but when I come to your room, you look like you're sound asleep so I haven't disturbed you. Shall I wake you the next time?"

"I hope there won't be a next time, Nan Nan. Maybe just talking to you will help me rest easier from now on."

"It may well, Muchie. You know we're all very fond of you. I want you to be happy here."

"Thank you, Nan Nan. You've been real good to me. But I miss my family. I wish Papa would let me go home."

"I'm sure he will once you're over your feelings for Teddy. One thing I know for certain: your papa is never going to let you marry him. You may as well put that right out of your mind."

I laid my head on the table and started crying.

"Hush, child. Don't take it so hard. I'm sorry you feel bad. Is there anything I can do to make you feel even a little bit better?"

"Would you talk to Papa for me? Try and get him to change his mind?"

"You know I can't do that, Muchie. It isn't my place to interfere with your papa's way."

"Then I guess there's no hope for me. I'll just die a broken heart," I said, crying hard enough to make my stomach hurt.

"That's no way to talk, Muchie. What you need is a nice beau to take your mind off this Teddy of yours. There are plenty suitable young men around here, some of them right in this house. Did you know Justice is sweet on you?"

"Yes, ma'am, he told me. But Justice and I are like brother and sister."

"Good marriages have been built on less. If you don't fancy Justice, I've got five other sons. Any one of them would be proud to court you, Muchie. It's something to think about, dear."

I thought about it enough to write cousin Helen and tell her what Nan Nan had said. Helen and I had devised a code before I left home. She knew the parts of my letter written in blue ink were meant for Teddy.

I couldn't write her very often because that would look suspicious. Helen was my only link to Teddy.

Twice, she'd managed to slip notes from Teddy inside her letter to me with no one the wiser. I kept one in the bosom of my dress to read whenever I was alone.

My darling, Muchie,

I don't know what kind of game your father is playing by sending you away from me, but rest assured I am playing for keeps.

He snatched you out of your childhood home because of your love for me. I know you crave the peace and security you grew up with. I promise you'll have it again, with me. Our home will be full of contentment and tranquility. I'll give you security if I have to work three jobs to do it.

You say you fear I'll forget you. That will never happen no matter how long I must wait for you.

And when you come back to me, as you surely must one day, you'll discover that not only did I wait, but I also made everything ready for your return.

I'll devote my life to your happiness, Muchie.

Teddy

Now that Nan Nan had stepped up her campaign to marry me off to one of her sons, I was desperate to get back to Teddy.

Late in the night, after I'd said my prayers and gone to bed, I remembered Nan Nan was already worried about me looking poorly.

It gave me an idea, a plan to get back home. I would stop eating and make myself sick. Even my loving godparents would not want the responsibility of a sick girl on their hands.

"You're getting thin as a switch engine, Muchie," Nan Nan said after two weeks.

"If you don't eat, you'll ruin your health," Parran said.

"Send that willful girl home. I'll straighten her out," Papa had written, in response to a letter that Nan Nan had sent him.

After nearly a year of pining, it took only three weeks of pushing my plate away to get me home.

When I returned from exile, Papa and Mother had not softened one iota.

"I'm ashamed of you, Muchie. Acting a fool about that man. Your stunt had your godparents worried to death. I won't stand for any such foolishness in this house. You mark my words," Papa said.

"Be a good girl now and listen to your papa. That man is not for you. You must stop being such a willful girl, Muchie. It isn't becoming," Mother told me as she loaded my plate with her good cooking.

"His name is Teddy, Mother. Why can't you even say his name? I'm not being willful. I'm in love. Do you even know what it feels like to be in love?"

My outburst left Mother speechless. For bullheaded Papa it was a red flag.

He jerked me out of my chair and shook me. Pins flew out of my hair, clattering as they hit the floor. Mother grabbed his arm to make him stop while I shrieked in terror.

I stumbled and fell, hitting my cheek hard on a corner of the table. Blood welled up and ran down my jaw to splatter the white collar of my blouse.

"Oh, baby girl, you know I've never laid hands on you in anger. I was wrong, Muchie. Please forgive your papa."

Hurt and anger left me mute. Papa scooped me up in his arms and held me close as he'd done when I was a little girl. I broke down and cried.

He rocked me gently, whispering comforting words the way he used to when I had a bad dream.

"Don't cry, Muchie. Papa's right here. I'm sorry I hurt you. Shhh, don't cry."

My head was on his shoulder and Mother was dabbing at my cheek with a wet cloth. "There, there, Muchie," she said.

"I just want to be happy," I cried.

"Darling girl, there's a whole lot more to living in this world than being happy," Mother said. "Forget about Teddy. Your papa and I love you. Trust what we tell you."

"I can't. It's like he's behind my eyes and in my head. I can't forget him any more than I can forget my name. Papa, I love you and Mother. I love Teddy too. Please let me love all of you."

I held the wet cloth to my face and stood up. My knees were wobbling a little and I had to hold the table to steady myself.

Papa and Mother looked at me as love, anger and pity struggled for a place in their eyes.

Then Papa kissed me on the forehead. Mother put her arm around me and helped me to my room.

Despite Papa's apology, I vowed this was the last night I would sleep in his house. Much as I loved him, for the first time in my life I feared him.

When I was alone, I packed my old school satchel with some of the clothes I'd brought back from my year at the mill. I wrote Teddy to tell him what had happened.

I asked him to take me away from here and marry me. I was of age. We didn't need my father's blessing.

Just putting those defiant words on paper made me shudder. I was scared and alone. But I knew what I had to do.

Nan Nan had been right. There was no changing Papa's mind. He and Mother were determined to stand in the way of my happiness.

The next morning, dear cousin Helen took my letter to Teddy. It wasn't the way either of us wanted to start our life together, but I knew he would do as I asked.

Right after cleaning up the supper dishes, I pleaded a headache and went to my room. A short time later I stepped through a big window opening on the wide porch of our house with my satchel, the gold hoops in my ears and a little bit of money I'd saved from my job at the mill.

I never looked back.

Chapter Sixteen

1927

I cried as I walked away from home and family and nearly everything I knew in the world. My school, my friends, even my church.

More than once I even thought of turning around, but I knew that would only prolong my troubles.

Papa called me willful and stubborn. All I could think was the apple hadn't fallen very far from the tree. I wasn't going to change my mind about Teddy and neither was Papa.

There was nothing else for me to do but leave if I ever wanted to be with Teddy.

He met me a few miles from the farm on a shady path that led to Buccatunna. Teddy carried a suitcase in one hand and a rucksack on his back.

"Muchie, I just want to know one thing. Are you sure about leaving your family like this? Shouldn't I talk to your father again and try to get his blessing?"

My answer was to step into the fading light.

When Teddy saw my cheek, he took my satchel and said, "I see. It's like that, is it? Well, you'll never have to worry about anybody hurting you again, Muchie. Not while I live."

We got to Buccatunna an hour before the train arrived. The dusty street running through the middle of town was deserted and the windows of the few buildings shimmered in the fading heat of a Mississippi evening.

When the train slowed down to get the mail, Teddy and I waved and shouted until it stopped. It waited just long enough for us to board. As we shook the dust of Buccatunna, Mississippi, from our shoes, I wondered when we might ever pass that way again.

"Where is this train taking us, Teddy?"

"I thought we'd try our luck in Mobile, Alabama. I've got some good friends who live there. They'll help us get settled. And I'm pretty certain I can find work in a city that size."

"I can work too, Teddy. Parran taught me a lot at the mill and I know how to cook and sew real well. I'll help us as much as I can."

"I know you will, Muchie, if it comes to that. But I imagine once we're married, you'll have your hands full keeping house and taking care of me."

The very idea made me blush.

Teddy and I rode the noisy, creaking train all night long. We talked for hours catching up on our year apart. When we were too tired to say another word, we slept snuggled together beneath Teddy's old army overcoat, holding each other like two friendless children.

Teddy believed in love the same way he believed in God. Passionately, and without question. He believed love bestowed power and strength and courage.

When we ran off to marry, Teddy's love sustained me. I had little else.

It was dawn when we got to Mobile. The streets were already bustling with delivery trucks. Even early in the morning, the air around the train station was full of the smell of roasting peanuts.

Newsboys hawked their papers at every intersection and whistles blew loud from boats lining the river. Everyone seemed to be going somewhere fast.

There were store windows full of anything you'd ever want to buy. I gawked at everything like the country girl I was.

Never in my life had I been in a town like Mobile. The sight of all those people riding in every kind of vehicle made me wish for eyes in the back of my head. I didn't want to miss anything. Teddy and I walked through the town to see the sights stalling for time so it would be a decent hour before we dropped in on his friends.

When I told him I was hungry enough to take a bite out of him, he changed course.

"Muchie, we'd better find Aaron Jasper's house right away." He laughed.

Like the old folks say about friendly people, Teddy had never met a stranger. He asked a man for directions and before I knew it, the man had walked us right to the front door of a cream-colored house with a deeply pitched roof.

"They call this a Creole cottage," Teddy explained. "You'll see plenty like it around here. See how it's raised off the ground? That's to keep it from flooding."

We knocked on the door. A smiling man wearing a suit grabbed Teddy by the hand and kissed me on the cheek. He propelled us into the house, talking the whole time.

"Teddy, you almost beat your telegram here. Dorali," he called, "Dorali, come meet my friend Teddy and his young lady."

"Welcome to our home. You must be famished after your trip. Let me fix you some breakfast," Dorali said.

She led us into a beautiful yellow room furnished with a round table, a polished sideboard and a glass-front cabinet filled with china and sparkling glasses.

The meal she fed us that morning was the best food I'd ever tasted. We had grits swimming in butter along with crispy fried fish, sliced muskmelon and hot biscuits. The table was set with delicate floral china on an embroidered cloth.

She and her husband soon surprised me with the extent of their hospitality.

"Now you listen to me good, Teddy. No sense in you trying to argue. This child needs decent chaperones right now if you want folks to accept her as a respectable woman once she's your wife," Aaron said.

"You can't up and marry Muchie today without even having a place to live as man and wife," Dorali declared as she laid more fish on his plate.

"Oh, Mrs. Jasper, I wouldn't dare impose on you that way." I blushed as I spoke, unsure if they, like my papa, already thought of me as a fallen woman.

"It's Dorali you must call me, dear. Now don't be silly. We have more than enough room and I can see you don't eat enough to keep a bird alive. So where is the imposition?"

Teddy looked at me. When I smiled my agreement, he nodded. With that it was settled.

Aaron and Teddy set off to visit Reverend Hill, a Methodist minister who'd served with them in France. Their plan was for Teddy to bunk at the parsonage for a while. What could be more respectable than that?

When they were gone, Dorali bustled me off to bed.

"You must be tired from all the excitement of traveling,"

Dorali said. "Make yourself comfortable and sleep as long as you want. We'll get acquainted later."

I smiled at the canopy above my head and before I knew it, I was sound asleep.

By week's end Teddy had a job for the fall teaching social studies at Mobile County Training School over in Plateau, Alabama.

Aaron was something of a local history expert as he demonstrated at supper that evening.

"You'll be teaching in a place that has direct links to Africa, Teddy."

"How's that, Aaron?" Teddy inquired.

"When the government outlawed the sale of slaves, a young, white fellow made a bet that he could bring in a ship full of captives. He landed *The Clothilde* right near Plateau. In a little place called Magazine Point."

"What happened to the people on board?" I asked.

"Every single one of them jumped ship. Their descendents live around there to this day."

"You think there might be any root doctors among them, Aaron?" Teddy winked at me as he asked the question.

"I imagine there may well be. Why do you ask a thing like that?"

"Muchie comes from a family of healers and unless I've forgotten everything I saw on the battlefield, she's something of a healer herself."

After that, nothing would do but for Teddy to insist I tell Dorali and Aaron about my family and healing.

The words spilled out of me so fast I hardly stopped to draw a breath. About how good Papa was when men were sick and scared. About Tyler Mama and all the babies she'd helped birth. About Theola and the little boy with his hurt arm. I hadn't even told Teddy about Moss Germaine, but he heard it that evening along with the Jaspers. Telling them about the herb garden, the farm and Mother's courage. When I started talking about her cooking I was half afraid they might laugh at me. City folks had different ways than we did in the country.

"You're blessed, Muchie, to come from a family with such gifts," Dorali said. "Your papa and mother sound like fine, decent people. Have you written to tell them no harm's come to you?"

"No, I have not. Papa and I parted on bad terms. I doubt he cares whether I'm alive or dead."

"Poor child, you can't possibly believe a thing like that. If your papa loved you before you left home, he loves you still. Let's go to my room and write him a nice letter. I think it's time to start healing his heart and yours."

Dorali wouldn't take no for an answer. To be polite I went with her to write my parents. She wrote to them as well, introducing herself to them and explaining that I was in good hands. Our letters finished, we went back to join Aaron and Teddy.

"I was just telling Aaron that I need to find a job to take care of our immediate needs until school starts in the fall, Muchie," Teddy said.

"You come with me Tuesday morning and I'll introduce you to the labor boss at the International Longshoremen's Association hall. There's plenty works at the docks, Teddy," Aaron said.

Teddy was at the Jasper's door first thing Tuesday morning. He and Aaron came back in high spirits.

"They hired me on the spot, Muchie. Some of the fellows tried to scare me off the union by saying how hard and dangerous dock work is, but I don't mind," Teddy said.

"Nothing can stop Teddy once he gets an idea in his head. He paid his money to join the union then and there," Aaron told us, slapping Teddy on the back.

"Here's my union card, look right here. It says Edward T. Preston is a member of Union 1410. This card is my ticket to work regular. The fellows said they always call the union men first."

"Mobile is a busy port, Teddy. Plenty of ships full of cargo dock here every day. You're young and strong enough to work double shifts if they'll let you. Won't leave any time for Muchie, though," Aaron teased.

"Muchie and I will have the rest of our lives together. I don't think she'll begrudge me the time, especially since I'll be making good money," Teddy said, kissing my hand.

Teddy took Aaron's advice, working 16 hours at a stretch. He'd sleep eight hours at the parsonage before going back to the docks for as much work as they would give him. He was working hard to earn enough money to rent a little house for us to live in when we married.

Dorali and I soon became fast friends. With Teddy practically living at the docks and Aaron driving all over three counties selling insurance we had a lot of time to get acquainted.

"I've always wanted a sister, Muchie, someone just like you," she said, fussing with my hair one morning.

Dorali inventoried the contents of my satchel and insisted I try on some old things she said she'd outgrown. I had such fun that morning preening in flowered dresses and pastel dresses and plaid skirts and linen blouses far nicer than anything I'd ever owned.

"You are the kindest person I know, Dorali. But these clothes don't look old to me. Why, some still have the store tags on them."

"It's like this, Muchie. Hammel's Department Store is happy to take money from colored women, but we can't use the dressing rooms to try on clothes. Most of these things just don't fit me. Would you do me the favor of wearing them? Otherwise, Aaron will chide me for wasting his hard-earned money."

"I've never had dresses as pretty as these. We made all our clothes back home."

"Then it's settled? You'll wear them for me?"

"I'd be proud to, Dorali. But I can't just sit around like a lady of leisure letting you do for me. Let me help out with the cooking at least."

"Don't be silly, Muchie. It's a treat for me to have company with Aaron away as much as he is. It *would* be nice to eat someone else's cooking for a change though."

In no time flat I made myself at home in their kitchen. One day Dorali took me to a fish market on the river. I saw sacks of oysters in the shell ready to shuck, baskets full of live crabs, mountains of shrimp in all sizes and more kinds of fish than I knew existed. I figured I was going to like Mobile just fine.

"Muchie, I've invited a few friends to have lunch with us so they can meet you," Dorali said.

They were nice women and we laughed and talked like old friends over shrimp salad and deviled eggs that Dorali taught me how to make.

"That Bevane is something else, isn't she, Muchie?"

"She sure does have a sharp tongue, but she's sensible and level-headed, like my mother. I liked her a lot, Dorali. Do you think she liked me?"

"I'm sure she did, Muchie. You're something else, yourself."

Dorali invited Teddy to eat with us whenever he wasn't working.

"I hope Teddy will come to supper today, Dorali."

"The way you've been showing off in the kitchen, he'll miss a good meal if he doesn't."

That night I cooked fried corn, smothered beef chops, and rice and gravy and turnip greens with hot corn bread.

"Lord, Muchie. You fixed so much rice I think you must have a bias against potatoes," Dorali accused.

"We'll just see about that. I'll make you a nice dinner Sunday that will change your mind," I promised.

She and Aaron couldn't say enough about my special Sunday meal of scalloped potatoes, country ham, tiny English peas and shrimp piled in puff pastry shells.

"I may never step foot in that kitchen again, Muchie. Your cooking puts mine to shame," Dorali laughed after the meal.

Over two months had passed since I'd written to my parents, and still no response. Whenever the postman came I pretended to be busy. That way Dorali wouldn't see my disappointment if there was no letter for me.

"Muchie! Muchie! Come quick, here's a letter for you from Mississippi and one for me too," Dorali said, tearing open an envelope.

"I'm scared to open mine. Read yours first, Dorali."

She did and at the sight of her tears, my heart just about stopped. I walked in a circle patting my chin with the letter, too nervous to stand still and hear the news.

"Don't you want to know what he has to say, Muchie?"

"I don't know. Is it bad, Dorali?"

She handed me the letter, and my papa's bold handwriting filled the page. He was glad to know I was safe and staying with respectable people. He sent his love and asked Dorali to look after me until *he and Mother arrived.*

"You invited them to come here? They'll make me go home

with them, Dorali. I can't do that," I cried, shaking so much I dropped my own letter.

"Settle down, Muchie, and read your letter before you get all upset."

"No, you read it, I can't see straight right now."

"Your papa says here that he's prayed and prayed for you. He's had a change of heart about Teddy. If you love him and want to marry him, he won't stand in your way. He'll come to give you away like a loving father should. That's what he says, Muchie. Like a loving father. What do you think of that?"

Dorali did not let any grass grow under her feet. Before the day was out, Dorali and I started making plans for my wedding.

I was nervous and excited the afternoon she took me to Hammel's Department Store to select my wedding attire. There were dresses of every color and style, and I got confused looking at all the pretty things in the store.

"This blue one is nice," I said, holding a dress up to myself for Dorali's verdict.

"It looks kind of plain to me, Muchie. Besides, you're entitled to wear white for your wedding. Aren't you?" she asked, not meeting my eye.

I blushed as red as the store's carpet before answering her. "Do you mean have Teddy and I . . . ? Well, the answer is no. We haven't. Not yet anyway."

Dorali laughed and pinched my cheek. "That's my girl," she said. After that, all the dresses she picked out for my approval were white. And very fancy.

"I wish you could try these dresses on, but there's no helping that. What do you think of this one?" She held up a tea-length white dress with a tightly fitted bodice. A row of embroidered buttons ran down the back and the cuffs were decorated with more embroidery.

"It's the most beautiful dress in the store, Dorali. Do you think it suits me?"

"A beautiful bride ought to have a beautiful dress. Let's find a hat and shoes to go with it."

Her taste for shopping led us to several more departments, then to the bakery and finally the florist.

When I got home and modeled my wedding outfit for her, she pronounced me the picture of fashion. I burst into tears at my reflection in the mirror.

"I hope those are tears of joy, Muchie. You certainly do look lovely. Now don't go splashing tears all over your wedding dress. That would be bad luck."

She replaced my hat in its box, stuffed my shoes with bags of lavender sachet and put my dress on a padded hanger.

"There, all done for now. The cake is ordered and flowers for the church. All that's left is for us to decide what to serve for your wedding supper," she said, leading me to her cookbooks in the kitchen.

I could hardly wait for Teddy to see me on my wedding day. It made me blush to think what wearing white really meant.

Chapter Seventeen

1928

Warren Street Methodist Church was beautifully decorated for our little wedding. Dorali had outdone herself festooning the pews with pink organdy ribbons and sweet-smelling lilies. Masses of flowers graced the altar and the front of the church held a wrought-iron arch woven with more ribbons and flowers and greenery.

True to his word, my papa was present to give me away. The organist began playing the "Wedding March" and Papa asked, "Muchie, it's time. Are you ready?"

Papa held my face in his hands and searched my eyes for an answer. I nodded and Papa kissed my brow. He linked my arm with his and patted my hand in a reassuring way. For some reason I felt tears prickling behind my eyes.

"Thank you, Papa," I whispered, gripping his arm and blinking back my tears. Papa winked at me and pretended to spit. My tears vanished as Papa led me to the floral arch where he paused to place my hand in Teddy's.

All twelve of the people in church were smiling when Reverend Hill asked, "Who gives this woman to be married to this man?"

Mother stood with Papa and together they happily announced, "We do."

Love really did make everything possible. The proof was that Teddy and I were married with my parents' blessing.

Teddy and I walked out of the church hand in hand. We stood for a moment on the landing and took in our first glimpse of the world as man and wife.

"Teddy, do you think there's a happier couple in the whole state of Alabama?"

"I doubt it, Muchie," he answered, giving me a thoroughly married kiss in the bright sunshine that knocked my wedding hat askew.

"Look how clear the sky is and how everything looks fresh and new. Even the birds are singing for us."

"It's as if the whole world wishes us well," Teddy said.

He helped me down the steep steps and our married life began with us skipping and twirling like the children we passed at play in their yards.

"Is it good luck for newlyweds to hear children laughing?" I asked.

"We'll soon find out," Teddy said, breaking into a big grin.

I giggled and kissed him as our wedding guests strolled down the street behind us.

Aaron boomed a question over the tiny group, "Are we ready for a nuptial celebration?"

Whistles and cheers answered him. Soon everyone was milling about the Jasper's garden in fine good humor.

"You make a truly beautiful bride, Muchie." Bevane hugged me and I could see tears in her eyes.

"You're a lucky man, Teddy," she said and gave him a kiss on the cheek.

Despite the restrictions imposed by Prohibition, Mr. In-Love-with-France Teddy had managed to get a case of champagne for our wedding day.

He offered the first toast, "To Mr. and Mrs. Tyler, Muchie's gracious and loving parents," he said, lifting his glass to salute Mother and Papa.

"To the bride and groom. May they always love each other as they do today," Papa responded with a catch in his voice.

Not to be outdone in his own home, Aaron gave his own toast, "To new friends and old friends and little friends yet to come," he said with a wink to Teddy and me.

My face got so hot I had to cover it with my hands, making everyone roar with laughter.

"That's enough toasting for now. We'd better eat before all this champagne goes to your heads," Dorali announced with a gesture to the table.

It was a lavish meal displaying both the generosity of the Jaspers and the bounty of land and sea. We feasted on fresh seafood from the Gulf of Mexico, ham and turkey, six different vegetables, fresh fruit with whipped cream and a wedding cake from Pollman's bakery.

After supper we danced and drank champagne and danced some more until the sun went down. Mother took me aside and pressed a tissue-wrapped parcel in my hands.

"I made this gown for you, Muchie. For your wedding night," she stammered. "Is there anything you want to ask me?"

"Are you happy for me, Mother? Truly happy?"

"I am, sweet girl. Teddy is a good man. He'll do right by you," she said placing her hand on my cheek.

Together, Teddy and I walked through the garden making the rounds to thank our guests and bid them good night.

"You take care of my girl, Teddy. If you ever get tired of her, you send her back home to me, you hear?" Papa told Teddy as he shook his hand.

"Yes, sir. I'll do my best," Teddy said, ignoring Papa's last comment.

We said our final farewells beneath a hail of rice. Teddy and I didn't say one word, suddenly shy with each other as we made our way to the house he'd rented.

At the door, Teddy broke his silence. "Did your mother talk to you about your wedding night, Muchie?" Teddy asked, concern or maybe champagne making his voice husky.

"Don't forget, I was once a midwife, Teddy. I think I know what to expect," I told him with a giggle.

He laughed and easily lifted me over the threshold to carry me through the parlor straight into our bedroom.

"Let's see how much you really know, my darling," he said, nuzzling my neck.

"I want to change my clothes, Teddy. Mother made me a beautiful nightgown for our wedding night," I said, showing him the little package. "Will you help me with these buttons?" I asked.

Teddy let me go long enough to undo the buttons that ran down the back of my wedding dress. Before I could object, he slipped the dress from my shoulders. I stood shivering in my slip at a loss for what to do.

"I want to hold you now, Muchie. I love the feel of you. Your hair smells like flowers," Teddy said as he removed my hat and unbraided my hair.

Despite my boasting, I was shaking like a newborn calf. I wasn't cold, I was just plain nervous about being alone with my husband.

Teddy turned me around to face the cheval glass standing in the corner of our bedroom.

"Look, Muchie," he said as he untied the ribbon straps of my slip. It fell to the floor, and Teddy stood behind me, holding my bare breasts in his dark brown hands.

"Muchie," he whispered in my ear, making me quiver even more, "your breasts are so sweet and round. My Muchie, my wife."

He took the longest time stroking my breasts and breathing warm, loving words into my ear. It felt like my breasts would take wings and fly off my chest from excitement.

Teddy stroked my hair. He kissed my neck and shoulders and back until I thought I would faint dead away.

I was long past shame. Never in my life had I stood half naked in front of a looking glass. Let alone half naked in front of a looking glass *and* a man. Teddy didn't mind my embarrassment as he caressed me.

"Your skin is softer than a breeze off the Gulf," he said when he turned me around so we were face to face. Teddy moved my hands to touch him. He showed me how to make him as breathless with yearning as he made me.

"Unbutton my shirt, Muchie, so I can feel your skin against mine."

When I opened his shirt, I had to bury my face in the soft, black down that covered his chest.

"You smell like cloves to me, Teddy. Warm and spicy. I want to gobble you up."

"Time enough for that later, Muchie," he murmured.

Though I was green as spring grass, it was plain to me that Teddy was not.

"Were there girls in France, Teddy?"

"Shh, Muchie. There's no one in the world for me but you," he said, sliding his tongue across my collarbones, around each ear and ever so lightly over my eyelids.

Teddy kissed me every place there was to kiss. When he slid my bloomers down to kiss me where I'd never touched myself save to bathe, I thought I would dissolve into a puddle of longing at his feet.

He carried me to our bed and I turned over to hide my nakedness. He traced a line with his finger from my neck to the curve of my bottom. Then he was gone.

I heard a pop and felt a tiny trickle of icy coolness down my back as it pooled at the base of my spine. Teddy lapped up the liquid before it spilled on the sheets.

"Your skin improves the flavor of champagne, my Muchie," he said to me. I nearly swooned.

I was no more good. He could have called in the neighbors to watch and I would not have objected. Passion made me shameless.

Teddy could have smothered me with a pillow and I would not have had the strength to offer any resistance.

He did neither. Teddy turned me over and kissed me again and again and again. I felt his smooth hardness begin to ease into me, gentle and insistent. Then, I found my strength.

Was I moving to him or moving away? Was I inviting him in or pushing him out? All I can say for certain is that out of our struggle he made me his own.

Teddy loved me with his body the first time and every time after as if I were a prize he dared to claim but feared to lose. I followed his lead. Not only because I didn't know where to go without him but also because anywhere he was taking us was good enough for me.

He was strong and gentle. Patient and insistent. Eager and

willing to wait. We were joined heart to heart. Mind to mind and spirit to spirit. Loving consumed every particle of who we were and ever wanted to become.

On my wedding night, my Teddy made me glad he was my first and only lover.

When I awoke the next day to find Teddy sleeping beside me I pressed my face against the warm curve of his back. He stirred in his sleep when I put my arm around him and stroked his belly. I discovered yet another secret of married life.

"I had no idea it would be like this, Teddy," I murmured in his ear.

He mumbled, "Thought you knew everything, Muchie."

Then Teddy snuggled his body into mine before dozing back to sleep.

I gave a luxurious stretch reaching far above my head and pointing my toes. My entire body tingled in the aftermath of Teddy's touch: I didn't want to be away from him for one second. Not today, not ever.

"I'll stay in bed all day and watch you sleep," I said to Teddy's slumbering form.

Looking at my husband's lean, dark body beneath the white sheet I realized nothing Tyler Mama taught me could have prepared me for loving Teddy.

True, she had explained what went where but she'd said nothing about how good it could feel. No wonder women endured childbirth when they had love. For the first time I understood it was a fair exchange.

Teddy and I loved and slept the day away.

"Muchie, I don't know if I'll have strength enough to stay married to you," Teddy declared, holding his throat and poking out his tongue.

"My throat is parched and I'm near to perishing from hunger."

"My stomach *is* grumbling, Teddy. I suppose even old married folks like us must still eat," I said.

Searching through the clothes strewn about the room I found Mother's gift and slipped the embroidered nightgown over my head. Teddy wrapped himself in a sheet and we marched off to the kitchen together.

Chapter Eighteen

1929

"Married life agrees with you, Muchie. You're pretty as a peach. My peach of a girl. Sweet and ripe and juicy," Teddy teased, giving me a loud, smacking kiss before he left for school.

"You're looking well yourself, dear heart. I love cooking for you and seeing you fill out. You worked yourself down to skin and bone at that shipyard," I said, handing him his lunch pail.

"I don't mind telling you teaching is a whole lot easier on me than the docks. But if they'll have me come summer, I'll work there during the months there's no paycheck coming in from teaching."

Ever since we got married, I'd been spending my days sewing curtains and doing what I could to make things nice for Teddy. The house we lived in was far from grand. It was already old when we moved in, with creaking shutters and a rickety back porch.

Our house was set far back from an unpaved street. We had to step over an open ditch to get to our door. Teddy built a narrow bridge of sturdy planks to keep our feet dry when the ditch filled up with rainwater.

He was handy with tools, securing the shutters and shoring up the porch. Out back, he helped me clear some space to plant a garden. We agreed growing our own vegetables would save us money. What we didn't eat right away, I could pickle, dry or can in Mason jars.

Teddy thought it was countrified to have laying hens for eggs, but I overruled him when I discovered that several of our neighbors kept chickens *and* geese in their yards.

Tyler Mama had been right. Love made everything possible. It was love that fueled our work fixing up the house. Nothing but love could have given Teddy the patience to teach me how to paint.

"Wait a minute, Muchie. Don't start slapping paint around that way. There's a system to painting," he said as paint dribbled from my brush to speckle the floor.

"Are you sure about that, Teddy?"

"Indeed I am. First thing we must do is spread newspaper over the floor," he instructed me, taking the brush from my hand.

"Then I'll paint the edges and the corners of the room. You can do the middle part, Muchie. Less chance for harm doing that."

Love filled our days and nights. When I noticed I hadn't been bleeding on schedule, it was love that brought me joy instead of fear. I had all the signs. Teddy and I were going to have a baby.

Before I could write to Mother, before I could even tell Dorali and Bevane, I had to share the news with Teddy.

After supper we often sat on the porch to catch a breeze. In the evening Teddy liked to read his newspaper and I enjoyed sitting beside him to work the crossword puzzle. We were quiet, enjoying the cool of the evening together as neighbors passed, nodding and smiling.

"I sure do miss the mosquito hawks we had in Mississippi," I told Teddy.

"These blasted mosquitoes nearly eat us alive when the weather is warm. I wish somebody would invent a way to get rid of gnats though. They're a year-round nuisance," Teddy said, swatting at the pests with his newspaper.

"I don't mind the fireflies. They're the only bugs with sense enough to stay to themselves. Don't bother a soul. Look how pretty they are spangling the bushes."

Next door there was a family with a radio. Often they played it loud enough for the rest of the neighborhood to hear. We listened whether we wanted to or not.

"You hear that, Muchie? They're saying banks are failing all over the country. Folks can't get their money out."

"It's a good thing our money is safe in this house. Anything in the paper about the banks?"

He handed me the paper. I read a front-page article that said our country faced a major economic crisis.

"Will it hurt *us*, Teddy?"

"I don't know, Muchie. But if the world is in an uproar, hard times are surely coming for colored people. It's always been like that."

"With all the bad news, do you feel like hearing some good news?"

"Sure I do, Muchie, good news would be mighty welcome right now."

"We're going to have ourselves a baby, Teddy. In about six months near as I can tell. How's that for good news?"

He didn't say anything for a long time. Teddy sat holding his newspaper and looking out toward the street.

"A baby you say? We're going to have a baby? Oh, Muchie, that is good news!" Teddy said, dropping the paper and gathering me up in his arms.

We were only half right.

Actually two babies were born in the Preston home during the first hard year of the Depression. Tyler Mama would have been proud that mother and babies were healthy and sound.

Dorali and Aaron honored us by standing as godparents for our twins. We named them Charlotte and Margaret after Tyler Mama and Mother.

"Look at their little feet, Teddy. Don't they make you think of turnover pies warm from the oven?"

"How will these little feet ever hold my plump girls upright to walk?" Teddy said, bouncing one baby girl on each knee.

"Be careful, Teddy. The soft place on the top of their heads hasn't closed yet. See that pulse throbbing on the top of Margaret's head? Nothing but a thin layer of skin is covering her brains," I said.

I couldn't stand looking at the soft spot. It always gave me a woozy feeling. The twins never went outside without their heads covered, because I sewed them bonnets and made knitted caps for every season.

Thinking about how fragile babies were could move me to tears. It was the reason I couldn't bear to leave Charlotte and Margaret for more than a few minutes at a time.

When I had clothes to hang on the line, I put my babies in a basket and toted them with me. They soon grew tired of being confined and started to whimper. Their crying made my breasts fill up with milk, and I'd have to stop what I was doing to nurse them.

"Muchie, you're piled up in the bed nursing the babies when I leave for work and you're still nursing when I get home. Is that what you do all day?" Teddy asked with an edge to his voice I didn't appreciate one bit.

"I'll have you know I do the housework and fix your supper while they're sleeping. And I read them stories and take them out for some fresh air too, Mr. Edward Preston," I said in a huff.

"Don't take on like that, Muchie. I know the girls need a lot of attention. I didn't mean any harm," Teddy said, kissing Charlotte and Margaret. Almost as an afterthought, he kissed me too.

Now and again, friends stopped by during the day to give me a hand with the babies. It was nice to have company, but I didn't like hearing their advice.

"Muchie, you spoil those babies rotten," Bevane complained.

"If feeding a hungry baby and holding her in my arms so she never has to cry is spoiling, then you're right, Bevane."

"You're so in love with those babies I wonder you have any time left for Teddy," she teased, hitting a sore spot.

"He wants his children to be happy, Bevane. But I'm real tired when I get them settled in for the night. It's all I can do to keep my eyes open long enough to sit with Teddy ten minutes on the porch."

"I'd be willing to keep them for a few days," Bevane offered kindly.

I looked at my baby girls and shook my head. It would be hard for me to let them go, even with Bevane.

"You and Teddy need to be alone for a change. But you have to wean them first. I don't have a thing for them and I've heard them cut up when they're hungry."

"In time, Bevane. They're too young to wean just yet. Wait until they can eat solid food and then they can stay with you."

"Can you at least put them on a feeding schedule, Muchie? I could keep the girls for a few hours and let you get some rest."

"I've tried to, Bevane, but I can't bear it when they cry. The poor little things depend on me for everything. Teddy said I ought to let them cry themselves to sleep some nights. He sees I'm worn out. But it breaks my heart to ignore them when they're lonely or scared."

"Have it your way, Muchie. But it won't hurt a baby to cry sometimes. Clears out their lungs, folks say."

Much as I hated to admit it, Bevane proved to be right. When the twins were a year old, I weaned them and started them on solid food. They had fun learning to feed themselves despite the fact that it seemed there was often more food on their faces than in their stomachs.

Eventually they were happy to toddle off with Bevane, and I was glad for the rest and the extra time to spend with Teddy.

Chapter Nineteen

1932

By the time the twins were walking and talking, I was pregnant again. It seemed as though there was always a baby at my breast or tugging at my skirt tail or swelling my belly rushing to be born.

In the mornings Teddy's voice would drag me out of my slumber, his body warm and insistent on loving mine.

"Wake up, Muchie. You plan to sleep the day away?" Teddy said as I burrowed under the covers.

"Five more minutes," I begged, pulling a pillow over my head.

"Arise, my love, my fair one," he quoted, sliding his hand beneath my gown and awakening me in more ways than one. No matter how sleepy I might be, no matter how much I wanted to put off the day, it was hard to resist Teddy in the morning.

"Oh, Teddy. I know I look a sight. How can you want me as fat and clumsy as I am these days? I don't even have a waistline anymore," I whined.

I sat up in bed rubbing the sleep from my eyes and pushing my hair back under my night hat.

"How could I not? I always want you, Muchie. Even when I'm teaching school. One thought of you and it's all I can do to get behind my desk before the students notice their teacher's pants are poking out."

"I don't believe a word you say, Edward Preston."

"Then let me show you how much I want you, Muchie," he said, tickling my ear with the tip of his tongue.

"You're even more beautiful when you're round and full of life, Muchie. Don't you know only a dog wants a bone?"

Teddy had a way of making me feel desirable even when my mirror told me otherwise. Maybe that's why we had four babies during the uneasy years of the Depression.

Nursing or toddling, I loved the sight of our babies. Their sweet brown faces as varied as a box of assorted chocolates. They took the best from each of us, our babies did. The fragrance of clean baby hair and the touch of soft baby skin only reminded me how much I loved their daddy. It was all I needed to be happy.

Our next baby was a boy. We named him Edward Thompson Preston, Jr.

"Does this mean I have to go by senior now? Makes me feel like I'm getting on in years," Teddy joked. "Are we going to call him Teddy too?"

"I don't know about that. One Teddy is more than enough for me." I laughed. "Having the same given name is all right. But to keep down any confusion let's call the baby Tom-Tom."

Our boy had such round and rosy cheeks I had to mind that his sisters didn't bite him when they were playing. From birth, he had double rows of thick, black eyelashes just like his daddy.

People believed it was bad luck for a boy to get a haircut before his first birthday, and Tom-Tom's hair grew in fluffy ringlets.

It made him look as pretty as his sisters. People often mistook him for a girl.

"I'm glad you're finally cutting this child's hair," I told Teddy.

"He's a handsome boy, Muchie. With his hair flat on his head like that and his big wise eyes, Tom-Tom looks like a baby seal, doesn't he?"

Almost before Tom-Tom was walking on his own, we had another baby. Teddy had a sweet tooth and he took one look at our fourth baby, kissed her and declared her name was Madeleine.

"She's as sweet as those little cakes I loved to eat in France," he said.

I'd learned my lesson about making time for my husband. When Madeleine was born, Mother came to help me for a few months until I got my strength back.

She had her hands full with four little children, but after raising 10 in her own house, she knew exactly what to do.

"It sure is a relief to have Mrs. Tyler stay with us, Muchie. I don't know when we've been able to take a walk alone," Teddy said one evening as we strolled about the neighborhood.

"I'm sorry about neglecting you, dear heart. I got so caught up trying to be a good mother, I forgot about being a good wife."

"That's all right, Muchie. I wouldn't love you the way I do if you weren't so hell-bound determined."

He kissed the top of my head, and we walked along holding hands. Every day after that we made time for each other, often walking for an hour or two until the sun went down.

Before we got married, we had joined Reverend Hill's church and managed to get there for service just about every Sunday. I liked Warren Street because Reverend Hill was a Bible scholar who taught during his sermons. The church also had good music and an active Sunday school program.

The first year our twins were big enough to stand up before

the church to say an Easter speech, Teddy helped them learn their parts.

"Now when you get up there, look at me. I'll be standing way back in the church. You must say your speech loud enough for me to hear it," Teddy told Charlotte and Margaret who nodded meekly.

"And don't fidget. Stand up straight. Make your daddy proud of you," I added, while putting the finishing touches on their Easter dresses.

Easter Sunday afternoon, Teddy was more nervous than the girls. But when it came time to say their speech, Teddy's face glowed with pure paternal rapture.

Our little lambs held hands in matching homemade dresses and brand-new patent leather shoes. Lace-trimmed socks hugged their fat little legs. Usually shy, they spoke their piece in unison with voices as clear as tiny silver bells.

Rabbits soft and cuddly. Baby chickens too.
Easter eggs in baskets, white and pink and blue.
Easter cards of greeting, music fills the air.
Lilies nod to tell us, it's Easter everywhere!

"Muchie, those girls are smart as they can be. If I get you a primer book do you think you can start teaching them to read?"

"I'll do my best, Teddy."

He had big plans for his family, my Teddy did. Before going to Mississippi to teach school, Teddy had been a traveling man.

In France for the Great War, he stayed over there to visit Austria and Flanders and Belgium and God knows what other foreign countries. But it was France he loved.

"You can't imagine the food, Muchie. I'd never eaten such good bread before. That crusty bread, some cheese and a glass of wine made a mighty satisfying meal. In France I saw entire streets lined with nothing but greengrocers and fish markets and butcher shops and little stores selling every kind of pastry and sweets."

"How did you keep from eating yourself silly, Teddy?"

"Who says I didn't?"

"You think I'll be stylish enough to keep you when we go to France?"

"No matter where we are, there's no one for me but you, Muchie. You ought to know that by now," he said.

"What's it like in France, Teddy? Are there any colored people over there?"

"Plenty of them, Muchie. But the thing you'll really like is people don't see color like they do over here. In France I was an American. Not a colored man. I felt free for the first time in my life. I want the children to know how that feels."

"So do I, Teddy. So do I."

"When the children are grown, we'll go to Venice and ride in a gondola. I'll pay the boatman to serenade you, Muchie."

Although Italian was a language neither of us understood it made me no less eager for the serenade Teddy promised me.

"When you tell me about Europe, Teddy, I can picture the fields of Alpine daisies and the grand opera houses you've seen. Is French champagne a lot different from what we drank at our wedding?"

"As different as Mobile is from Paris, Muchie. Everything in France is different than here."

It wasn't only foreign countries Teddy wanted his family to visit though. Taking an atlas from the bookshelf, he traced a route for me that followed the railroad line from Mobile to parts north. He showed me the cities where we'd stop.

Atlanta, Richmond, Washington, D.C., Philadelphia and New York City were just the beginning.

"One day we'll get on the train and take a tour of the entire United States of America, starting on the east coast. Wait until you see New York City, Muchie. There's nothing in the world so dazzling as Broadway. You've never seen such lights."

Teddy knitted together enough stories and dreams and plans for the future to wrap me in the warm luxury of his imagined possibilities.

"You remind me of Tyler Mama sometimes, Teddy. She could talk up relatives like you talk up new places. The way a conjure man talks up spirits."

"Just don't let Reverend Hill hear you say that, Muchie. He might put me out of the church for a heathen," he laughed.

When Teddy wasn't making plans for the future, he was busy doing things all the time. I could barely keep up with that man and all his energy.

Every December, Teddy loaded the children up for an expedition to the woods where they searched for the perfect Christmas tree. When they settled on one they loved, Teddy chopped it down to bring home and decorate.

We spent an evening cutting out stars and making construction paper garlands. Each branch held its own tiny candle. The tree made our parlor as lovely as a dream.

I was crazy about Christmas and my husband and children were full of holiday excitement. The children danced around like moonbeams.

My own preparation for Christmas started the day after Thanksgiving. That's when I made my fruitcakes. The children helped by cracking pecans and picking out the nutmeats, eating as much as they put in the bowl. Teddy had to stir the batter for me because it was heavy with candied fruit.

I baked three cakes and wrapped them in cheesecloth to soak

in bourbon until Christmas Day. One was a gift for Dorali and Aaron, one for Reverend Hill and one for us to enjoy through the winter.

Long before sunup the children ran to the tree searching for the few little presents Santa Claus left them. The Depression made money scarce and their gifts were homemade.

Teddy carved wooden dolls for the girls and I sewed a wardrobe of miniature dresses for them. He fashioned whistles and spinning tops for Tom-Tom.

We always found a way to buy each child a book and a peppermint candy cane. Bags of oranges and boiled peanuts completed our gifts.

"Go clean yourselves up and get out of your nightclothes," Teddy told the children. "Your mother is cooking a special breakfast. Hurry now or you'll miss it."

No matter how meager our funds, Teddy always brought home a sack of oysters to shuck for Christmas breakfast. I fried the oysters and made a big pot of grits for our holiday meal.

Dorali and Aaron came knocking on our door laden with parcels. An early morning visit with their godparents was a treat for the children.

Teddy and Aaron were in rare form, joking and laughing throughout the meal.

"Muchie, this coffee is not sweet enough," Teddy announced with his devilish grin, winking at Aaron as he handed me his coffee cup.

"Aaron, please pass the sugar," I said, rushing to do my husband's bidding.

"I don't need any sugar, Muchie. If you'll just put the tip of your sweet little finger in my cup, I think the coffee will be just fine."

Aaron roared at that old joke. I laughed too and pursed my lips to lecture Teddy, "You don't have do-right on your mind, Edward Preston."

"I declare, Muchie, you've got yourself one trash-talking man there. Teddy, you're as bad as Aaron and he can talk a snake out of its skin," Dorali giggled, blowing her husband a kiss.

Right after breakfast, people started dropping by to pay pop calls. Nobody stood on ceremony waiting for a special invitation to run in and holler at you on Christmas Day. It was taken for granted that folks would hold open house and extend hospitality to any guest who walked through the door.

"All right, Muchie. Time you learn how to make gumbo for your company," Dorali announced.

"We bought live crabs and shrimp too," Aaron pitched in.

"Just don't let those crabs get me, Aaron. I'm scared of them live. Help Dorali get them in the pot and I'll chop the seasoning."

"Wait just a minute now," Teddy interrupted. "A fellow down at the wharf showed me how to clean crabs live."

The children all shrieked and ran as he took the lid off a basket full of crabs. "Hand me my work gloves, will you please, Aaron?"

"Now watch and learn, ladies. Watch and learn. You must clean them live, to keep the meat sweet tasting."

"Crabs can pinch hard enough to draw blood. How in the world are you going to clean them unless they're good and dead?" Dorali asked Teddy.

He pulled on his heavy work gloves and picked out the biggest crab in the basket. Then he ripped off the two big pincher claws.

"You see. This crab is now powerless to hurt me or anyone else," Teddy intoned with his best teacher voice.

"It is now a simple matter to pry off this flap of shell called the apron. With a paring knife you scrape out what is known as dead man's fingers. All the other mess inside too. *Voila!* Your crab is ready for the gumbo pot."

We responded with a round of applause. Dorali admitted the sweet, fresh crabmeat smelled good enough to eat it raw right out of the shell.

"You've made a believer out of me, Teddy. I'll never go back to my old way of fixing crabs," she said.

"That Teddy can do anything, can't he?" Aaron asked.

"Just trying to be like you, Aaron," Teddy said, nudging Aaron with his elbow.

"You go on now with your foolishness, Teddy," Aaron said.

"I believe in giving credit where it's due, Aaron. The credit for the crab lesson goes to the man at the wharf. For everything else, I can either ask you or go find myself a book."

Their banter made Christmas that much merrier for us all. Standing in our kitchen, I was proud my husband taught me everything I know.

Teddy was a summertime stevedore, but he was a year-round member of the International Longshoremen's Association. He voted with his union brothers to have Oscar DePriest as the speaker for the Emancipation Day Celebration on January first.

"He's the first colored man elected to Congress this century," Teddy told me. "I sure hope he won't be the last."

"What makes you say that, Teddy?"

"Look at this flier. The Klan is passing it out all over town."

"Oh, Teddy, how ugly and hateful this thing is."

"KKK Will Kill the Nigger Congressman from Illinois on the First Day of the New Year," read the headline over an ugly caricature of Oscar DePriest.

"The union is asking the mayor for police to protect DePriest," Teddy said. "If the mayor doesn't come through, we'll have to take care of it ourselves."

The Emancipation Day Celebration was part church service and part political rally commemorating Lincoln freeing the slaves. Most of all it was a matter of pride for colored people.

Teddy and I put on our Sunday clothes to go hear Mr. DePriest's speech along with much of the colored community. We arrived to find a crowd already up in arms.

"There's not a policeman to be found," people complained.

"That lying roach of a mayor is afraid to buck the Klan."

"Mayor's word is no good. He's not worth a damn himself."

"He's shown his true color is yellow."

Longshoremen guffawed at the joke and in a manner of minutes organized themselves into defense units. They stationed themselves around the podium, around the ILA hall and around the block to protect Oscar DePriest from the Klan.

"Don't worry, Muchie. There won't be any trouble today." Teddy patted my hand before taking his place among his union brothers.

The longshoremen were not known for starting fights, but no one doubted they could hold their own if the need arose.

A few cars holding white troublemakers cruised down the street jeering at the men.

During the course of the afternoon each time that happened I saw longshoremen put one hand to their hip in what looked like a casual gesture. The movement brushed aside coattails and revealed pistols and buck knives stuck in nearly every man's belt.

Mr. DePriest gave his speech as scheduled. Without incident.

Chapter Twenty

1936

"Teddy, wake up, Charlotte is burning with fever. She's struggling for breath. I don't know what's wrong. Help me get her in a tub of water to cool her down."

He ran to fill the washtub. Before we could get her into the water, Charlotte started to writhe and twist, her small body contorted and then shaking with spasm after spasm. Charlotte's eyes rolled back in her head and flecks of saliva covered her mouth.

"My God, Muchie, what's happening to her? Is she having a fit?"

"It's the fever, Teddy. We've got to cool her down, help me . . ."

Even cool water didn't stop the horrible contortions rippling through poor Charlotte's little body. I prayed as I bathed her, asking God to let me use the healing gift to save my child. Pouring cool water over Charlotte, I begged for healing to reach her through my hands.

Margaret and Teddy and Madeleine stood in the doorway. They were wide awake and crying, "What's the matter with Charlotte?"

"Go get in our bed, children. I'll come see about you in just a minute. But you must go right now," Teddy told them.

"Oh, God. Oh, God. Help Charlotte. Please help her. Give me the healing gift again, please God. Give it to me now," I prayed.

"What are you saying, Muchie? Why is Charlotte so still? Does it mean she's better?"

"I don't know, Teddy. I think she's worn out from the spasms. Pray with me, Teddy. Pray for healing. Tyler Mama said I had healing hands. Pray I can save my baby."

Teddy took Charlotte's hand and mine, and began to pray with me.

"Please God, help me, help me now," I prayed. Charlotte had another convulsion, more wrenching than the last.

"I'm going to fetch a doctor. I'll be back fast as I can," Teddy said. I heard him running to the door.

My eyes were fixed on Charlotte. She grimaced and shuddered and went limp in the water. I scooped her up in my arms, screaming for help.

"Teddy! Teddy, Charlotte's not breathing."

He grabbed Charlotte and put his ear to her chest. "Oh God, Muchie, I can't hear a heartbeat. What should we do?"

Sucking the phlegm from Charlotte's nose, I breathed into her mouth. Once. Twice. Again. Praying to rescue my baby from death the way Tyler Mama had when her blue baby came into the world not breathing. I got light headed and dizzy, but the healing gift did not come no matter that I prayed with every breath.

Teddy touched my shoulder. "It's no use, Muchie. It's no use."

"I tried to save her, Teddy. Why couldn't I make the healing gift work?" I moaned, "It's been so long, why wouldn't it come?"

He didn't answer.

In the morning, Reverend Hill came to the house. "You have my deepest sympathy," he said, gripping Teddy's hand and patting my shoulder kindly. "Shall we have a word of prayer together?"

Teddy nodded his agreement.

Reverend Hill took our hands to make a prayer circle. I could feel Teddy's hand trembling in mine as we stood in silence for a moment.

"Dear heavenly Father, bless this man and this woman in their hour of need. Bless their family. Please comfort them in their time of loss. Strengthen their faith. Oh Lord, make them obedient to your will. Lift the hearts of these grieving parents as they mourn the passing of their child. Welcome little Charlotte into your bosom where she will have everlasting life. Encourage this family and enable them to once again give you praise for your love and mercy. These and many other blessings we ask in the matchless name of your Son, Our Lord, Jesus the Christ. Amen."

I started to cry and Teddy bowed his head to hide his own tears.

"I can only imagine how hard this is for you," Reverend Hill said. "Parents don't expect to outlive their children, and I know this must be doubly hard because your loss was completely unexpected."

"It's worse than that, Reverend Hill. Muchie comes from a family of healers. I've seen her heal once before, but she couldn't help Charlotte."

"I see. What a terrible cross to bear! Yet the Bible says healing is one of the spiritual gifts and calls it a blessing."

"What good is a healing gift if it didn't save my child?" I snapped.

"Muchie, please. It isn't Reverend Hill's fault," Teddy said.

"I'm sorry, Reverend Hill. It's just I loved Charlotte so much."

"I know you did, Muchie, but losing our loved ones is part of life."

"Why, Reverend Hill? Why is it that way? What good will it do God to take Charlotte?"

"Sometimes God breaks our hearts so we can be open to even greater love, Muchie. Suffering tests our faith. If we can only hold on, God always gives us new blessings. Can you accept that?"

"I don't know what to believe anymore, Reverend Hill. If God gave me a gift, why wouldn't it work when I needed it?"

"That is a question I cannot answer, Muchie. Perhaps healing isn't like an oil lamp you can turn up or turn down at will. All I can tell you is what I believe. The Lord works in mysterious ways, his wonders to perform."

At Charlotte's funeral, Teddy sat on the edge of her small grave with Margaret cradled in his arms.

"Your sister is in heaven now, Margaret. She's an angel in heaven."

Margaret cried without making a sound. Her little face reflected the pain stamped on Teddy's face. I feared they would both topple into the grave to be with Charlotte.

Six weeks after we buried Charlotte, poor little Margaret gave up grieving for her twin and died in her sleep. We could only think it was from a broken heart.

I do believe Teddy loved our sweet baby girls even more than he loved me, but I never felt any jealousy. The twins *were* our love. Charlotte and Margaret were the first walking, talking, living proof of our love.

When Margaret died, our house became silent except for the sound of Tom-Tom and Maddy crying. Teddy and I couldn't talk to each other. Our pain was too great for words.

I went to sleep before Teddy came home. He left for work before I woke up in the morning. We each grieved alone.

There was no more laughter. No more evenings on the porch together. No more plans for the future. Not even wondering how he was and what he felt could break through my own silent grief.

My baby girls were dead. Nothing could change that. It was too much to bear. My prayers for the healing gift to save Charlotte had gone unanswered. After Moss Germaine I'd had no sign of the healing gift. Did that mean it had left me?

Charlotte's death made me believe as much. Despite Reverend Hill's counsel, I couldn't understand why God would bless me with a gift at one time and then curse me with failure each time I called upon it.

Perhaps I had no gift at all. Could it be that Tyler Mama and Papa had been wrong about me? Or was I to blame for turning my back on the gift?

Prayer brought me neither comfort nor answers, so I stopped praying since God only ignored me.

Late one night as I lay wrapped in sadness, Teddy crawled into bed and took my hand. I turned to kiss him. His face was wet with tears.

"What will become of us, Muchie?"

"I don't know, Teddy. I just don't know."

"Why did our babies die, Muchie?" Teddy sobbed in his grief. "What did I do for God to take both of them?"

"Don't talk like that, Teddy. You did nothing wrong. If anyone is to blame, it's me. I lost faith in my healing gift after Tyler Mama died. When I needed it to save Charlotte, it wouldn't come to me.

I couldn't make it work. If I could have saved Charlotte then Margaret would be alive too," I said, tears spilling down my cheeks.

"Please don't cry, Muchie. I love you. I love you with all my heart. It's not your fault that Charlotte died, or Margaret either."

Teddy and I held each other for the first time in weeks. During the night we shared what was in our broken hearts.

"I miss Charlotte and Margaret so much, Teddy. I feel so guilty that they're gone."

"So do I, Muchie. So do I."

We were sad and confused as we cried together remembering details of our daughters' short lives.

"Remember how they were about their favorite stories, Muchie?"

"Nothing would do but for me to read both stories every night, no matter what."

"And when they played, it was like they had their own private world. I can see them now, singing and twirling around in that ring game they made up. They were such little angels, with their sweet faces and happy smiles."

"Yes, they were. Our two little angels."

I heard the neighborhood rooster crow and noticed the darkness was beginning to fade. Snuggling into Teddy's arms, I kissed his neck, pressing my nose into the warm spot behind his ear.

"We better get some sleep, Teddy. It'll be time to get up soon."

"I'm getting up now, Muchie," Teddy said, putting my hand on him.

"What do you think about having another baby? Would a baby make you happy, Muchie? Not to try and replace Charlotte and Margaret . . . just because," he muttered into my hair.

"Shh, not now. We have plenty of time for that," I whispered. "Love me for myself, Teddy, love me for myself."

Neither of us got a wink of sleep but it didn't matter. Love made everything seem possible. Even banishing the silence and sadness that had enveloped our lives.

The next morning I made pancakes for breakfast. Using raisins for the eyes and bacon strips for smiles, Teddy turned the children's pancakes into happy faces. Maddy sat on her daddy's lap to eat. Tom-Tom couldn't stop grinning. Neither could I.

Chapter Twenty-one

1937

"Muchie, you see any problem with Tom-Tom going to my school when he turns six? It would give me more time to spend with him."

"He'd enjoy that, Teddy, and it would be nice for him to be right there with you, just in case. But won't his teacher spoil him rotten with you being on the same faculty?"

"I'll ask her not to play favorites. But I expect teachers will always take a liking to our boy on account of his good home training. Tom-Tom's got winning ways and he's smart as a whip."

"Just like his daddy," I said, giving Teddy a kiss on the cheek.

It was quite a change for me to have only one child at home during the day. With Tom-Tom in school, Maddy and I made good use of our time together.

In the morning we tied on our aprons and set about cleaning the house back to front. Maddy liked to dust, and I had to ration out the furniture polish because her tendency was to pour it on until it ran down to the floor.

After we swept the porch and made a design with the broom in the dirt walkway in front of the house, I sat Maddy down between my knees to comb her hair. That was one task I did not relish.

Maddy squirmed and wiggled as I pulled a black Ace comb through her hair. She had brown hair like me and it tangled easily.

"I want my hair to be short like Tom-Tom's," Maddy told me just about every day. "I could comb it myself, then. He combs his."

"Short hair is fine for a boy. But little girls look pretty with ribbons in their hair. What would I do with all your nice ribbons if I cut off your hair, sweetness?"

She puzzled over my question before coming up with a solution that tickled me.

"You could tie them around my head and I could stick a feather in the back. Like the Indians in the book, Miss Muchie."

Maddy was a great one for studying her lessons with me. She could already read and print neatly formed letters. By the time she started school next year she might be able to skip a grade and catch up with Tom-Tom.

In nice weather we worked in the garden, pulling weeds or staking the beans. I had a little plot of herbs for cooking and making simples. Maddy liked to pinch the leaves and smell them. It always made me think of Tyler Mama.

After we had a bite to eat, I put Maddy down for a nap. The rest of the day lay heavy on my hands.

I didn't know what to do with myself. After years of trying to keep house while tending to four small children, it felt funny to be able to sit still and think without interruption.

The deaths of Charlotte and Margaret were often on my mind although I was blessed to still have two children and a husband, all three loving and healthy.

While Maddy napped, I tried to pray. Daily, I asked God to help me understand and accept the loss of my children. All that came to me was the memory of Tyler Mama saying, "Use your gift."

But I *had* tried to use it with Charlotte and I failed. There was no way around that sad fact. Why did Tyler Mama's words continue to haunt me? My halting prayers gave me no answers.

Tom-Tom thrived in school and rushed home to share his adventures with Maddy. She was on pins to start school and be with him every day.

"Muchie, I'm planning to work at the docks again this summer," Teddy told me over supper one evening.

"I wish you wouldn't, Teddy. Can't you take your three months off this summer like the other teachers? It would be nice to have you home with me."

"I'd like that too, but we can't live on my teaching salary. Not if we're ever going to be able to buy a house, Muchie. I want better for our children than growing up in a rented house. Don't you?"

"Of course I do, it's just that I get so lonely with only Maddy for company."

"Tom-Tom will be here with you soon enough. What about teaching Vacation Bible School at the church this year, Muchie? Reverend Hill would be glad for the help."

"I suppose I could do that. But it only lasts two weeks. Will you at least give some thought to what I said?"

"I will, Muchie. But it won't change my mind. We need the money."

Our house was about a mile from the state docks. In the summer Teddy walked to work every day. Sometimes the children and I walked a way with him in the morning. Tom-Tom carried his daddy's dinner pail and Maddy collected rocks along the way.

"What are you planning to do with all those rocks, Maddy?" Teddy asked her as she stuffed the pockets of her pinafore.

"Tom-Tom told me boys at school tease him sometimes. If they do it when I go to school, I'll hit them with my rocks and make them stop," she said with a frown.

"Now, Maddy, it's good to stand up for your brother. But I don't think hitting boys with rocks is the right way to do it," Teddy said.

"Yes, Daddy," Maddy said, dropping the rock she held in her hand. When we got home, she emptied her pockets, dumping her rocks into a sack she kept beside the front door.

I was fixing dinner for the children when I heard three disaster bells followed by six long whistles wailing from the docks. I grabbed Tom-Tom and Maddy by the hands and started running.

An explosion nearly knocked us off our feet. I never shall forget a woman who was struggling to run with a baby on her hip and a toddler by the hand. One breast was hanging out, round and swollen with milk. She pulled at her dress as she ran, but she wouldn't stop to cover herself.

The closer we got to the docks, the more women there were dashing to get to their men.

What I saw that day was worse than my worst nightmare. Men came running out of the ship, staggering, holding each other up. They were covered with soot, with ash, with blood.

Some were on fire, choking and burning as they ran. Others were slumped in heaps on the ground. Still, except for their groans and screams.

I ran from man to man searching for my Teddy. I finally found him as they were fixing to take him to the hospital. He was unconscious, with burns all over his body.

"That's my husband. I have to go with him," I shouted over the din.

"We can't let those children in the ambulance. You'll have to meet him at the hospital," the attendant said.

Thank God, someone said, "I'll watch your children for you."

"Take them to Mrs. Jasper's house," I yelled, climbing into the ambulance with Teddy.

All the way to the hospital, I knelt next to the stretcher and talked to Teddy, "You're all right, dear heart. I'm with you. I won't let anything happen to you. Just rest, Teddy, you just rest now."

I pressed my cheek to his chest, whispering loving words of comfort. The sound that Teddy made as I held his shoulders was the most horrible thing I've ever heard.

Deeper and more heartrending than a cry for help, it was the groan of a man struggling with unbearable pain.

It scared the breath out of me. My poor darling was suffering torments I could only imagine.

I gently released Teddy and with infinite care laid him back on the stretcher. That's when I saw the damage my touch had done. Every place I'd laid my hands on Teddy, his clothes and skin had pulled away to reveal new wounds. Patches of raw, dark red showed all over his poor burned body. Pieces of Teddy's charred skin were stuck to me. My hands were bloody. I nearly gagged.

"Marine Hospital is full. So is City. We're taking him to Providence," the attendant shouted over his shoulder.

"But he's not Catholic," I answered.

"Don't matter, every hospital in town is taking these men today."

At the hospital a doctor gave Teddy medicine for the pain. Two nuns wrapped him up in bandages like a mummy. Said it was to keep the air off Teddy's burns.

"Whatever you do, don't touch him," they ordered. "If those burns get infected, it could kill him."

Teddy didn't scream like some of the men in the ward. But his quiet moans tore the heart out of me. I sat with him all day.

"Please get well, Teddy. Please don't leave me. Tom-Tom and Maddy love you. I love you with all my heart. You'll see. When you get well we'll buy our house and we'll do all the things you ever wanted to do. Please, Teddy. Please get well."

I sweet-talked Teddy. I repeated every single word we'd whispered when we were alone.

Come evening, a doctor made his rounds of the ward checking on every patient and giving instructions to the wives and mothers who sat with their injured menfolk.

"If he regains consciousness, he might have a fighting chance. Keep talking to him. Maybe that will bring him around," he advised me.

"Teddy, think about our trip to Italy. You promised me a ride in a gondola, remember? And France. You said we'd go there too. Oh, Teddy. I'll happily walk all the way to New York City on my hands. If you'll just wake up for me. Can't you just see that, Teddy? Petticoats covering my head. Wouldn't that make you laugh?"

I told him how much our children needed their daddy. I even lied to him.

"We have another baby on the way, Teddy. Doesn't that good news make you want to wake up?"

I talked to my darling Teddy until I didn't have any voice left. When my voice was gone, I whispered.

But it didn't help. He remained unconscious, groaning and grunting with each breath.

I had to do something. Fearing to touch Teddy and cause him more pain, I held my hands just a hair above his bandages.

I prayed, struggling for the right words to make God hear me, "Heavenly Father, please forgive me for doubting you. Please God, please send my gift back to me. Let me use it to save my husband. Dear God, please, please help me, just this once."

I prayed until I was blue in the face, but nothing happened. I swallowed my fear of hurting Teddy to rest my hands on his body for an instant. The deep, guttural sounds he made tore a hole in my heart. But still, nothing happened.

The healing gift failed me again.

Right before dawn broke, Teddy finally opened his eyes, soft brown like melted milk chocolate. I smiled at him.

Then I began to sob because I saw that his eyelashes were burned clean away.

I spoke his name again and again, "Teddy. Teddy. Teddy. Teddy."

He heaved a great big sigh then, like he used to do at the end of a long day when he'd come home tired as a dog from working at the docks.

Days like that, all he wanted was to sink into a tub of hot water so I could wash the stink of fertilizer out of his hair and rub the tightness from his shoulders.

I leaned close to kiss his beautiful eyes. Though it was the softest, most tender kiss, he flinched.

"I'm sorry, Teddy. I didn't mean to hurt you. I love you, dear heart. I love you."

He gasped, one word at a time, "I. Love. You. Muchie."

Then he was gone.

For half a day and the night long, as he lay suffering, I'd ignored the nursing nuns and priest in their endless processional through the ward, rustling and shifting like a ghostly congregation.

When a priest came to Teddy's bed, I jumped up from my vigil chair.

"He's not a Catholic. Don't touch him. Leave him alone."

"My child, please allow me to bless your dead husband. He is a child of God, whatever his faith," the priest said kindly.

"No. I won't let you make him dead." I pushed the priest aside. He was clumsy, swathed in the flowing draperies of his office. My push sent him tumbling.

I climbed into the hospital bed with my Teddy, shielding him with my own body from the priest, from the world, from Death itself. I held onto Teddy, hoping to force the warmth of my own body onto his body. I cursed anyone who tried to come near us. Swearing from Amazing Grace to Rock of Ages and back again.

"You get away from my husband. Don't you dare touch him," I snarled, trying to shake Teddy awake.

"Sit up, Teddy. Wake up, Teddy. Don't let them make you be dead, Teddy. Sit up. Please don't be dead, Teddy," I moaned hoarsely as I rocked my husband, my tears splashing into his closed eyes.

I rocked him back and forth, dislodging bandages, revealing his horrible wounds. Loosening pieces of burned flesh.

I don't know how long I rocked Teddy, keeping everyone at bay. The next thing I knew, Dorali was standing beside me.

"Come along now, Muchie. It's time to go. Come along with me," she said softly. I almost couldn't hear her over the sounds of men suffering in the ward.

Dorali stroked my hair like I was a feverish child. She pried my fingers from Teddy's body to lay him back on the bed.

"But I can't leave Teddy. He's hurt, Dorali, and he needs me. I can't leave him alone."

Dorali pulled me off the bed and held me tight.

"You can't help Teddy right now, Muchie. You come on along with me. It's all right, Muchie, come along with me."

I didn't have any strength left to push Dorali away like I'd done the priest. I was tired. All the fight in me was long gone. Dorali helped me straighten Teddy's bandages so he'd look decent. She held me steady as I bent to kiss him. And she kept her arm around me as she led me out of the ward.

When I turned to blow kisses at my darling Teddy, I saw the priest anointing him. The sight made no sense to me and I would have run back to stop him, but Dorali wouldn't let me.

"Come along with me, Muchie. Your children need you," she said.

Chapter Twenty-two

❦

1937

God bless my friend Bevane, she was always the practical one. She met us at the front door and handed me a tall iced tea glass full of clear brown liquid.

I was thirsty from talking to Teddy. Gulping down the contents, I didn't even notice what it was until Bevane said, "Hold on now, Muchie, that's sipping whisky you're guzzling. Take it easy, baby girl."

It didn't matter to me whether it was ice tea or bourbon or rat poison. I kept drinking as long as Bevane filled my glass.

I refused to believe that Teddy was really dead. I kept telling Bevane and Dorali he was just gone away for a time. That's why I didn't fuss with them about any of the arrangements. None of it really mattered to me because it wasn't my Teddy they were burying.

The day of the funeral, Bevane bathed and dressed me. While she was combing my hair, I listened tolerantly to her confusion.

"Muchie, I know this is hard for you. You must look nice to-day. There'll be a lot of people in the church and you don't want to shame Teddy by having your hair wild all over your head and acting the fool."

"There's really no need for me to go to church, Bevane. I'll just stay right here and wait for my Teddy. Go on and pray without me."

"Baby girl, Teddy won't be coming home anymore. Don't you remember? He passed five days ago, Muchie. Today is his funeral. Don't you remember, Muchie?"

"I think you are mistaken, Bevane. I talked to Teddy last night. He got hurt and he's in the hospital, but he's getting better. He'll be home, you watch, he'll be home when he's well."

Reverend Hill met me on the steps of the church. "I'd like to speak with you a few moments if I may, Muchie," he said, taking my arm to lead me into his study.

"There's really no reason for me to be here today, Reverend Hill," I protested.

"I'm sorry you feel that way, Muchie. I was hoping you would feel differently by now. I want you to know my eulogy for Teddy comes from the *Song of Solomon*. Here let me show you the verse in my Bible."

I read the passage where Reverend Hill pointed and smiled to see the familiar words, words Teddy had quoted to me time and again.

"That's Teddy's favorite book of the Bible, Reverend Hill. The first time I met him he recited a verse from it."

"I know, Muchie. Teddy and I often discussed the Bible to-gether. He told me the *Song of Solomon* had special meaning for you. That it was one of your favorites as well as his."

"Many mornings Teddy would say to me, 'Rise up my love, my fair one and come away.' Reverend Hill, I thought he was quoting poetry to me. But Teddy told me it was from the Bible. It wasn't until I read it for myself that I believed him. Not that he was in the habit of lying, you understand. But you know how Teddy loves to joke."

"Yes, Muchie. I remember Teddy's sense of humor. I selected the *Song of Solomon* because you know it well, Muchie. I hope it will bring you some measure of comfort. Now if you will excuse me?"

I left Reverend Hill and walked into the church. People turned to stare at me and whisper. They were shaking their heads and wiping their eyes.

An usher led me to the front of the church and when I saw the coffin I wanted to scream. Too many coffins in my life. Too much dying. I refused to look inside the box.

When it was time for him to speak, Reverend Hill didn't stay behind his pulpit. He walked down the steps to stand beside me where I sat scowling and muttering in the pew. He gripped my shoulders and then laid his hands on my head.

"God bless you, Muchie, and give you strength," he whispered.

Had he not done so, I would have run from the church. The scent of flowers, the sound of people crying and the sad music swirled around me reminding me of everyone I loved. Everyone I had failed to save with my fickle healing gift.

Poor little Tom-Tom and Maddy sat huddled together next to me. They cried and cried believing their daddy was dead. But I knew better.

"Teddy," I screamed, needing him to comfort me and assure me all was well. "Teddy," I moaned, until Papa and Mother came to sit on either side of me, holding me upright as Reverend Hill sadly shook his head.

With a weary smile of resignation Reverend Hill began to speak in a resonant tone that filled the church.

"I take my text today from the fifth chapter of the *Song of Solomon*, sixth verse. It is a text that spoke to my heart as I contemplated the devastating loss of our brother in Christ, Edward Preston. The text reads, 'I opened to my beloved, but my beloved had withdrawn himself and gone: my soul failed . . . I sought him, but I could not find him, I called him but he gave me no answer.'

"Brothers and sisters in our Lord Jesus Christ, we come today to pray for the soul of our departed brother Edward Preston. He has gone from this vale of tears to be with our Father God in heaven. He has gone to prepare a place for us. Today, in the fullness of our faith we know that Edward Preston's suffering is at an end. And for that blessing, we must all rejoice. But even in the security of our Christian faith, we find our hearts are heavy within us today, because the earthly light of our brother is now extinguished. His life was a beacon to many of us. Without him, the way seems dark indeed.

"Those who were blessed to know Edward Preston as teacher, as friend, as citizen, as son-in-law and as father know he was a man who could be depended on to do his duty where he saw it. He did so quietly with never a thought of glory or reward.

"There is yet another important fact you must know about Edward Preston's exemplary life. It is a fact that makes this celebration of his life and death in Jesus Christ especially poignant. Our brother, Edward Preston, was devoted to his wife, our dear sister Charlotte who sits before us overwhelmed by her loss. I look at Charlotte, known to all who love her as Muchie, and I say to you, the bright candle of their love reflects the scripture I read. Solomon uses earthly love to illustrate God's divine love for us, his people.

"The verse speaks to us of God's pure love for his chosen people. Love that protects and sustains and yes, love that tests us.

" 'My beloved has withdrawn himself and gone,' the text reads. Indeed, it would appear to any not nourished by the word of God, that Edward Preston has in fact withdrawn himself and gone. We see here before us his earthly remains, burned in the explosion of a ship where he worked to support his family. We see and we grieve, for his pain and for our loss. But our faith tells us that Edward Preston is no longer with us in a physical sense. He has been reunited with our Father God in heaven.

"I implore all of you who loved Edward Preston to let him rest in the fullness of his salvation. I pray you will find strength to lift your souls from despair. And, dear Muchie, I entreat you not to fall victim to a crisis of faith. Do not let the harsh fate you have suffered embitter you and rob you of your sweetness. Do not demand from God an accounting for the working of his will. I say to you, we must believe the Lord does work in mysterious ways his wonders to perform. Let us accept the death of Edward Preston, not as a punishment to be endured, but as a wondrous miracle God has done for his own reasons in his own time. Amen."

Leaving the church, I struggled to understand how anyone could say Teddy would ever leave me. It wasn't possible. He would never do such a thing.

Teddy was not the kind of no-account, shiftless colored man to leave his wife and children. He was too good and decent for that.

I kept shaking my head, no, no, no.

Chapter Twenty-three

1938

"How you doing, baby girl?" Bevane asked when she brought me a box of canned goods courtesy of the Benevolent Club at the church. She unpacked the box to put the cans into my cupboard.

"About all I can say is I'm doing, Bevane."

"Doesn't look like you're doing too well with your nightgown on this time of day, Muchie. And look at your hair. It's a rat's nest. When was the last time you combed your hair?"

"With my Teddy gone away, what's the use in me fixing up? Nobody cares how I look, least of all me."

"Well, I care, and I imagine your children care too. You're all they've got now, Muchie. I know it's hard, but you've got to try. For them."

"I'm tired, Bevane. At night I can't sleep. All I want to do is curl up in the chifforobe and hide," I confessed, not even making the effort to hide my secret. It was all I had to give me any comfort.

"You sound crazy as a road lizard talking like that. You've got to do better, Muchie. You owe it to Teddy. He wouldn't want you letting yourself go, and he sure wouldn't be happy with the house like this."

"It's real hard, Bevane. Losing Charlotte and Margaret and then Teddy going away. All in less than six months. I just feel beat down from everything that's happened. I keep waiting for the next bad thing to come along, and it keeps me jittery."

She rummaged around in her purse. "Somebody gave me this years ago. I'm giving it to you. Maybe it will help you some. Here, read it out loud."

I took the card Bevane offered. It read: "Forgive me, Father, for the times when I am anxious. You have promised to take care of all my needs."

"Read it when you feel bad, Muchie. It will calm you and give you strength."

I put the card in my pocket, promising to do as Bevane asked.

After she went home, I looked around my home with her eyes and saw how many things I'd let slip. The furniture was covered with dust. There was a fine layer of grit on all the floors. I looked out the window. The garden was wilting and overgrown with weeds.

It had been weeks since I'd even remembered to wash Maddy's hair. When I called her in from playing with Tom-Tom I could see her long braids were matted and dirty, badly in need of my attention.

Left on their own, Tom-Tom and Maddy would spend the whole day running and ripping outside, climbing trees and scooting over fences.

Brave little Maddy still collected rocks to defend her big brother. Once or twice she even used a few. But it was usually Tom-Tom who had to take up for Maddy because children teased her unmercifully about her skin.

It started with red, rough patches on her arms and legs that spread to her face and head. I warned her not to, but she would scratch, making ugly scabs. I doctored on her the best way I knew how with one of Tyler Mama's remedies, but my poor baby looked a sight.

Holding her head underneath the tap to rinse out the soap, the water revealed sores oozing yellow slime.

"Come sit down, Maddy, so I can rub this salve on your scalp."

"Will it hurt, Miss Muchie?"

"I hope not, sweetness."

As I smoothed medicine into Maddy's scalp, I felt the lovely shape of her little head beneath my hands. It filled me with tenderness.

"You're a beautiful child, Madeleine Preston. I'm happy you're my little girl."

She giggled at the compliment and sat still instead of squirming the way she usually did when I combed her hair.

The feel of her head beneath my hands was such an unexpected pleasure that I was lulled into a lovely calmness.

Suddenly, I got a dizzy spell and felt like I was going to faint. My hands tingled and burned, like I'd picked up a pot hot off the stove. I lost all sense of myself.

Then Maddy was struggling and shouting, "You're pulling my head off, Miss Muchie. Stop!"

I let Maddy go. Strange as it sounds, there were no red patches of roughness on her skin. Her face was smooth and even toned. When I parted her hair to check, the sores were gone.

I was truly glad Maddy's skin was healed. I was also terribly confused. God used my hands to heal Maddy, that was plain as day. Just as he'd done for others.

But never for anyone I loved. Until now. What made Maddy

different from Tyler Mama and Charlotte? Why was today different from the times I'd begged God for the healing gift to come?

Her life had not been in danger. Was that why God let me heal her? I thought of Theola and her baby, the little boy at school and Moss Germaine. Had I tried to heal them or had the gift merely worked through me? So much had happened to me that I simply could not remember.

It made me angry to think there was a showboat God sitting up in heaven turning my healing gift on and off when it pleased him. But it was pointless to be mad with God.

Choking back my rage, I thanked God for healing Maddy and prayed again for understanding. The only sound I heard was the breeze blowing through the trees.

At night it helped me sleep if I had the children in bed with me. I piled pillows like barricades on either side of the bed, making a nest for us.

Tom-Tom and Maddy were all sharp knees and pointy elbows. I dubbed them my little birds.

"You're the strongest little bird, Tom-Tom. You must help me protect the nest," I told him.

Though he and Maddy got along fine during the day, at night they would thrash and squirm and bicker about who was pulling the cover and whose turn it was to pick the bedtime story.

To settle them down, I recited a verse Tyler Mama had taught me.

Birds in their nests agree
And it's such a shameful sight to see
Children in the same family
Fall out and fuss and fight.

Then I'd stretch out with my dear little ones next to me and listen to their prayers. The slow steady sound of their breathing lulled me to sleep. But if I heard a sound in the night it startled me awake and I couldn't fall asleep again.

It made no sense and I knew it, but I roamed the house, pulling on all the doors to be sure they were locked, checking every window and screen. I must have cried two rivers of tears those long nights wandering through our little house.

I felt abandoned and alone, it made me want to howl like a dog. But I didn't dare wake my sleeping children.

When I could bear my loneliness not a second longer I retreated to the safety of the chifforobe that still held Teddy's clothes. Pushing his things aside, I made room to curl up in the little closet. I held one of his worn shirts to my face, breathing in the fragrance of my husband.

It was the only comfort I could find in the world.

"Teddy, please come home. I need you, Teddy. Please come home soon."

Blinded by my tears and nearly out of my mind with grief, I heard a little sound. It was Tom-Tom standing in the darkness watching me. At first I pulled back to hide in the chifforobe, unwilling to give up my haven. Then I heard my baby sobbing.

"Oh, honey, don't cry. Come here and snuggle with me. It's all right, Tom-Tom. There's room for both of us."

I reached out for him, but Tom-Tom shook his head, refusing to climb into the chifforobe with me.

He stretched out his thin little boy arms and grabbed my shoulders with his bony little boy hands. Tom-Tom held me, digging his fingers into my skin. He wouldn't let me go. No matter how hard I tried to pull away, he kept holding me with strength I did not know he had, tears running down his face all the while.

Something happened. I can't explain it, but everything

changed. I felt like a drowning woman being pulled to shore. My little boy pulled me out of my grief when he pulled me out of the chifforobe.

It was a come to Jesus moment for me.

Tom-Tom made me leave my refuge and lay my sorrow to rest in the old-fashioned closet full of his father's clothes. He poured out his childish strength for me and he saved me from grief.

He was shaking from the effort. I closed the chifforobe door and never crawled into its depths again.

The next morning, I woke up feeling good for the first time in months. My body didn't ache and I wasn't afraid or anxious the way I'd been since Teddy went away.

I jumped out of bed, snatched open the curtains and pulled up the window. Soft air blew in on my face, tender as a kiss. I laughed out loud, hardly recognizing the sound of my own voice.

Dropping to my knees in the sunlight I said my morning prayers.

"Thank you, God, for giving me this hopeful day. Dear Lord, please tell me. Is what I'm feeling temporary? Will I go back to feeling bad again?"

It was the first time God ever answered me. "It's permanent enough for today," he said.

Chapter Twenty-four

1939

Must have been a good seven months after Teddy went away when Mr. Ernest Winston came to call. Mr. Winston was an older gentleman who owned the biggest funeral home in town.

Something about him reminded me of Papa. He was tall and well set up like Papa with a nice, easy manner about him. He even had a neatly trimmed moustache, just like Papa did.

Although I'd never actually met him, I knew who he was through my friend Bevane. She was a cousin on his mother's side.

"Good morning to you, Mrs. Preston. Lovely day, isn't it?" Mr. Winston took off his hat when he greeted me. I was on my knees weeding my flowerbeds.

"Indeed it is, sir. Hot though for this time of year. I expect we have another scorcher of a summer ahead of us."

I wiped my hands on my apron and stood up to face Mr. Winston, who blushed when I smiled at him.

"Mrs. Preston, your garden is simply beautiful. Takes a lot of work to maintain a garden like this one. Your peonies are exceptional."

I snipped off a few fat blossoms. "I'll just wrap the stems in damp paper and you can take them home with you, Mr. Winston."

"I wouldn't think of troubling you that way, Mrs. Preston, though I know my mother will enjoy these flowers. Let me just put them in my handkerchief," he said as he reached into his back pocket.

Mr. Winston's first name and the earnest way he wrapped the stems forced a laugh out of me. Soon I was laughing like a ninny.

He looked startled and then he began to laugh along with me.

"Please forgive me, Mr. Winston, I haven't laughed in such a long time."

"No need to apologize. I like to laugh myself and in my line of work, there aren't very many opportunities."

That set me off again and I laughed until tears ran down my cheeks. My giggles turned into sobs and Mr. Winston wasn't laughing anymore.

He was observing me with concern. Brushing his thick salt-and-pepper hair off his brow, he put his hat back on and took my arm to sit me down in the shade of the front porch.

Mr. Winston handed me yet another handkerchief. This one was starched linen and it came from his breast pocket.

"Here you go, Mrs. Preston. Wipe your face for me. May I get you some water?"

As I dabbed at my eyes I caught a peek of a discrete blue monogram embroidered in the corner of the handkerchief.

Mr. Winston's no-nonsense manner made me take a deep breath and try to regain my composure. I looked up, but I was too embarrassed to meet his eyes.

"Ever since my Teddy went away, it's been really hard, Mr. Winston. Just. Well. I'm sorry about carrying on like this."

"Actually, your husband's death is the reason for my visit, Mrs. Preston."

He reached into the inside breast pocket of his navy blue jacket to pull out a fat white envelope. He handed it to me with an apologetic smile.

"Mrs. Preston, the shipping company finally paid all the expenses for the men killed in the explosion. You're due this refund on your late husband's burial policy."

It didn't seem prudent to try and clear up his confusion about Teddy right then. I knew in my heart Teddy would come back to me one day. But so far I had been unable to convince anyone else of that. Everybody kept telling me Teddy was dead, but I just wouldn't believe it.

God knows I needed money so I simply accepted the envelope Mr. Winston offered with good grace.

"Thank you kindly, Mr. Winston. I sure do appreciate you bringing me this money. Right now, it will come in handy."

"I imagined you could make good use of it, with Mr. Preston gone. I came by as soon as I could. Do you mind me asking about your plans, Mrs. Preston? Have you given any thought to going back home to your people in Mississippi?"

"The thought has crossed my mind, Mr. Winston. But I like living in Mobile. I expect what I'll have to do is find myself a real job," I said without really thinking.

"Why isn't that a coincidence, Mrs. Preston? I'm needing some help right now myself at the mortuary," he told me with yet another smile.

Mr. Winston had a nice face with fine features. His practiced charm and serious demeanor were very persuasive.

"I don't know a thing about the burial business, Mr. Winston.

The only paying job I've ever had was working my godfather's sawmill. I ran his office for him, did the payroll, kept all his accounts and such."

"Then you may be the answer to my prayers, Mrs. Preston. My accountant has taken sick, and I've been doing all his work as well as my own, but it occupies a powerful lot of my time. Do you suppose you'd be willing to come help me out? It would mean working every day excepting Sunday but I'll pay you well for your time."

"I'd need to be home before too late in the evening because of my children, Mr. Winston, and I don't see how I could work all day every Saturday and keep things up around the house. But if you're offering me a paying job, I'd be proud to take it. There's just one condition."

"And what might that be, Mrs. Preston?"

"You must call me Muchie. Everybody does."

Mr. Winston and I shook hands on the deal. "Don't you worry about a thing, Miss Muchie. We'll work out fine together."

I was giddy as a goose about getting a job. I didn't even ask him what he'd pay me. How ever much it was would sure be more than I had now. Turned out he was more than fair about my wages. And everything else too.

My first day on the job, I found fresh-cut flowers waiting on my desk. I thought it was just a nice, friendly gesture from somebody who'd pulled a few blooms out of a funeral spray to make me feel welcome.

"I know the flowers aren't as nice as the ones you grow in your yard, but do you like them, Miss Muchie?" Mr. Winston asked around the middle of the day.

"Why sure I do, Mr. Winston, I've always been partial to flowers and these smell so sweet I can enjoy them without even looking at them. Thank you for your kindness."

"It's no more than you deserve, Miss Muchie."

After that, there were fresh flowers on my desk even on the days we didn't hold a wake or a funeral. Mr. Winston brought them to me from his own yard, which got us to talking about aphids and other garden pests.

He knew his flowers, Mr. Winston did. When there were none blooming at his place, he'd bring in bulbs he'd forced. They brightened my desk through the dead of winter. He was mighty thoughtful that way.

Not much got past Mr. Winston either.

"You're very good with people, Miss Muchie. Can I persuade you to take over the supervisory responsibilities for the funeral car drivers?"

"I don't know about that, Mr. Winston. I've never been the boss of anyone before. Do you think the men will listen to me?"

"Why, sure they will, if they want to keep working for me. The main thing you'll need to do is post the schedule for funerals each week. Let them know who is to drive, which vehicles will be used and such."

Mr. Winston's confidence gave me courage that grew as the months passed.

"I think I have a good idea, Mr. Winston. Do you mind if I tell it to you?"

"Not at all. Please, go right ahead."

"You have the biggest funeral home in town and you've built up a fine reputation over the years. But the drivers don't look as nice as they could. My suggestion is for your drivers to start wearing black suits with white shirts and dove-gray ties. That will make them look better than everybody else's drivers. It will give you an edge over the other mortuaries. What do you think, Mr. Winston?"

"It's a fine idea, Miss Muchie. Make it like a uniform. We can get crests with the mortuary's name on it for their breast pockets to really dress them up."

"I'm glad you like the idea, Mr. Winston. There's one more thing."

"Yes?"

"Will you ask the men not to smoke cigars when they're on duty? The smell makes some people sick."

"Well, now. That's something I won't do," he said. "I approve of the idea, and I'll back you up on it. Don't get me wrong. That's something they should hear from their supervisor though," he offered with a wink.

One or two of the men balked at the changes I suggested. When they went to Mr. Winston with their complaints, he set them straight in a hurry.

With Mr. Winston in my corner, not a soul gave me any trouble again.

Chapter Twenty-five

🌸🌸

1940

I'd been working for Mr. Winston more than a year when he asked me to stay a few minutes after work. He hemmed and hawed a good bit, straightening the papers on his desk and not meeting my eyes.

That made me nervous. I was afraid I'd done something wrong, and he was going to fire me.

Eventually he got down to cases.

"My club holds a costume ball every year, Miss Muchie. It's a few days after Christmas. Kicks off the Carnival season. Since I'm president, I feel like I ought to have a partner for first dance. I would be mighty happy if you'd consider going to the dance with me, Miss Muchie."

"Oh, Mr. Winston, thank you kindly. I do love to dance. But I'm still in mourning for my husband. I don't go to dances and things like that anymore."

"I understand," he nodded sadly.

His invitation took me by surprise. I knew about his dance because Dorali's husband, Aaron, was a member of the same club as Mr. Winston. She began planning their costumes early in the summer.

It was sweet of Mr. Winston to ask. I'd never heard of him squiring anybody around. I was flattered but also worried.

Even with the generous wages Mr. Winston paid, money was still as tight as Dick's hatband. I had barely enough to make fee for stockings after taking care of the children's needs and paying rent and utilities.

Had refusing his offer offended Mr. Winston? The last thing I needed was to get on his bad side. I needed to keep my job.

He never said another word about it. Things went on with us the same as before.

The details of my financial condition were no secret. Every few months, Mr. Winston drummed up a new reason for a raise.

It was a true fact I worked as hard for him as any two people might. I tried to repay his kindness by coming up with ideas to help his business make money. Even with that, he paid me way more than I thought I deserved.

I tried to talk over the situation with Dorali and Bevane, but they had other ideas.

"I think Mr. Winston is trying to court you in his own quiet way," Dorali said.

"Ernest is a good catch. You could do a whole lot worse than encourage his attentions," Bevane told me.

"Mr. Winston is just a Christian gentleman trying to help a poor widow woman raise decent children," I told them.

They hooted with laughter.

"Don't play crazy, baby girl. Talking like one of the early Christian martyrs doesn't fool me. You know what Ernest is up to," Bevane insisted.

"Muchie, you're as full of stuff as a Christmas turkey. Ernest may be older than you, but he's still a man. You're a good-looking woman. You spend six days a week together. What do you expect?" Dorali said.

"He's got his nose wide open for you, Muchie. Can't you see how he lights up when you're around? And why do you think he brings you flowers all the time? He's like a schoolboy with his first crush. You better open your eyes, Muchie, and see what everyone else sees."

"Did it ever occur to either one of you meddling busybodies Mr. Winston might just respect me for pulling more than my weight at the funeral home? Maybe he treats me good like he does because I work hard for him."

"Nobody disputes you work hard, Muchie. There's not a lazy bone in your body, never has been. And you're smart too, God knows. All I'm saying is long as I've known Ernest Winston I've never seen him carry on about anybody the way he does about you."

"You tell her, Bevane. Tell her how he's always asking you about her. Wait. Listen to this. Aaron told me Ernest is forever singing your praises at club meetings. All he can do is talk about how Miss Muchie did this and how Miss Muchie said that. Why he was so tickled the time you complimented his tie he couldn't wait for club meeting to tell Aaron."

"You can say what you will or may. I'm not about to listen to any of your matchmaking nonsense. Not one word of it. Besides, you know Teddy is the only man for me. There's nothing left for anybody else."

After the New Year rolled around Carnival was in full swing. Mr. Winston brought me a box of sweets from the Three Georges Candy Shoppe.

"Your candy was made fresh today," he told me.

"May I offer you a piece?"

"No, no. It's all for you, Miss Muchie."

"Thank you for the candy, Mr. Winston. If you don't mind, I'll take it home to share with my children. Store-bought candy will be a real treat for them. You are very kind."

"It's no more than you deserve, Miss Muchie."

One Sunday after church, Tom-Tom, Maddy and I walked down the steps to find Mr. Winston standing beside his big car.

"Good morning, Mr. Winston. What in the great wide world brings you all the way from Point Clear to our neck of the woods this bright and sunny day?" I asked.

He smiled sweetly and tipped his hat to me. Then he opened the car doors.

"I just happened to be in the neighborhood, Miss Muchie. Would you and the children like a ride home?"

A ride anywhere in an automobile was a special occasion for us. The children enjoyed it no end. For once they were quiet. Sitting in the back seat they gazed out the windows making swooshing sounds.

"Why don't I take you the long way? Then you can see the azaleas in bloom down Government Street," he said. "We'll pass right by McKinley's. How do you children feel about an ice cream cone?" he asked over his shoulder.

The light in Tom-Tom and Maddy's eyes gave him the answer.

Seems like Mr. Winston popped up everywhere I went after that day. I'd be haggling with the greengrocer and there was Mr. Winston, buying tomatoes or beans.

When I visited the butcher's stall, Mr. Winston leaned over my shoulder. "The liver looks especially good today," he commented.

He refused to let me take out my money to pay for one single thing. Mr. Winston was always the perfect gentleman, carrying my parcels and insisting on driving me home.

"If you keep this up, I'll be spoiled rotten, Mr. Winston." I laughed.

"It's no more than you deserve, Miss Muchie," he said.

"How is it that you shop the same time and the same place I do, Mr. Winston? Don't you have any markets in Baldwin County?" I teased after another one of our impromptu meetings.

"Indeed we do and very fine ones at that. I'll have to show them to you one day," he answered, ignoring my first question entirely.

Although he was practically supporting my children and me with his generosity, Mr. Winston never asked for so much as a handshake in return.

He helped me with such graciousness I never felt cheap accepting his charity. It made me work all the harder helping him at the funeral home.

Come summer, Mr. Winston told me he'd never been sick a day in his life.

"It's that pure, sweet air blowing in off the water, Miss Muchie. Do your children like the beach? I hate to think of them suffering all summer long in this heat."

"The only time they've been to the beach is for church picnics. I keep meaning to take them out on the ferry one Sunday for a ride."

"I have a better idea, Miss Muchie. Why don't I bring you all out to the house for dinner some Sunday? My mother would enjoy the company, and so would I."

"Oh, we wouldn't dare impose on you, Mr. Winston."

"Don't you worry, Miss Muchie. It won't be a bit of trouble. If you like, I can come for you after church."

The very next Sunday that's just what he did, striking up conversation with Tom-Tom and Maddy and charming them from the minute they got into his car.

"My house is in Point Clear, Alabama, on the eastern shore of Mobile Bay," he told them. "The area is famous for something called Jubilee. You ever hear of that?"

"No, sir," Tom-Tom replied.

"What's Jubilee mean?" Maddy asked.

"Late in the night, fish and crabs flop right on the beach for you to scoop up as many as you want. Folks load up buckets and pails, even whole boats, with more seafood than they could catch in a month. That's a Jubilee," he said.

"For real? I sure would like to see that sight," Tom-Tom said eagerly.

"Mr. Winston, you mustn't fill my children's heads with such nonsense," I scoffed.

"I know it sounds strange, Miss Muchie. But I've seen enough Jubilees to assure you it *is* true. Jubilees happen mostly through the summer. Folks ring Jubilee bells up and down the shore to wake everybody up for the bounty."

"What makes a Jubilee, Mr. Winston?" Tom-Tom asked.

"No one really knows, son. Some speculate that freshwater from the river and saltwater from the bay change places and the fish come to shore looking for air. It might be the tides or something about the moon that causes a Jubilee."

"Fish really come to shore like you said, Mr. Winston?" Tom-Tom sounded a bit unsure.

"Indeed they do. You can pick them up with your hands and crabs too. They won't even bite you when it's a Jubilee." He laughed.

At his house, my children tumbled out of the car and stared.

"Look, Miss Muchie! A candy cane house!" Tom-Tom announced in amazement to see a red-and-white striped house.

"Let's go see the candy cane house. Candy cane house. Let's go see the candy cane house."

Maddy sang until Tom-Tom caught my eye and poked his sister into silence.

"Mind your manners now," I said to the children. They stood stock still, waiting for me to tell them what to do.

"I like your name for the house, Tom-Tom. Do you think I ought to get a sign for the gate, Maddy?" Mr. Winston asked with a twinkle in his eye.

"Yes, sir. That way everyone will know what to call your pretty house," Maddy replied. Tom-Tom nodded his agreement.

"Then I'll do just that. Tell you what. We can go in the candy cane house right this minute. Or, we can take a trip down to the beach first. It's up to you," Mr. Winston said.

Two little heads turned to me for permission. Before I could open my mouth, Mr. Winston said, "Miss Muchie, it's been fifty years since that poor lonely beach had the pleasure of children playing on it. You'd be doing me a great favor if you'd let the children walk down there."

They were wearing their Sunday best, but I didn't have the heart to refuse him. He sent the children on ahead telling them to stay away from the water until he got there.

Lord, I'd never even thought about the dangers lurking in the bay. When I started to sputter, Mr. Winston took my arm and escorted me to the porch where he deposited me into his mother's care.

What he did touched my heart. Mr. Winston handed me his navy blue suit coat, rolled up his pants legs and pulled off his shoes and socks to set them neatly on the steps. Then, off he ran to where my little ones were chasing the seagulls and shrieking like banshees.

I could hear the three of them laughing and having a high heel good time on the beach.

"I can't remember the last time I saw Ernest enjoy himself so much," Mrs. Winston laughed as I walked into the kitchen with her.

"He thinks the world of you, Mrs. Preston."

"Oh, please, Mrs. Winston. Call me Muchie, everybody does," I told her as she led me to a table where a pile of vegetables awaited us.

"You have a beautiful place here. I just love your garden. Your flowers are a sight to behold."

Mrs. Winston dimpled at the compliment. "The vegetables are from my garden too, Muchie. I like having fresh vegetables for the table."

"I keep a little garden behind my house for that very reason, Mrs. Winton."

She was friendly as could be. Much nicer than I'd ever expected because Mrs. Winston had quite the reputation of being a dragon lady clinging to her only son all his life. But she seemed genuinely glad we were visiting and pleased about my friendship with Mr. Winston.

As we sliced tomatoes, green onions and bell peppers for a salad, she told me, "My son talks about you all the time, Muchie. He thinks you are just the smartest, prettiest thing. Ernest thinks you hung the moon and I can see why."

"You are too kind, Mrs. Winston. I am very grateful to Mr. Winston for his generosity. If he hadn't given me a job after my Teddy went away I don't know how we would have made it."

We puttered around together putting dinner on the table and chatting about one thing or the other for the better part of an hour. When she saw Mr. Winston and my children come straggling up the path to the house, she didn't say one word about their appearance.

My formerly tidy children looked like the very wrath of God. Loaded down with driftwood, piles of seashells and their shoes and socks.

There was sand all over their clothes and sea grass sticking out of their hair. Mrs. Winston smiled and pointed to a stack of towels on the porch.

"Let Ernest run the garden hose over their feet and be sure they dry off real good so they don't take cold."

"I apologize for how they look, Mrs. Winston. You must think we're a bunch of vagabonds."

"Don't be silly, Muchie, they're just children. Let them have their fun." Not a word about tracking up her house. No fear they would smell like the great outdoors, which they surely did after running and jumping in the hot sun. I could see where Mr. Winston got his gracious manner.

It was the best dinner I'd eaten in many a year, even more so because someone else cooked it. Mrs. Winston made a lemon pound cake with fresh lemon sauce for dessert.

"Lemon pound cake is my favorite, Mrs. Winston, and this is better than any I've had. Would you mind sharing your recipe with me?" I asked timidly.

"Nothing fancy about it, Muchie, just a plain old pound cake. Half a dozen nice-sized eggs, a pound of butter, three cups of flour, three teaspoons of lemon flavor, grated lemon rind, three cups of sugar, baking powder, salt and a little sweet milk. It's the lemon sauce that makes it good. That's my secret."

By the time we'd eaten our fill and cleared the table, Maddy felt right at home. She volunteered to sing while our food digested. As she stood and curtsied, her smile was as bright as the highly polished baby grand in the corner of Winston's parlor.

When Maddy exhausted her repertoire, Mrs. Winston suggested we sit on the wide wraparound porch to enjoy the breeze.

In no time, Maddy dozed off for a nap, but Tom-Tom was getting fidgety.

"Son, I forgot to ask if you like to fish when I was telling you about Jubilee," Mr. Winston said. "I've caught some good eating fish right off that jetty out there."

"I don't know how to fish, Mr. Winston, but I've caught crawdaddies out of the creek near our house. Cooked them myself, didn't I, Miss Muchie?"

"Indeed you did, Tom-Tom, and they were delicious too."

"Well that's mighty fine, sounds like you've got the making of a fisherman in you. Maybe you and I can strike a deal. You show me how to catch crawdaddies and I show you how to fish. What do you say to that?"

"Can I, Miss Muchie?"

"Don't you mean 'May I,' Tom-Tom? And the answer is yes, long as you're no trouble to Mr. Winston."

"How about Saturday, son? You want to come fish with me next Saturday morning early?"

"Yes sir, I sure do!"

"But Mr. Winston, Saturday is our busiest day at the funeral home. I wouldn't want to inconvenience you."

"Don't you worry about that, Miss Muchie. You just make sure this young man is ready to go before day in the morning so we can get the fish while they're still sleepy. I'll take care of the rest."

Tom-Tom talked about going fishing all week long. Turned out Mr. Winston was as good as his word. He came for Tom-Tom before the sun was up Saturday morning.

When I got home from work I found two tired fishermen who proudly presented me with a mess of nicely cleaned ground mullet.

"You sure you didn't get these from the fish market?" I teased them.

"Miss Muchie, these fish were swimming in the bay this very morning. If you'll do us the honor of cooking them, they'll be our supper tonight."

Mr. Winston stayed to eat with us. Maddy helped by stirring up batter for hush puppies. I fried them along with the fish, crisp and golden brown. Tom-Tom pulled three ripe tomatoes off the vine outside the kitchen and sliced them for our meal.

"I'm sorry I didn't have time to bake a cake for dessert, Mr. Winston. I hope you like rice pudding," I said apologetically.

"I can't tell you when I've had a supper like this," Mr. Winston said, full of praise for the simple meal.

Mr. Winston and Tom-Tom went fishing together once or twice the month. Those two would fish every day if nobody stopped them.

Chapter Twenty-six

1941

I never stopped missing Teddy the longest day of my life. Despite that, I responded to Mr. Winston's attentions.

It charmed me that he cared enough to court me in his old-fashioned and gentlemanly way. Piled one upon the other his kind gestures began to win me over and build my confidence.

"My mother is quite ill, Miss Muchie. There's little hope of a recovery considering her age," he said.

"Oh, I'm so sorry, Mr. Winston. Is there anything I can do?"

A brief thought of the healing gift flickered in my mind and then it was gone.

"As a matter of fact there is. Do you think you can run the funeral home for me? I trust you to take care of things, Miss Muchie. With you in charge I'll be able to spend whatever time is left with my mother."

"Of course I will, Mr. Winston. Don't you worry, everything will be fine here," I said.

Mrs. Winston died in January and Mr. Winston grieved hard, staying away from work for months. My heart went out to him and I tried to find ways to console him.

I dispatched one of the funeral home drivers to Mr. Winston's house over the bay once a week with something good I cooked for him to eat. Chicken and dumplings, bread pudding, a pot of beef stew, apple dumplings, anything I could think of that was warm and comforting.

The first holiday after his mother's death was Easter Sunday. Far as I knew, Mr. Winston had spent every holiday of his life with his mother.

Not to mention every Sunday and indeed, every weekday as well. He had to be missing her something terrible.

I invited him to Easter dinner to keep him from being alone on a holiday so soon after his mother's death.

He arrived exactly on time, with a pot of Easter lilies for me. On either arm he carried baskets of chocolate bunnies and gum-drops from the Three Georges Candy Shoppe for Tom-Tom and Maddy.

"Thank you, Mr. Winston," the children shouted, tearing into their baskets with delight.

"Save your candy until after dinner," I said to my children. "The lilies are lovely, Mr. Winston. Thank you for thinking of me."

Right after Tom-Tom blessed the table, Mr. Winston leaned over and whispered to me, "I'd like to sit at the head of your table, Miss Muchie."

"Oh, Mr. Winston, I'm sorry. I didn't mean any harm. You're welcome to change places with Tom-Tom. I've just gotten into the habit of letting him sit at the head of the table," I said, getting up to make the switch.

Mr. Winston's hazel eyes were bright as he gave me the oddest smile.

"No, no," Mr. Winston told me, patting my arm, "That's not what I meant. I'm happy with my seat today. I was just trying to say I want to marry you, Miss Muchie."

I sat at the table dumb as cake dough staring at Mr. Winston like one of us had lost our minds. He smiled again and reached to touch my hand. He must have thought better of it because he folded his hands in front of him.

"You don't have to give me an answer now, Miss Muchie. Please consider the matter. That's all I ask," he said.

The rest of the meal, not to mention the rest of the day, passed me by like a bank of storm clouds.

I couldn't sleep that night thinking about Mr. Winston's proposal. I sat up in bed wide awake turning his question over and over in my mind.

If only I could get some advice. Teddy had a way of seeing right to the heart of things and I talked to him that night as I did whenever I was alone. But it was always a one-way conversation.

I could feel his presence, but for the life of me, I could never hear his voice. It was probably asking too much for my husband to counsel me on a marriage proposal from another man anyway.

Dorali and Bevane had made their opinions clear. My children were too young to know anything about life. There was no one to talk to about my predicament.

I was on my own. I knew I didn't love Mr. Winston. It didn't seem right to marry with a man without loving him. And I would never love any man but my Teddy.

Here I was, missing my husband every day of my life. How could Mr. Winston ask me to marry him knowing me as he did?

Mr. Winston had recently lost his mother. Perhaps it was grief talking when he proposed, not good sense.

He'd never been married. What would he want with a woman and two children at this time in his life? Why would he want me?

The only thing I could think to do was draw a line down the middle of a sheet of paper. I labeled one side "positive" and the other side "negative."

To be fair, I listed the positive things about Mr. Winston first.

He was free to marry any woman in town. Even I could see he was handsome and everybody knew he was well to do. People liked him. He was generous, intelligent and hardworking.

Mr. Winston had been good to my children and me. I was indebted to him for giving me a job and for treating me with unfailing courtesy and respect. I liked Mr. Winston more than any man I knew. I valued his friendship and I admired him tremendously.

His manners were perfect and he knew how to have a good time. He lived in a house that proclaimed happiness with its cheery red-and-white paint. Mr. Winston was a generous man with a kind heart.

The only two things I could find to write on the negative side were that I didn't love Ernest Winston and he wasn't Teddy.

If I had never known Teddy, I'd be on my knees thanking God for sending me a man like Ernest Winston. Indeed, I would do almost anything for him, but I could not marry him.

I was afraid hurt pride might cause Mr. Winston to fire me. That worried me.

Refusing an invitation to a dance and turning down a marriage proposal were two different things.

Colored men and women, even educated ones, were still the last ones hired and the first ones fired. I would have a time trying to find another good-paying job like the one I had if Mr. Winston let me go.

About the only other kind of work I was qualified to do was domestic work. Lots of women smarter and better educated than me did that kind of work every day.

But I'd be damned if I'd throw away a steady job I loved in a respectable colored business to go work in Miss Anne's kitchen.

I had to find a way to refuse Mr. Winston's proposal without hurting his feelings or his pride. All I could do was tell him the truth. Maybe not the plain, unvarnished truth, but I had to tell Mr. Winston enough of the truth to convince him I was serious about never marrying again.

I decided I'd reveal my secret hope. One day Teddy would come home to me. I couldn't marry anyone else as long as that was a possibility.

The funeral home was closed for Easter Monday, giving me one more day to build up my nerve. Bright and early Tuesday morning I marched into Mr. Winston's private office and shut the door behind me, holding on to the knob for courage.

"Good morning, Mr. Winston, how are you doing today?"

"I'm just fine, Miss Muchie, thank you for asking. Won't you sit down?"

"No, thank you, Mr. Winston, I'd rather stand. I was very flattered by my request for your hand, I mean by your request for my hand in marriage. But I regret I cannot accept."

"Why is that, Miss Muchie?"

"I can never marry again because I am still married to my Teddy. I am still his wife."

There. I'd said it like I meant it, which I did. Now I was braced for the worst. Ernest Winston got up from behind his desk and came over to where I stood clutching the doorknob for dear life.

"Miss Muchie, please, won't you sit down for just a moment? Look how pale you've gone. You're shaking like a leaf. Are you all right? Here, sit down before you fall over dead."

I was cold with fear, but I had no idea it showed. Mr. Winston guided me to a chair and took my hands. He stroked them lightly, bringing warmth back into me. He had a gentle touch as soothing as a bowl of pudding.

I began to feel better until I realized we'd never touched skin to skin before except for the first handshake when he'd offered me my job. Then I got nervous all over again.

"Miss Muchie, please believe me when I tell you I understand your feelings and respect your honesty. Will you allow me to be honest in return?"

I nodded, not trusting myself to speak.

"You've told me many times how you grieve for your husband. It's perfectly natural and normal for a young woman to feel the way you feel. Everyone in town knows what a terrible shock you suffered. You loved each other. He was a fine man and all who knew him say he was devoted to his family. He was intelligent and sensible and he loved you very much. What do you think he wants you to do?"

"I've been thinking about that since Easter Sunday, Mr. Winston, and all I could come up with is Teddy would want me to do what's right. He'd want me to do what was best for all of us."

"That is exactly my opinion, Miss Muchie. And what is best for your children? Is it best for them to do without nice things because you cannot provide for them by yourself the way your husband did? He did everything he could to take care of you and those children.

"Isn't that why he worked at the shipyard? He knew it was dangerous, but it paid well and he needed money to take care of his family. Is that the truth, Miss Muchie?"

"It is God's own truth, Mr. Winston, and I've reproached my-self more times than you can know. I've blamed myself every day and every night for letting him work at that damned shipyard. Is that what you want to hear? It was my fault that he got burned so bad, Mr. Winston, all my fault and I'll never forgive myself."

"I don't want you to feel guilty, Miss Muchie. You've been hurt enough. It wasn't your fault. It was nobody's fault. All I'm trying to make you understand is that Mr. Preston wanted good things for you and your children. That's why he's gone, Miss Muchie."

"Don't say that, Mr. Winston! I can't bear it. I would give every inch of my skin, all the blood from my heart. I would give my very soul to bring Teddy back. Please don't say I made him go away."

"Poor dear girl, that's not what I'm saying. Listen to me good now. You're not the reason your husband is gone. The explosion did that. You're doing the very best you can, but it is hard for a woman alone to provide for two children. They deserve to have nice things and so do you. Look at that dress you're wearing."

I looked down, thinking I'd spilled something on myself or ripped my hem, but that wasn't what Mr. Winston meant.

"You are always neat as a pin and just as pretty as you can be, Miss Muchie, but you've been wearing that same dress and two others as long as I've known you."

It was a fact. I had three dresses to wear to work. There was no money for new clothes what with the children's shoes and doctor bills and rent and all. I tried to crochet new collars and cuffs to spruce up my outfits when I had time but I suppose for someone with an eye for style like Mr. Winston, I looked rather shabby.

"A fine-looking woman like you should have all the pretty clothes she wants. When was the last time you had a new dress or even a new hat?"

"Well, it has been a while Mr. Winston, I must admit. But I don't need any new clothes, really I don't."

"Need and want are two different things, my dear. I don't need a wife but I want you." He paused then as if startled at his own admission.

I blushed.

"Why not let me give you pretty things, Miss Muchie? Let me take care of you the way you should be taken care of. Let me buy your children all the books and toys and music lessons they want.

"I'm not asking you to do anything dishonorable, Miss Muchie. I am not asking to be your sugar daddy. I know you are too decent for anything like that. I am asking you to do me the honor of being my wife. Would that be so terrible?"

"It wouldn't be terrible at all, Mr. Winston. Except, I don't love you. It wouldn't be fair to marry you without loving you, would it?"

"Oh Muchie, sometimes you seem very young. I know you don't love me now but maybe one day you will. You like me, don't you? You like to be around me, don't you?"

"You know I do, Mr. Winston. Nobody could help but like you, good and kind as you are. And I do enjoy your company very much, there's no getting around it."

"Then we have a lot to work with already, don't we? Don't worry about love. I'm pretty sure I can find enough love in me for the both of us. Will you at least let me try?"

"Mr. Winston, I have to tell you something. I believe, that is I know Teddy will come back to me. That's the real reason I can't marry you. Teddy is coming back to me one day."

"I see. That's what it is. You poor little thing, you really believe that, don't you?"

I nodded, too close to tears for speech.

"Well, I tell you what. Why don't we just cross that bridge when we come to it?"

By this time I was crying hard. How could any man be as loving as Mr. Winston? How could any woman be as fortunate as me? I wiped my eyes and gave him a watery smile.

"Mr. Winston, I don't know if I have anything left to give another man, even one as sweet as you. But I promise you. I'll do my best to be a good and loyal wife to you. Please, just let me keep Teddy in my heart. Don't try to make me forget him. You'll let me hold on to him?"

"Of course I will, my dear."

"And my children?"

"Put your mind at ease. I am extremely fond of them already. That Tom-Tom is quite a fisherman and Maddy is a treasure, like you, Muchie. They come from good stock and have a lot to be proud of. If you will marry me, your children will have me. I'll do everything I can for them. Will you please say yes, Muchie?"

"Yes, Mr. Winston. Yes, I'll marry you."

"I have a little engagement present for you, Miss Muchie. Actually, it's from my mother. She wanted you to have it," he said, handing me a slip of paper.

"Oh, oh my. Oh." I burst into tears again. "It's her recipe for the lemon sauce."

"Yes, she wanted to be sure her secret wasn't lost. I told her I was going to ask you to marry me and she gave it to me then."

Overwhelmed by yet another example of Mr. Winston's kindness I threw my arms around him and kissed him on the mouth right there in his formal business office.

I think it surprised us both.

When I married for the second time, it was for reasons more practical than love. Mr. Winston and I decided to have a small, private wedding with only a few friends present and of course my children.

Reverend Hill married us in the parsonage parlor and this time, when he asked, "Who gives this woman to be married to this man?" my children announced, "We do!" with big grins on their faces.

Movers had already taken my things out to the house on the bay. All that remained was for me to shut up the house and return the key.

It was raining the day I went to my little rented house for the last time. I walked through each room, saying good-bye to bare spaces that once held my life. If only I could hug Charlotte and Margaret again and kiss their fat, dimpled cheeks.

If only I could sit across the kitchen table from Teddy and hear him speak his morning nonsense to me. But the table and all the other furniture had been taken away.

All that remained were scuff marks on the floor.

In the kitchen I noticed the movers had left my little hand mirror hanging over the sink. I'd kept it there all the years of my marriage. When it was time for Teddy to come home I would peek into the mirror to tidy my hair so I would look nice for him.

Tucking the mirror into my pocket I stood in the kitchen and closed my eyes. Remembering. Happy times. Sad moments. Work-filled days. Embraces in the night.

I held my breath trying to bring back the sound of voices I loved. In the dim stillness of my empty house, I thought I heard him. Then I was sure.

"Arise, my love, my fair one. Arise and live. Live for both of us."

I turned around and around searching for the source of the words. I ran from room to room calling, "Teddy, Teddy, Teddy." But he was nowhere to be found.

I was alone in the house and I stood watching rain slide down the windows.

When I was able, I walked out of the kitchen locking the back door behind me for the last time.

The rain had let up a little and the sun was making a valiant attempt to shine. Charlotte and Margaret used to say it was the devil beating his wife when the sun and rain showed up at the same time. I smiled at the memory of my little girls.

Somehow, I couldn't bring myself to say good-bye to the garden.

Maybe the next family to live in the house would take care of my flowers. The roses were in bud and the yard would soon be filled with color and fragrance if someone cared enough to tend them.

Perhaps the new tenants would enjoy the tomatoes, greens and butter beans I'd planted.

I hoped some of the happiness I'd felt shelling peas on a warm summer night might remain for them.

Chapter Twenty-seven

❀❀❀

1942

The Second World War was in full swing as Mr. Winston and I settled into married life. Gasoline rationing kept us close to home and work left precious little time for a honeymoon.

"When this war ends we'll go somewhere, Muchie. Maybe Cuba or Bermuda, would you like to do that?"

"I've always wanted to go to Europe, Mr. Winston, France especially."

"Then that's where we'll go, if there's anything left to Europe after this war," he said with a worried frown.

Younger men at the funeral home had enlisted right after Pearl Harbor. To replace them we hired men past fighting age and women who couldn't get jobs at the aircraft carrier plant. The demands of war left no one idle.

We worked long hours to keep the business going. Tom-Tom and Maddy even gave us a hand, doing what they could to help. It was hard going, but the only thing we lost was sleep.

Other folks were not so lucky. The town was full of Gold Star Mothers brokenhearted in their pride. Every week there were reports of boys we knew dying in places we had to search a map to find.

Dorali, Bevane and I volunteered at the canteen for colored soldiers. There were plenty of pretty young women flirting with the soldiers while they served coffee and donuts.

A lot of the young GIs were lonely and desperate to talk to someone about home and family. We helped them write letters and spent a lot of time simply listening. The hard part was sending the boys off with a substitute mother's kiss on their cheeks.

"How many will ever see their mothers again?" Bevane asked.

"It makes me shiver to hear them talk about going into battle," Dorali said.

"They think it will be a grand adventure," Bevane noted.

"The saddest thing is some of the boys don't even know how to read and write, yet they're going off to war," Dorali commented, shaking her head.

"Uncle Sam took them straight off the farm," I said. "They're really just boys, only a few years older than Tom-Tom. Many have never even been away from home before now."

The three of us did our best to let the boys know someone cared. Working at the canteen left me drained, and at home I often cried thinking about boys going off to war.

"Muchie, you're too tenderhearted for that canteen. Isn't there some other way for you to help win the war? Find something easier on you," Mr. Winston suggested.

"Colored boys are shipping out of Mobile every day to get shot at all over the world, Mr. Winston. The least I can do is share a smile and a kind word before they go."

No matter that Mr. Winston had been an only child as well as a bachelor all his life. He immediately stepped into the role of caring for a wife and a ready-made family.

"Son, we've all got to do our part to help the war effort. Your mother's been helping at the canteen. I've signed up for Civil Patrol. Have you thought about what you might do?"

He asked Tom-Tom after supper as they studied a map of the south Pacific together.

"Some of the boys at school are collecting scrap metal. But I want to plant a Victory Garden."

"That's a mighty big job for a young fellow like you. What say I get a patch of the yard plowed and planted. Then you and Maddy can tend to it for us?"

"I'd like that a whole lot, Mr. Winston," Tom-Tom replied.

Each night, I thanked God my son was too young and my husband too old to be called up by the draft.

I can't say I loved Mr. Winston, but I was comfortable with him. I did not rush into his arms at the end of the day full of joy at the sight of him. But the sound of his voice was a comfort to me although it never made my pulse race as Teddy's had.

We shared a world of trust and respect between us, and I depended on his strength and unfailing kindness.

In the evening when the children were busy with their schoolwork, Mr. Winston and I enjoyed walking on the jetty that stretched far into the bay. He liked to drop a few crab traps in the water just for the fun of it.

Come morning, Mr. Winston would send Tom-Tom racing out to check the traps. It delighted him to find enough crabs for dinner.

"Muchie, you know before we got married, I lived a fairly quiet life here with my mother," Mr. Winston said.

He unwrapped a sheet of newspaper and started cutting chicken necks into chunks with his pocketknife.

Greedy seagulls squawked at the prospect of an easy meal and settled to wait on the jetty's guardrails.

"I imagine you still miss her a lot, don't you, Mr. Winston?" I asked as I tied string around each raw chicken piece.

Stooping down, I baited the traps and snapped into place the square of wire that held them shut. Mr. Winston slid the traps into the bay with a gentle plop and dusted off his hands.

"I do, Muchie. Sometimes I think I can feel her spirit around here though," he said. "I think she's happy to have children in the house."

"I'm glad of that, Mr. Winston. Do you ever miss your quiet life?"

"Not at all, Muchie. I actually enjoy the bustle Tom-Tom and Maddy make. Their prattle is like a tonic to me."

"You certainly do seem younger and more sprightly than you did when I met you, Mr. Winston."

We laughed together and walked back to the house for Mr. Winston to listen to the children's lessons. He beamed like a lighthouse at what they were learning and how well they were doing in school.

Mr. Winston went overboard trying to spoil Maddy, but it was Tom-Tom who thrived under Mr. Winston's care.

Every chance they got, he and Mr. Winston went fishing together in the bay at the crack of dawn. They often sat on the kitchen steps talking while cleaning their catch.

"Tom-Tom, I think I'm fixing to cross words with that mailman of ours."

"Don't you mean cross swords, Mr. Winston?"

"No, indeed. I said just exactly what I meant, son."

"How are you planning to cross words lest it's a puzzle? For the life of me, I can't see you and the mailman working a puzzle together."

"Son, you've known me long enough to know I'm a peace-loving man so it's doubtful I'd ever cross swords with a living soul. That's for young fellows like you. But I tell you the truth, I'm ready to give that fool mailman a piece of my mind about the way he's taken to messing up delivering our mail. I've lived in this selfsame house my entire life. You'd think the United States Post Office would know that by now."

"I don't rightly know much about the Post Office, Mr. Winston. But Miss Muchie told me to be careful before giving somebody a piece of my mind, just in case maybe I can't spare it."

Their laughter boomed out over the yard while they prepared their fish for my skillet.

"Miss Muchie, will you fry these fish for breakfast that Tom-Tom caught?" Mr. Winston asked.

"I didn't catch all of them, Miss Muchie. Mr. Winston did his part," Tom-Tom added.

"It would be my pleasure, gentlemen. All I ask is for you to wash up while I cook. You're a bit smelly, the both of you," I said, wrinkling my nose.

When the four of us sat down to eat, Tom-Tom and Mr. Winston continued telling the whoppers of true fisherman.

"Tom-Tom, I need to teach you a thing or two about playing the dozens. Don't ever forget, a smart man can talk his way into or out of just about anything."

"But that's not playing the dozens, Mr. Winston. At school, we call it playing the dozens when one boy says something bad about another boy's mother."

"That's right as far as it goes. The thing is, you boys are

friends. You ought to know what you can get away with saying," he said, taking a big bite of fish.

"Mr. Winston, if boys say bad things to Tom-Tom about Miss Muchie, I can pull a big rock out of my pocket to make them stop," Maddy offered.

That tickled Mr. Winston. He laughed until he got red in the face, then he began to choke. He pulled at his throat, gasping for breath, pointing at the fish bones piled on his plate.

"Maddy, run get the vinegar," I shouted.

I pounded Mr. Winston on the back to try and dislodge the bone.

"Move, Miss Muchie," Tom-Tom said.

He put his hands on Mr. Winston's neck as Maddy returned with the vinegar.

"Here, Mr. Winston, take a spoonful of this," I said.

"It will dissolve the fish bone."

He coughed and swallowed, "What for, Muchie? Seems Tom-Tom has fixed me up good as new all by himself."

Mr. Winston cleared his throat again and drew a deep breath.

"I don't know how you did it though, son."

"Me neither, Mr. Winston. Something just told me to put my hands on your neck. I'm feeling kind of dizzy now."

"Sit down and rest yourself, Tom-Tom. I'm grateful for your help. Man my age ought to know better than laugh and talk with my mouth full. Isn't that right, Muchie?"

"Indeed it is, Mr. Winston."

After breakfast I asked Tom-Tom to stay and sit with me for a bit at the kitchen table.

"Honey, you don't look like you're feeling so good. You upset about what happened with Mr. Winston?"

"No, Miss Muchie. It makes me real tired though."

"What makes you tired, honey? Tom-Tom?" I asked.

"When I help someone who is hurt, it makes me feel like I'm going to fall out. Afterwards I'm tired for a long time."

"Has it happened before, sweetness?"

"Yes, ma'am. I was scared to tell you, but Maddy fell and cut her leg real bad coming home from school one day. It was bleeding and I didn't know what to do. I put my hand on her cut and then I got a funny feeling."

"I haven't seen a cut on Maddy's leg, Tom-Tom."

"Because it went away when I was touching her, Miss Muchie. Just like the fish bone in Mr. Winston's throat went away."

I held him tight until he squirmed from my embrace, giving me an awkward peck on the cheek.

"Are those the only two times you've had this funny feeling? Think now, it's important for you to remember."

"I don't know if I dreamed it or if it was real, but one time when we were living at the old house?"

"Yes, honey, what about the old house?"

"I thought I saw you sitting in Daddy's chifforobe. In the middle of the night. You were crying. You tried to make me get in with you, but I didn't want to. I grabbed you and held on until you climbed out."

"Can you tell me anymore about what happened that night, Tom-Tom?"

"No, Miss Muchie, only it was the first time I can remember getting the dizzy feeling in my head. Was I dreaming, Miss Muchie?"

"You weren't dreaming, Tom-Tom. It really happened and you helped me. Like you helped Mr. Winston today. Like you helped your sister."

"All I did was pull you out of Daddy's chifforobe though."

"It may not seem like much to you, but when you made me get

out of that chifforobe you saved me from being sad and lonely. It was a mighty big job for a little boy, but you did it. You have something very special inside you, dear heart."

"What is it that's in me, Miss Muchie?"

"My grandmother Tyler Mama called it the healing gift. It's time you know what that means."

I poured the last of the morning's imitation wartime coffee into a cup for me and gave Tom-Tom a big glass of water.

"If I say anything that doesn't make sense to you, you stop me and I'll do the best I can to explain it better, all right, Tom-Tom?"

"Yes, ma'am, Miss Muchie."

"You remember when you went up the country to stay with your grandparents in Mississippi for the summer?"

"Yes, ma'am. Your papa let me help him tend to the horses. One got sick and Papa helped make him well."

"Papa is a healer, Tom-Tom. Did he tell you that?"

"I don't think he did, Miss Muchie. He just said sometimes he could help folks that were sick and animals too."

"That's true, Tom-Tom. Lots of men in Wayne County depend on him."

"For what, Miss Muchie?"

"My papa is known for raising the finest cattle for miles around and other men come to him for help with their livestock. He knows what to do so even thin and puny cows can drop healthy calves. Some of it is skill and some of it is a gift from God. Like the gift you have, sweetness."

"How do you know, Miss Muchie? That I have a gift from God?"

"Everyone has some sort of gift from God, Tom-Tom, but your gift is different. I saw it when Mr. Winston was choking on that fishbone. You laid hands on him and his choking disappeared."

"But I didn't do anything, it just happened, Miss Muchie."

"Sometimes it's like that with healing, honey. Hard to tell when it will come and when it won't. My grandmother, Tyler Mama, had it. So does my papa. They said I did too when I was your age. It was just about the only thing they ever agreed on."

"Do you have it now, Miss Muchie? Can you heal like Papa can?"

"I simply do not know. There have been times I've tried with all my heart to heal and nothing happened. Other times, the healing just came."

"That must make you feel bad," Tom-Tom said sadly.

"Yes, it does, son. But don't worry about me. It's you who have all the signs of the healing gift now unless I am badly mistaken. God has blessed you to help the ones you love. I was never able to do that."

"Do you mean healing is different for every person and I can only help the people I love, Miss Muchie?"

"Healing is a funny thing, Tom-Tom. I can't explain how it works, or why a healer can help some folks and not others. The healing gift is strong in you even though you're only 11. I can't tell you the reason though, because I don't know it. I don't even know why healing runs in our family, but you're living proof it does."

"No disrespect, Miss Muchie, but you don't seem to know very much about healing," Tom-Tom said.

"I'm afraid you're right, sweetness. Perhaps one day you'll help me learn more. This much I know for certain. You have the healing gift."

Tom-Tom looked as puzzled as I was feeling. How could I explain healing to him when I didn't even understand my own sometimey gift?

Time and again healing had failed me when I prayed for it to come. I didn't want my child to suffer such pain, but how could I protect him?

There was no denying the signs. Tom-Tom *was* a healer. All I could do was watch him with care and pray his gift would never betray him as mine had.

Chapter Twenty-eight

❧

1947

Every good mother swears she loves her children equally. Quiet as it's kept, that doesn't mean a mother can love each child exactly the same. No two children are alike, and mothers have to be nimble in their loving, changing course with a child's needs. Charlotte and Margaret's deaths led me to love Maddy and Tom-Tom even harder than I might have ordinarily, pinning my fondest hopes on their small shoulders.

Having two children die made the remaining two even more precious to me. Tom-Tom and Maddy were only a year apart in age, but their hearts were close enough for them to be twins. My son and my daughter called forth love from me, different from what I intended, but more or less what each seemed to want.

Maddy was comfortable being loved at a slight remove. Like Tyler Mama, she didn't like to have a lot of people in her face all the time. She was an affectionate child, but strictly on her terms. Much as she adored her brother, she needed time away from everyone, even him, and would not allow anyone to intrude on her solitude.

It was easy to understand Maddy, since I'd been a girl myself. I halfway knew the right words to say as she moved from little girl to young lady. When her body began to blossom and she became vain about her appearance, it was no surprise because I had experienced that stage myself.

"Miss Muchie, I look like a peach head," she complained when her hair rose up in rebellion against the humidity off Mobile Bay.

"You are my peach of a girl, Maddy, but your hair needs some pomade and a thorough brushing to make it lay down," I suggested.

"Will you do it for me?"

Maddy sat patiently while I sprinkled a bit of water on the brush and insisted on giving her hair a hundred strokes. Afterwards, she seemed pleased at her reflection in the glass.

"That looks a lot better, Miss Muchie. Thank you," she said very politely as she had been taught.

All the temptations a girl might face were familiar to me. It was second nature to advise and protect Maddy.

Tom-Tom was a different story. Watching my little boy turn into an almost man, I was at a loss for what he needed to prepare him for the challenges ahead of him. I didn't even know what they might be.

Boyhood was alien territory to me. I didn't speak the language or understand the customs. I had no idea what Tom-Tom experienced as his body began to change and his voice to deepen. How could a mother shield her boy from danger, harm and woe?

Like his daddy, Tom-Tom had never met a stranger. He was fresh faced and openhearted with anyone and everyone, talking without a thought to any dangers they might present.

He demanded attention and filled up whatever space he was in with his charming ways. Loving him was easy. Understanding him however was close to impossible for me.

It made me ever more grateful for the presence of Ernest Winston in Tom-Tom's life.

"Muchie, you can't ride herd on a boy. He's got to be free to roam a bit. Let him make his own mistakes. Boys learn by doing," Ernest told me.

"I just don't want any harm to befall him, Ernest."

"Don't worry, Muchie. I won't let him go too far. He'll be all right."

The healing gift didn't trouble Tom-Tom or me as he grew older. I was glad to be free of the burden, but I kept watch over my son just in case.

"You'd tell me wouldn't you, Tom-Tom?"

"Sure I would, Miss Muchie, the way you worry. I'd come to you right off the bat. But I've never felt a thing since the day Mr. Winston was choking."

"Back home they used to say healing ran mother to son, father to daughter. I wonder what happened to my gift?"

"Maybe the healing gift did what it was supposed to and moved on to someone who needed it more than you, Miss Muchie."

"I hope you're right, Tom-Tom. And don't forget . . ."

"I know, I know. Tell you if anything unusual happens. Anything at all. Did I get it right?"

"You're a scamp, making fun of your poor mother's fears. But, yes, that's right."

My tall stripling wrapped his long arms around me. It made me feel very short, very female and almost unbearably tender toward him. Tears filled my eyes.

"I just don't want the healing gift to hurt you or frighten you, dear heart. Even though you're big now with your new whiskers and all. I look at you and still see my fat baby who got food in his many chins. I tried never to let anything hurt you when you were little. I could protect you then."

"I know, Miss Muchie. Don't worry so much though. Healing won't do either of us any harm, I promise."

For a sixteen-year old boy, Tom-Tom seemed mighty sure of himself. Since I had faith in his good sense and wanted to believe him, that's exactly what I did. Putting my worries aside until there was good reason for them.

"This country is on the move, Miss Muchie. Jackie Robinson is just the beginning. Things are opening up for Negroes, you watch and see," Mr. Winston said.

"I'm glad Tom-Tom and Maddy's world will have more opportunity than mine, Mr. Winston," I said wistfully.

"Miss Muchie, the children are older now. Why not get started on that college education you're always talking about."

"I'm over forty years old, Mr. Winston. People would laugh at a woman my age in college."

"Now don't sound so pitiful, Miss Muchie. Age is not an obstacle. Look at all the soldiers taking advantage of the GI bill. Plenty of older students."

"I'll give it some thought, Mr. Winston."

"Don't think too long now. Before you know it those children will be going to college. Smart as you are, you'll put them to shame," he said proudly.

Ernest Winston and I plowed through life like a team, yoked together and pulling in the same direction. Neither one of us was money hungry, but we enjoyed the excitement of doing business.

Parran's example taught me not to waste a thing. He made money even from scraps at the sawmill. The mortuary business lacks the versatility of a sawmill, but it can still open the door to opportunities.

Besides, as the old saying goes, there's often more than one way to skin a cat.

"Mr. Winston, I heard about a parcel of farmland we can get for little or nothing."

"You miss being a farm girl that much?"

I poked him playfully. "No, you silly man, I do not. Didn't you say just last week that the colored cemetery is nearly full?"

"I did. And rundown too. What are you thinking, Miss Muchie?"

"Land is cheap right now. We can turn that parcel of land I was telling you about into a new cemetery. Landscape it nice. Make it look like a garden. People will want to put their loved ones somewhere like that. What do you think?"

"I think you've got a good head for business, Miss Muchie. Let's look at the land and see what they'll take for it."

The land was heir property and tied up in a conflict among six adult children who had no interest in farming. They wanted to sell real bad and were happy to cut us a good deal when we offered them cash money for the land and outbuildings. As it turned out, we bought twice as much land as I thought we needed.

"We can't go far wrong by planning ahead. People keep dying every day, Miss Muchie," Mr. Winston said.

"Well, at least we've got somewhere to put them now when they do," I replied.

That gave me another idea. I decided to do my research before discussing it with Mr. Winston. What I found convinced me it was time to act.

"You spend a lot of money buying caskets from that company in Tennessee, Mr. Winston."

"You're right about that, Miss Muchie. My travel and shipping costs add up."

"Have you ever thought about running your own casket-building business?"

"Can't say that I have. I don't know anything about building caskets, and I doubt you do either, Miss Muchie."

"But I bet we can locate somebody who does, what with all these fellows coming back from the war and needing jobs."

The man I found was a skilled cabinet-maker who immediately impressed Mr. Winston with his confidence.

"I don't see that building a coffin is much different from building any other kind of chest," the man said.

"Do you think you could build them fast enough to supply a busy mortuary like ours?"

Mr. Winston handed the man a sheet of paper that showed weekly and monthly funeral tallies.

"Sure I could, with help to do the finishing. I tell you what, give me a day and a half and I'll build you a casket. Then you decide."

He was good as his word. He presented Mr. Winston with a gleaming, miniature mahogany coffin complete with brass handles. It was a beautiful piece of work and finely detailed.

"Look here, I padded the inside and lined it with fabric like a real casket. Maybe your wife can use it as a jewelry case," he said.

"That is an idea," Mr. Winston said, winking at me.

"Your workmanship is very impressive," I said.

It seemed ghoulish to set a coffin on my dressing table, but I didn't want to sour the discussion by being squeamish.

"I think we have ourselves a deal," Mr. Winston said to the man.

They shook hands, dickered for a while about money and next thing I knew Mr. Winston and I were in the casket-building business with our own small factory running at full speed.

"You ought to be proud of yourself, Muchie," Mr. Winston said as we sat in his office finishing our year-end record keeping.

"Why is that, Ernest?"

I stood up and took a most unladylike stretch. Poring over pages of numbers gave me a stiff neck, and we'd been at our work for hours.

"Thanks to you, several Negro families now earn their livelihood working in two new Negro-owned businesses. You deserve all the credit for the cemetery and the casket factory, Muchie."

"You hush, Ernest Winston. All I did was tell you my ideas. It was your skill that turned them into reality."

Stretching again, I walked behind his desk and draped my arms around his neck, resting my chin on the top of his head.

"We make a good team, Muchie. A real good team."

"I won't argue with that, Ernest. Now, can we please go home before I have to curl up under your desk and go to sleep?"

With a laugh, he slammed shut the ledger, picked up his hat and took me home to our candy cane house on the bay.

Chapter Twenty-nine

1949

"Muchie, you stay so busy these days it's a wonder you know whether you're coming or going," Bevane said.

She and I had spent half the day downtown shopping. We'd already gone to three stores in our search for something to wear to Tom-Tom's high school graduation and were now in a fourth.

"I don't think I've ever worked this hard in my life, Bevane. Between the funeral home, the cemetery, the casket factory, Ernest and my two children, it's rare for me to have a minute to myself. This is the first time in months I've even been in a store," I admitted.

"You've come a mighty long way since we met, Muchie," Bevane said with a smile.

"Isn't that the God's honest truth? I thank you for sticking with me, Bevane. You know, I've kept the card you gave me years ago. The one with the prayer asking God to forgive me when I get anxious. It helped me more than I can tell you."

"It's funny, isn't it, Muchie, how a person never knows what's important until it's too late to do anything about it? Why is one person a friend for life and another just passing through? You ever think about that?"

"No, Bevane. What I do think about is you and Dorali making me welcome when I felt like I didn't have a friend in the world other than Teddy. I'll never forget that."

"When you're in the middle of living your life, it's hard to reflect on what you're doing or get a clear idea of what anything really means. It's only later when the dust settles that you can step back and say, 'Oh, yes, now I understand.' At least that's what I think, Muchie."

"You're very serious today, Bevane. Is everything all right?"

"Everything is fine, Muchie. I'm just a little hungry. Let's buy our dresses and then go home to have some lunch. If I don't eat soon I'm likely to fall out," she said.

At home that evening Tom-Tom and Maddy were immersed in yet another debate about where Tom-Tom should go for college.

"What about Washington, D.C.? We could both go to Howard University."

"That's too far from home for me, Maddy."

"If you go to A&T in Greensboro, I could go to Bennett when I graduate."

"Maddy, there's no law saying we have to go to college in the same place, is there?"

"Of course not, smarty pants. It would just be nice if we were together. Have you considered Atlanta? Morehouse for you and Spelman for me?"

"I don't know, Maddy. I haven't made my mind up yet. Let's wait and see what happens," Tom-Tom said, trying to put an end to what seemed to have become a daily discussion.

"What do you think, Miss Muchie?" Maddy asked, shooting her brother a look that nailed him to his chair.

Roping me into the conversation made it clear Maddy wasn't ready to let the subject rest. Tom-Tom rolled his eyes and twiddled his thumbs until Maddy pinched him.

"Ow, Maddy. Did you see that, Miss Muchie? This girl is moving from rocks to brute force." He laughed.

"All right, you two. Settle down. Here's what I think. Each of you ought to pick a school depending on what you want to study and where it seems you'd enjoy being the next four years. If it turns out you end up in the same place, that's fine and dandy. But college is a big decision. Don't limit yourselves."

Tom-Tom already had a stack of acceptance letters and was looking forward to graduating in a few weeks. Maddy still had one more year of high school to go.

It didn't surprise me for Maddy to base her college plans on her brother's choice. No matter what I said, I expected her to follow Tom-Tom to college as she had been following him all her life.

With graduation less than a week away, Tom-Tom finally put Maddy's mind at ease, managing to surprise Mr. Winston and me in the process.

"I'd like to stay home and attend the Branch for two years if that's all right with you and Mr. Winston," Tom-Tom announced over supper.

"Most of my friends are doing the same thing. We'll get real good grades at the junior college and then transfer somewhere big."

"I'll be glad to have you home with me for a while longer, dear."

Maddy's grin was too wide for words. She practically danced in her chair.

"Sounds like a fine plan, Tom-Tom. Get your legs firmly under you before you venture forth," Mr. Winston said, doing a good job of hiding his satisfaction and relief.

Too excited to sleep, I was up at dawn the morning of Tom-Tom's high school graduation. I tipped into his room and saw my child sprawled across the bed, sleeping soundly as if this day was no different from any other.

Eventually, the smell of breakfast roused the household, and then it was time for the mad scramble of four people bathing and dressing for a special event.

"This is a big day, Muchie. You doing all right?" Ernest asked, zipping the back of my dress.

"I'm nervous and I have to admit to feeling a little weepy too. I'm happy for Tom-Tom, but I can't help thinking about his daddy today."

"He'd be proud of that boy. I know I am."

"Oh, Ernest. When we got married, I didn't have any idea what having a stepfather would be like for Tom-Tom and Maddy. But I tell you the truth. After God made you, he threw away the mold. You've been a good father to my children. I'm grateful to you, very grateful."

I tried my best to hold back the tears.

"Come on now, no need to thank me for doing what any decent person would have done. It came naturally because I love you, Muchie, and I love your children. They're not mine by blood but most certainly by choice," he said, putting his arms around me.

"You can cry if you want to, Muchie. I don't mind one bit."

It was a toss-up who shed the most tears at Tom-Tom's graduation. Dorali and Aaron did their share of crying. There was no consoling Maddy, although Bevane tried her best, fanning the child and offering tissues throughout the ceremony.

Ernest and I sat together like the proud parents we were. We held hands and put on a brave front although both of us got misty when Tom-Tom walked across the stage to get his diploma.

I was looking forward to going over every detail of the commencement with Dorali and Bevane at our barbecue that evening.

While Ernest and his cronies tended ribs and chicken on the grill, my children and their friends laughed and played on the beach beside the bay. For the fiftieth time that day, I thought of Teddy.

"What a grand day, Dorali. I wish Teddy could have seen his son graduate though."

"I know, Muchie, and I don't blame you for feeling that way."

"All day I've been wondering how things would have been different. I mean if Teddy hadn't gone away."

"Muchie, there's no sense denying life could have been different for you. Any number of reasons, little and big, could have made it different. But that doesn't mean it would necessarily be any better."

"I don't mean to complain, Dorali, especially not on such a happy day. Where is that Bevane? I expected her to be here by now."

"She's not coming, Muchie. Bevane has gotten some bad news from the doctor. She didn't want to tell you and spoil Tom-Tom's graduation."

"I thought she was talking kind of strange when we went shopping, but she told me nothing was wrong. What can we do to help, Dorali?"

"That's what I want to ask you, Muchie, if you're willing to hear me out."

"What are you talking about?" I asked.

"Years and years ago, Teddy said you were a healer. Remember, it was at suppertime? Don't start shaking your head now, let me finish. I know you tried to heal Charlotte. With my own eyes I saw you trying to help Teddy when he was in the hospital. And you told me yourself what happened with Maddy's sores."

Dorali paused and looked me straight in the eye. She took both my hands in hers and asked me, "Can you try and help Bevane?"

"Oh, Dorali, I wish I could. But I can't. I've lost the healing gift. It never comes for me when I try to help. I'd hate to get Bevane's hopes up and then disappoint her."

"I don't know anything about healing, but I know this much. You love Bevane. She trusts you and she loves you. You do what you think is best, Muchie. That's all I ask."

Dorali was dead serious. She had never asked me for one single favor, not ever. In all the years we'd known each other it was always me asking her help. If I *could* still heal, if the gift would only come, then I owed it to Dorali to honor her request.

It took me several days of praying through doubt to get up my courage, but I went to see Bevane. We sat on her screened porch and sipped lemonade as we talked. After half an hour of idle conversation I was able to get to the point.

"Well, my dear. What's this I hear about you being under the weather?"

"I'm afraid it's worse than that, Muchie. I didn't want Dorali to tell you, not with all you've got on you these days."

"Shame on you, Bevane. What kind of fair-weather friend do you take me for?" I pretended to pout, poking out my lip and glowering with my head lowered.

That made Bevane laugh, "You're a good friend, Muchie. A friend forever."

Bevane shifted in her wicker chair and twisted around trying to get comfortable.

"Here, let me help you," I said.

I fluffed up the cushions behind her back and brought her a footstool so she could stretch out her legs.

"That's a lot better. Thank you, Muchie."

I didn't have the heart to tell Bevane what I was going to do. Instead, I stood behind her, put my hands on her shoulders and closed my eyes. She leaned back to rest her head on me.

Heaving a sigh, Bevane said, "Oh, Muchie, you just don't know. I am so tired."

With all my might, I concentrated on healing her body, on making her strong and vigorous again, blooming with energy and good health.

Through my hands on Bevane's shoulders, I felt life coursing steady inside her. The infinite goodness in her heart and the accepting nature of her spirit were plain to me as never before.

I struggled to call the gift and I prayed for it to work through my hands, but there was none of the confusion, none of the dimness I experienced in the past. For the life of me I could not feel the weakness that always came with healing. The gift would not come, refusing once again to respond to my heartfelt plea.

But the deep trust and abiding love between us filled me, blocking out everything else.

My hands didn't do a single thing but sweat no matter how long I laid them on Bevane's shoulders. After a while, I took my trembling hands away and opened my eyes.

I had failed my friend.

Bevane turned to look at me with an odd expression on her face. She wiped her eyes and blew her nose before speaking.

"I feel better, Muchie. Just having you here makes me feel better."

"I wish I could do more, Bevane."

"You did fine, Muchie, just fine."

Chapter Thirty

1950

"Muchie, I've been thinking. What with the war and then being busy at work I haven't done a thing to the house since before we got married, and it's starting to look a bit shabby. Showing its age. How do you feel like a little remodeling project? Just get one or two things done to spruce up the house," Ernest said as we rode to work together one morning.

"That's a good idea," I replied, only halfway paying attention.

"What do you think of putting in a swimming pool, Muchie?" Ernest had my full attention now.

"We've got the whole bay to swim in, Ernest. What do we need a pool for?"

"The bay is fine for fishing and wading, but the children need a pool. Think how they'll enjoy inviting their friends over to swim. It wouldn't hurt us any to get some exercise either. You can't swim laps in the bay, Muchie."

"I guess you've got a point, Ernest," I said, warming to the idea. "Let's fix it up to look like a Hollywood celebrity's with plants and patio furniture and bright-colored umbrellas. Wouldn't that be too grand for words, Ernest?"

"It's no more than you deserve, Muchie," he said.

The swimming pool took up a third of the backyard, but it soon became our favorite place. Tom-Tom and Maddy practically lived in the pool. Ernest often had his breakfast there and I enjoyed sitting beside the pool and reading on Sunday afternoon.

One major success under his belt spurred Ernest on to even more home improvement plans. He was just getting warmed up and it seemed like every day he had another new, and costly, idea.

"Let's knock out the wall upstairs between those two small bedrooms. Make one big room with space enough for a sofa and a desk and a record player on one end. Put the bed on the end. It faces the bay. We'll see the sun come up every morning."

"Maybe *you* will, Ernest. I've never been much of an early bird myself."

"Don't I know it," he chuckled.

Workmen were soon banging and hammering all over the place. The constant disruption got on my nerves, but all it did was give Ernest more ideas.

"When you shop for furniture, look for rattan and bamboo, Muchie, and pick out some tropical fabrics and colors to make the room bright. I'd like our room to have an island feeling. After all, we do have a beach right outside our door," he said.

The construction displaced Tom-Tom and he moved into our old bedroom.

"Muchie, the boy won't be comfortable with the old-fashioned things in that room. Let him pick out furniture more to his taste."

"But our old furniture is perfectly good, Mr. Winston. I hate for it to go to waste."

"It won't, Muchie. Use it in the room facing the driveway and make that a guest room. All we do now is store junk in there."

Ernest encouraged Maddy to get into the spirit of renovation. They put their heads together and decided she needed to redecorate her room too.

"But I thought you liked your bunk beds."

"They were fine when I was a little girl, Miss Muchie. But now I think a more grown-up room would suit me better. With a canopy bed."

Maddy fancied periwinkle with white trim for her bedroom. I bought billowing Priscilla curtains for her windows and had a settee and dressing table that belonged to Ernest's mother redone for her.

The thing about fixing up one part of a house is that it makes you notice how many other things need attention. Before we were done, we remodeled the kitchen, put in another bathroom, painted every room in the house, refinished the floors and installed new windows.

I refused to replace the wooden hurricane shutters though. They had protected the house from raging storms for many a year. No doubt we would need them again. But they were in dire need of a fresh coat of paint along with the rest of the exterior.

"Those painters want an arm and a leg to keep this house red and white," Ernest announced.

"Now you're quibbling about money? I thought you were determined to spend every dime we had," I told him, only half joking.

"If we go with a solid color, they can spray the paint on instead of doing all that expensive hand work. It would cost a whole lot less, Muchie."

"And it would break my heart, Ernest Winston. I like living in our candy cane house. Please don't ever change it."

Our house sits far back from highway 98 at the end of a winding drive lined with crepe myrtles that bloom the color of ripe watermelon in the summer.

It is a two-story southern Victorian with a wraparound porch graced with white railings and solid columns that gleam against the big ferns hanging above them.

Between each white vertical board is a wide ribbon of red paint and all the windows are framed in red. The blue sky above and the greenery around the house make it strikingly beautiful.

The house has something ladylike about it, delicate and refined like Ernest's mother was in her lifetime. When it rains, I imagine the house daintily lifting its skirts to avoid the mud left by sudden storms blowing in from the bay.

Until our whirl of remodeling we had always treated the house with the dignity such a lovely structure deserves.

If Ernest and I don't have enough energy for our walk on the jetty, we saunter barefoot down to the beach and toss stale bread to the seagulls while the sun goes down.

"Look at the funny color of the water, Muchie. I bet you money there's a Jubilee coming before long. I can tell by the water and from how soft the breeze is off the bay," he said when our bread bag was empty.

"You and your Jubilees. I have yet to see one after living here all these years."

"That's because it would take Gabriel blowing his horn to wake you once you go to sleep, Muchie. The children have been in plenty Jubilees with me and we filled up the freezer with flounder, catfish and crabs to prove it."

"So you say, Ernest Winston, so you say." I laughed.

"I tell you what, Muchie. The next time that Jubilee bell rings, I'll get you out of bed if I have to drag you," he said.

"You just do that, otherwise I'll go to my grave doubting your word," I replied.

I squatted in the sand picking up an assortment of tiny shells. When I hit him with a volley of seashells, he let out a yelp and began splashing me with water from the bay. Our mock battle ended quickly and we sat on pieces of driftwood, digging our toes into the still-warm sand.

"Muchie, I'm glad Tom-Tom decided to stay in town for college. It makes me feel good to have the children and their friends in the house."

"I was worried about that when we first got married. Thank heavens, this house was built to survive anything, including my children and your renovations," I teased.

"I didn't do it any harm and neither have they. This is their home, Muchie. I rest easy at night knowing there's someone who'll take care of the house when I'm gone. You will, won't you Muchie? And the children after you?"

"Of course, Ernest. But that's a long, long way off. Please don't talk about dying today. Let's just try to enjoy what we have."

He smiled and put his arm around me as I nestled my head on his shoulder.

As Ernest predicted, Tom-Tom and Maddy made good use of the swimming pool. They had parties nearly every week through the summer and, in August, a back-to-school party for their school friends.

Several of Tom-Tom's buddies stayed overnight on the promise of a morning fishing expedition with Ernest. I could hear them laughing and telling lies when I went to bed.

The lights were flashing on and off and my bed was shaking like a ship at sea. I almost fell on the floor from all the commotion.

"What in the world?" I shouted, dazed at the sight before me. Ernest was wearing wading pants over his pajamas and Tom-Tom clutched a stick with a nail at one end. Maddy stood behind them with an empty sack over her shoulder.

"Is it the Russians? Are we being invaded?" I asked.

"Get up, Muchie, it's a Jubilee," Ernest said with a big grin on his face.

"Put something on and come down to the beach before the fish are all gone, Miss Muchie," Tom-Tom ordered.

"What is that in your hand, Tom-Tom? It looks dangerous to me."

"They call it a gig, Miss Muchie. It's to spear the fish we *won't* catch up here wasting time talking," he said.

Maddy tossed me the pedal pushers I'd worn the night before, gave me a rubber band for my hair and said, "Come on, Miss Muchie, I don't want to miss all the fun."

I followed my impatient fisher folk down the stairs, stopping to get a flashlight from the closet. The beach was full of people grabbing the endless number of sea creatures littering the beach.

"Careful of those sting rays, and look out for the catfish too," I warned.

No one paid me the least bit of attention. They were too busy piling up mountains of fish and crabs.

I gingerly lifted a big crab and to my surprise, it made no attempt to snap at my fingers when I tossed it into Maddy's sack. Neither did the next one and the next one until the sack was brimming with slightly dazed crustaceans.

I was hooked then, laughing and shouting as I filled buckets and then laundry baskets with more crabs than you could shake a stick at.

When we ran out of containers, we lugged our Jubilee catch to the house and began the tedious task of sorting and cleaning crabs and fish sufficient to feed the five thousand.

"We can eat crab for breakfast, can't we, Miss Muchie?"

"I don't see why we can't eat crab right now," I answered.

"That Jubilee gave me a big appetite, how about you?" Mr. Winston inquired of the young people crowding our kitchen. They bellowed their agreement.

I took a box of salt from the cupboard along with red pepper flakes and celery seed. Grabbed a handful of lemons from the fruit bowl and beckoned Ernest to come relieve me of my burden.

"It will be a darn sight easier for us to boil as many crabs as we can eat on the spot than to clean all these," I said.

My sweeping gesture took in nearly every pail, pot, basket and sack we owned.

"Son, dump those fish in the sink and help me get this crab pot boiling outside," Ernest directed.

He took the seasonings from the counter and collected three bottles of beer from the refrigerator on his way out the door.

"To flavor the crabs," Ernest whispered with a wink.

"Ow, that stings," shouted one of Tom-Tom's friends, clutching his hand as blood seeped through his fingers.

"What happened?" I asked.

"Must have grabbed the wrong fish," he admitted, showing me his hand.

There was an ugly gash across the palm, ragged and bloody.

"It was probably one of those devilish catfish. They have spikes, Jubilee or no Jubilee," I said in a soothing voice to the anxious young man.

"Come on, let's get some peroxide on that hand," I said, leading him to the bathroom where I cleaned and bandaged his wound.

As the sun was coming up, Ernest covered the picnic tables with old newspaper and dumped piles of spicy boiled crab in front of us.

We ate our fill until the only decent thing left to do was wash the stink of crabs from our faces and hands and go back to sleep.

It started to pour down raining sometime during the day. Good sleeping weather, especially after our exciting night. I didn't open my eyes until I heard Ernest get up.

"Where you going?" I asked, squinting with one eye open.

"Well, sleeping beauty, I thought one of us should get up to see about our company."

"With all the fish from the Jubilee, I imagine they can manage to feed themselves," I said.

Ernest snorted and swatted my fanny on his way out of the room. I turned over to go back to sleep and saw the clock on his side of the bed. It was already late afternoon. Feeling like a sluggard, I reluctantly got out of bed.

Downstairs, Tom-Tom and Maddy were holding court with their friends over a meal of fried fish.

"I love living out here on the bay. There's just one problem. A heavy rain like this can leave us stranded for days at a time," Tom-Tom said.

"I never thought of that, Tom-Tom. But you're right, there is only the Causeway to link your place with the bridge," one of his friends remarked.

"That road is so low it floods when five people spit on it at the same time," another commented.

The boys laughed and slapped hands, nodding their heads in agreement.

"So what you're saying is we're stuck here with you? Heaven forbid."

They made faces and held their hands to their heads at the prospect, pausing only to stuff more fish into their mouths.

"Maybe not, if our gracious hospitality doesn't suit you," Maddy intoned, shaking her finger at Tom-Tom's friends in pretend anger as they ginned at her lecture.

She was clearly the group's pet, being the only girl and their host's baby sister too.

"Sometimes, if the bay isn't too choppy, we can take a boat to town. But it looks too bad for that today," Maddy added.

The rain continued through the day and into the night. Tom-Tom's friend developed a high fever from the catfish wound.

"Miss Muchie, he's pretty sick. Can you do anything?" Tom-Tom woke me up to ask me, clearly worried about his friend.

"I can give him some aspirin. Sometimes that will break a fever."

"You know what I mean, Miss Muchie. What about your healing gift?" Tom-Tom whispered.

"I don't know, Tom-Tom. There's no telling if it will work or not. But we can try. You have a healing gift too. Maybe one of us will be able to help him."

Sitting beside the feverish boy, I took his injured hand in mine and tried to summon the healing gift the way I had tried with Bevane, with Charlotte, with Teddy and with Tyler Mama, but nothing happened.

"I'm sorry, Tom-Tom, I can't help him," I confessed.

"That's all right, Miss Muchie. I know you tried," he said, kissing my forehead. Something in his gesture gave me a sense of peace, as if I had been forgiven.

I got up to leave the room, turning to look sadly at my son and his friend from the doorway.

Tom-Tom lifted the boy's head to give him a sip of ice water. He smiled as the boy gulped down the glass.

Then Tom-Tom gently wiped the sweat from his friend's forehead and sat beside him, cradling the wounded hand in his own as rain pounded against the windows.

In the morning I woke to the sound of laughter and splashing in the pool. Outside, all the young folks, including the one who had injured his hand, were enjoying another beautiful day by the bay.

Chapter Thirty-one

1951

Maddy graduated from high school and Tom-Tom got his junior college degree the same week, giving us two reasons to celebrate.

Bevane made an unexpected appearance at the buffet luncheon I gave for Maddy's graduation. She was in good spirits and even had a brand-new hairstyle.

"You look radiant, Bevane, especially for a woman supposed to be sick," Dorali said with none of her usual diplomacy.

"I *was* sick, Dorali. For quite some time, as you well know. Muchie visited me frequently and every time she did, I started to feel a little better. And Reverend Hill visited too."

"Did he now? Is our bachelor preacher the reason for those roses in your cheeks?"

Bevane got flustered and dropped her fork. Then she dimpled and blushed, which made us know we were on the right track.

"It's a distinct possibility," she said, breaking into delighted laughter.

"Well, do tell," I prompted.

"Come on, Bevane, this is no time to be shy," Dorali said.

Bevane could hardly talk for all the smiling she was doing. But before the luncheon ended, Dorali and I had the whole story. And yet another reason to celebrate. Reverend Hill and Bevane were to be married the day after Thanksgiving.

My friends were 10 years older than me, and Bevane had never been married before. Dorali teased her unmercifully about waiting until she was over 50 to take a mate who was even older than she was.

"I've always heard it's better to be an old man's darling than a young man's slave," Bevane said.

"You better ask Muchie about that, Bevane. Ernest is a good fifteen years her senior, you know," Dorali noted.

"I wouldn't exactly call Reverend Hill old, now, Dorali. He's the same age as Aaron, isn't he? Although that does make him rather mature," I said, ribbing both my friends.

"I wonder if you'd let Maddy come help me some this summer, Muchie. I want to get the house in order and sort through my things before I get married. She's a wonder at cleaning out closets and cabinets, you know," Bevane said.

"Did I hear my name?" Maddy asked, putting her arm around Bevane's waist who gave her a big kiss on the cheek.

"I have news for you, Maddy," Bevane said and whispered in her ear like they were both schoolgirls.

Maddy clapped her hands and squealed.

"I think that's the most romantic thing I've ever heard," she said as she and Bevane wandered off together.

The next thing I knew, Maddy asked me if she could move in with Bevane for the month of June.

It wasn't until hours later that I remembered what Bevane had said about feeling better after I'd visited her. Let it be the gift, dear Lord, I prayed. Let it be the healing gift that has come back to me.

"Do you still have your heart set on us going to college in the same town?" Tom-Tom asked while Maddy opened her graduation presents.

"Not so much anymore. I think I'll do what you did and go to the Branch for two years. It will be nice to have Miss Muchie and Mr. Winston all to myself for a change. You really hog up a lot of their time, Tom-Tom," she said.

He hooted at that comment and gave Maddy an affectionate jab on her shoulder.

Ernest spent the rest of the summer getting Tom-Tom ready to go away from home for the first time. He made it his business to tell the boy how a gentleman should behave in a wide range of circumstances.

Right off, he bought two dozen white linen handkerchiefs and two dozen white cotton ones for Tom-Tom.

"The first time I met your mother, I needed two handkerchiefs to take care of her, son. My advice is keep two on you at all times."

"Why'd Miss Muchie need so many handkerchiefs, Mr. Winston?"

"Well, Tom-Tom, that's a long story. But it was a good thing I had a starched linen handkerchief in my breast pocket and another clean one in my back pants pocket. You do the same and you'll never be caught short."

"That sure seems like a lot of trouble, Mr. Winston. What about tissues?"

"Tissues are fine and good in their place, son, like when

you're home sick with a cold. But, I've always believed a gentleman should have his handkerchief ready for when he might need it."

Tom-Tom took Ernest's handkerchief advice as law.

"When it comes to being a gentleman, you know everything worth knowing, Mr. Winston."

My boy proved to be a quick study, accepting Ernest's pronouncements without question.

He had the most fun though when Ernest described the kind of clothes he should wear as a gentleman and a scholar.

"Clothes don't make the man, son, but they sure do make a powerful impression. Look here, let me show you a thing or two you need to know about neckties."

"Oh, you showed me how to tie a tie a long time ago, Mr. Winston."

"That may be so, but you still want a little variety in your knots. If you wear a spread collar, look here, this is the way you want to wear that tie."

"I'm all thumbs when it comes to bow ties, Mr. Winston."

"Nothing to it, son. It's all in the wrist. I'll show you if you go ahead and put on your blue striped shirt and hand me the paisley tie we bought yesterday."

In July, to allow plenty of time for fittings, Ernest took Tom-Tom over to Mobile to visit his tailor. They spent the better part of a day examining fabrics and patterns before they selected the clothes Ernest deemed appropriate.

"I want him to know the difference between quality and everything else. Best way to do that is learning the feel of good suit material," Ernest told me after the trip.

Tom-Tom and Ernest could go on like that for hours, trying this knot or that shirt and tie combination, this suit style or that casual sport coat and slacks. Ernest was a thorough teacher. He shared his extensive male fashion advice with my eagerly attentive son day after day.

I'd listen in awe to them talk. Men's clothes were a mystery to me. I never knew the cut of a suit or the weave of a fabric or the quality of a tie could reveal secrets of the wearer's character.

The afternoon they brought home a complete set of monogrammed alligator luggage and a big leather steamer trunk, I thought it was time to put my foot down.

"You're spoiling him rotten, Ernest. What in the world does a boy his age need with expensive luggage?" I asked annoyed at what I considered an extravagance.

"The boy will be able to use luggage and a trunk most of his life, Muchie. It's only right for a young man to have a decent set of luggage when he goes out into the world."

Tom-Tom left for college with enough kisses from his sister and me to turn his cheeks red and a bear hug from Ernest to hold him steady. None of us doubted that Ernest's instructions would keep Tom-Tom on the straight and narrow path.

He knew he carried the blessings of his entire family with him and he left home certain of being loved.

There was nothing about Tom-Tom's departure to compare with the awful day I ran away from home to marry his daddy. But for some reason, it made me think of my parents and how worried they must have been when they found my bed empty and my satchel gone.

Mother and Papa had been badly hurt because I was hell bound and determined to have my own way.

Shame filled my heart when I realized that I'd made my parent suffer. Sending my son to college with promises to write often made me understand how cruel it had been to leave my parents without a word.

I prayed God would protect my son and keep him safe. I asked God to repair any damage I might have done to him or anyone I loved.

I looked with a woman's heart and a mother's heart at the willful girl I once had been and asked God to forgive me and spare me from ever reaping what I had sown when I betrayed Papa and Mother's trust to start my life with Teddy.

Chapter Thirty-two

1951

"Ernest, I know we're pretty well stretched to the limit right now, but I have an idea I'd like to discuss with you," I said as we tallied our September expenses.

"Does it cost any money, Muchie?"

"Not very much at all, Ernest, which is why I think it's a real good idea for us now."

"All right, let's hear it then," he said, taking off his glasses to rub his eyes.

"At first I was going to talk to you about starting a headstone business. It will have to wait because we don't have the capital for that now. But we do have quite a bit of money already tied up in rolling stock."

"We certainly do, Muchie. There's the hearse and all those funeral cars just sitting in the garage gathering dust when we don't have a wake or a funeral," Ernest agreed.

"Exactly. We can use those cars in a limousine service, Ernest."

"And who is it you think will need a limousine to ferry them around, Muchie? There's not much to do around here for tourists besides sit on the beach. Folks with money looking for beach vacations go to Bermuda or Cuba and the other islands where they have casinos and the like."

"Well, I tell you, Ernest. A lot of white people are actually starting to come south for the mild winters. Gulf Shores is calling itself 'America's Riviera' and Fairhope gets more retirees every year. You said the country is on the move and it is, Ernest. People are traveling and they are willing to pay for service."

"What are you saying, Muchie?"

"We situate ourselves at the train station and the airport to ferry passengers wherever they want to go."

"Sort of like a luxury cab service?"

"That's what I'm thinking, Ernest. A shining Cadillac shows up at the airport with a driver in uniform. Who wouldn't want to hop in the car and go to a hotel or home? We set a flat rate and make it known. In no time, I can just about guarantee we'll have all the passengers we can handle."

"Will white people ride in a Negro car though, Muchie?"

"How will they know who owns the car, Ernest? White people are used to being catered to by Negroes. All they'll know is they'll get a comfortable and courteous ride for a fair price."

"So you envision each passenger paying his own way?"

"That's what I can't decide, Ernest. Should we make the hotels pay up front or should we charge everyone who wants a ride?"

Ernest scratched something on a piece of paper and showed me his list before answering.

"The way I figure, there are four or five major hotels in the area, Muchie. It would be a real struggle to get the LeClede, the

Bienville on the Square, the Battle House, the Admiral Semmes and the Grand Hotel in Point Clear to do business with a Negro car company, though."

"Then maybe our best bet is to charge the passengers instead of the hotels. Have two cars at the airport and two at the train station so we can ride Negro and white passengers separately to keep down any confusion."

"This could work, Muchie. I think it could actually work, although I just can't visualize a lot of Negroes flying to Mobile, Alabama, for any reason."

"All in due time, Ernest. You wait and see."

"We'll need to take a look at the flight schedules and the train schedules. I don't expect we'll have much of a problem sending one car to the airport, but two might stretch us too thin, Muchie."

"I guess the best thing is for us to sketch out a plan, Ernest. If everything adds up do you think we might be ready to start the car service after the first of the year?"

"Let's see how the plan looks, Muchie. Then we'll know what we can do."

My hands were full with my regular work and getting things ready at home for Tom-Tom's Thanksgiving break and Bevane's wedding the day after that.

For some reason, Bevane didn't think it was seemly for a woman her age to have a real wedding.

"You don't have to wear a long dress and a veil, Bevane, but there's no harm in your having a small church wedding. You *are* marrying a preacher after all."

She dug in her heels and no matter what I said, she held to her position. I brought in the big guns, but even Dorali was unable to move Bevane. It took Maddy to do that.

"Miss Muchie, I asked Bevane about her wedding and she

started crying. She said she'd feel like a fool walking down the aisle with a bunch of flowers in her hand."

"I know, Maddy. I've been trying my best to convince her to have a private ceremony, but she's being unusually stubborn about it."

"Let's double team her after church Sunday, Miss Muchie, and make her change her mind."

Sunday afternoon we went to Bevane's house with our arms full of presents and a box of petit fours from Pollman's bakery. She laughed as Maddy set the little cakes on china plates with a flourish.

"I knew you wouldn't let us give you a bridal shower," Maddy said.

"But a bride deserves to get a lot of presents anyway," I added.

Bevane smiled to see Maddy's excitement and opened box after box, giggling with Maddy as she saw the pretty things inside.

"Maybe you should be the one getting married, Maddy, with all your romantic fancies about a wedding," she said.

"Miss Muchie would kill me if I got married before I finished college, Bevane. You know that. Here's what I want to tell you. There's a pretty little chapel over on the bay near our house. You can look out the church door and see the water. Since Reverend Hill can't marry the two of you himself, it doesn't matter if you're in Warren Street or not. I think the little chapel is just perfect for your wedding."

"But I don't want to have a wedding, dear. Didn't I tell you that already?"

"No, what you said was you didn't want to walk down the aisle. That's not the same as saying you don't want to have a wedding, is it?"

"I suppose you have a point, Maddy."

"The thing about the chapel is that it's too small to walk down the aisle. All you and Reverend Hill will have to do is stand together and be married. And I want to stand up with you and be your maid of honor. Please say I can, Bevane."

She looked at Maddy with years of affection reflected in her eyes and slowly nodded her head.

"Maddy, you're a hard one to resist. All right, I give in. We'll have our wedding where you say. Are you satisfied now?"

"She will be if you allow her mother to give your wedding reception," I said.

"Now, Muchie. I told you I don't want to look like a fool. I'm too old for all that."

"There's nothing foolish about celebrating joy, Bevane. Happiness is rare and it should be acknowledged regardless of age. I promise I'll have a reception that is dignified and in keeping with your new position. May I please?"

"You girls are something else. Since how I get married is officially out of my hands, what can I tell you but, yes?"

Maddy was utterly delighted with Bevane's decision. Her face wreathed in smiles, Bevane took our hands.

"My forever friends," she said.

Chapter Thirty-three

※❦❧

1951

Despite being pleased for a few days about persuading Bevane to have a wedding, Maddy was at loose ends. Without Tom-Tom to pal around with, she didn't seem to know what to do with herself.

"I miss him something awful, Miss Muchie."

"I miss him too, sweetness. But he'll be home for Thanksgiving before we know it. And his Christmas break lasts more than a month."

"That's a long time away. And I don't have anybody to talk to," she whined.

"You can talk to me, Maddy. And Ernest too, he's always enjoyed your conversation. I know it's not the same, but we're right here anytime you need us."

Maddy rolled her eyes and sulked. She was already much too sad for me to reprimand her for bad behavior. Instead, I offered another suggestion.

"Have you written to your brother? I know he likes getting mail."

Ernest did his part to cheer her up. He bought her four boxes of pretty stationery and enough stamps to send mail for a year.

But Maddy was inconsolable and remained moody and bad tempered despite our best efforts. I was close to losing patience with her.

On a dreary October afternoon, I invited Maddy to help me bake a double batch of peanut butter cookies. They were Tom-Tom's favorite, and I thought it might brighten her gloom to make something special we could send her brother.

"Maddy, remember how it was before you started school? You stayed home with me, and we had lots of fun together cooking and working in the garden while Tom-Tom and your daddy were gone during the day. It could be like that again, Maddy," I said, dropping scoops of dough on a cookie sheet.

"No it couldn't, Miss Muchie. Everything is different now," she said as she pressed the balls with a fork to flatten the cookies for baking.

"We're both a little older now, but otherwise, what's all that different?"

"For one thing, Tom-Tom won't be coming home from school every afternoon to play with me. And Daddy will never come back."

"What a thing to say, Maddy."

"Why do you keep pretending, Miss Muchie? I know Daddy is dead. I was at his funeral, don't you remember? Tom-Tom knows. Mr. Winston knows. Everybody but you knows Daddy is dead and he can't ever come back."

I felt like I'd been kicked in the head. It hurt me for Maddy to say such a thing. How dare she, when Ernest, Dorali and Aaron, even Bevane had let me hold in my heart the dream that Teddy would return one day?

Anger and grief drained all the blood out of me and I was cold, so cold that I began to shiver. Then I looked at Maddy and saw her crying silently. Her face was very much like Teddy's had been when he sat at Charlotte's grave holding Margaret in his arms.

I forgot my own pain at the sight of my little girl suffering.

"You poor lamb, how long have you wanted to tell me that?" I asked.

"I don't know, Miss Muchie. A long time," she sobbed.

Holding the table, I put one foot in front of the other until I could stumble the few steps it took to reach Maddy. Wrapping my arms around her, I held her, rocking to and fro as I used to do in the chifforobe.

"I'm sorry, Maddy. Please forgive me for not thinking of you. I am very sorry, darling."

We held each other and cried, finally able to talk about the loss we had hidden deep in our hearts. Maddy made me understand that Tom-Tom's departure had awakened all her fears about her daddy's death.

Her sorrow made me accept the fact that my Teddy was really and truly gone. It was a bitter pill to swallow, but for the first time I was able to say, "Teddy is dead."

Only love for my child, for Teddy's sweet Madeleine, could have ever made me give up the hope that Teddy would come walking through my door again. For years, the only thing that got me up in the morning was the thought that this might be the day I would be reunited with my Teddy.

But my dream had become a terrible barrier that kept me from knowing what was in my child's heart. Much as I needed my foolish hope, Maddy needed me more.

Maddy's moodiness seemed to lift, but around Halloween we faced a new worry. The child started complaining of severe headaches that left her exhausted and unable to function. She couldn't eat or sleep for the excruciating pain in her head.

"Maybe it's eyestrain the way you sit up reading all hours of the night. You might need glasses," I suggested.

But the eye doctor said her eyes were fine.

She cried pitifully when the headache hit her. Hearing the child in pain was pain itself for me.

I didn't know what to do besides the obvious remedies. Headache powders, quiet, cool compresses and dark rooms helped only a little.

Sometimes I would rub her face and neck to ease her suffering. Unfortunately the relief was short lived.

The Tuesday evening before Thanksgiving, Tom-Tom came strolling up to the kitchen door with a suitcase and a big grin.

"I only have one class on Wednesdays and it was cancelled this week. I got a ride home with one of the fellows to surprise you," he said giving me the biggest hug.

"It's a wonderful surprise, Tom-Tom. I'm glad you're home early. Let me look at you. Why, I think you've grown a few inches. Have you put on a pound or two?"

"The cafeteria food isn't bad, but it's nothing like your good cooking, Miss Muchie. Where's Mr. Winston and Maddy?"

"He'll be in soon. Maddy's in her room, honey. She came home from school with a bad headache. Said she couldn't see straight. Poor thing keeps a headache lately."

"That's odd. She never mentioned headaches in any of her letters, and believe me, there sure have been plenty of those." He laughed.

Maddy walked into the kitchen to get some ice for her head.

When she saw Tom-Tom she burst into tears and threw herself into his arms.

"You don't know how glad I am to see you, Tom-Tom. I've missed you so much," she sobbed on his shoulder.

He winked at me, suddenly acting every bit the grown man he nearly was.

"Me too, Maddy. You and your rocks," Tom-Tom joked.

He kissed Maddy's cheek and stroked her back like she was a little kitten.

I wrapped my two nearly grown children in a hug, wanting to share some of their happiness.

"Let me have some of that sugar," I said as Tom-Tom and Maddy linked arms around my shoulders.

Tom-Tom staggered, bumping Maddy's head with his own as he righted himself.

"What's wrong?" Maddy and I asked in unison.

"For a minute, I felt like I was falling. All this hugging and crying must be too much for me," he said, shamefaced.

"Are you sure that's all it is, Tom-Tom?"

"It was like that time Maddy cut her leg. You, remember Maddy?"

She nodded.

"I got light-headed just now. The same way I did then."

"How's your head feeling, Maddy?" I asked, although I was fairly sure of her answer.

"Well, my headache is gone, if that's what you mean. But this clumsy brother of mine nearly knocked me out with his big apple head." She laughed.

"I declare, Tom-Tom."

"We've got a lot of catching up to do," Tom-Tom said. "Let's talk later, Miss Muchie."

He hurried upstairs with Maddy.

I sat down at the kitchen table with my head in my hands. Tom-Tom seemed utterly unconcerned about his apparent gift.

Why had my gift plagued me with failure while his healing came as natural as rain? What made us different?

Each time I tried to heal someone I loved, the healing gift abandoned me. But Tom-Tom *never tried to heal*. All he ever tried to do was give comfort.

It was like the Bible said, "And a little child shall lead them."

My son's example led me to understanding that the healing gift had never failed me. It was me who had failed the gift.

I closed my eyes to pray. This time I didn't tell God what to do. I asked him to forgive me for doubting his goodness and his mercy. I thanked him for his many blessings. And while I prayed, God gave me the courage to face the truth about myself.

My willfulness, the stubbornness my papa tried to break with his own. Always demanding God work on my timetable. My stiff-necked pride was what had diminished the power of my healing gift, nothing more.

God had never turned his back on me, he had only waited for me to put aside my hurt, my grief and the need to have my way.

It was a painful revelation, nearly as painful as admitting that Teddy was dead. I had never been able to heal the ones I loved because I tried to use God's gift instead of allowing God to use me.

Too much time had passed to torture myself with "what ifs." All I could do now was accept God's will and set my own will aside.

"You look mighty somber, Miss Muchie. You feel like some company?"

Tom-Tom pulled a chair close to mine and put my head on his shoulder. My son was home and I felt absolutely content simply being with him.

The love we shared shimmered over me bright and warm. Without thinking, I closed my eyes, breathing in the fragrance of my child's healthy young body.

I felt the gift, not working through me, but working *for* me this time. My son's love was palpable, pulling me toward a place I had never been.

In an instant, they were all there with us. Mother and Papa sitting on the porch, Tyler Mama with her birthing bag slung over her shoulder, Charlotte and Margaret playing in the sunshine with Teddy.

The weight of loneliness lifted from me as their love and forgiveness set me free. I smiled while the ones I loved danced and danced and danced together.

"Miss Muchie? Miss Muchie? You all right?"

I opened my eyes to see my son's worried expression.

"I'm just fine now, Tom-Tom. Perfectly fine."

Chapter Thirty-four

1951

"Do you want to talk about what happened, Miss Muchie?"

"There's no need, darling. It was the healing gift, but I'm not afraid of it anymore. You don't have to fear it either."

"It never scared me, Miss Muchie, but you did. I was worried about how you felt. You always seemed so mad when you talked about healing. Like it had done you dirty or something."

"Honey, for years, I really did believe healing had done me wrong. That it betrayed and abandoned me. I blamed God for blessing me with a gift and cursing me with failure after failure."

"That's a heavy load to bear, Miss Muchie."

"Listen to you, my wise old man."

"Aw, now, don't make fun. You *have* been through a lot, more than most people could get through and still keep going. That makes you pretty special, Miss Muchie."

"And you are just about the sweetest boy in the world," I said, giving him several more hugs and kisses in case he was operating under a deficit after his months at school.

"What you did for Maddy helped me too. All these years I've tried to *make* my gift work, instead of simply letting it happen the way you do, Tom-Tom."

"Just like that, I helped you? Maybe I had a double play today and healed both my girls, huh?"

I reached for my dishtowel, rolled it up and snapped it at him. He pretended to cower and we laughed until tears ran down our cheeks.

"When I had my head on your shoulder a few minutes ago, did you feel anything unusual?"

"Now that you mention it I did, Miss Muchie. But I wasn't dizzy or fuzzy in my head like the other times. Nothing like that. I felt good. Safe somehow."

"You know what, Tom-Tom? So did I. It was like being back home on the farm only it was our old house. I wasn't sad though. I saw your daddy and Charlotte and Margaret and Tyler Mama. They were all together and they seemed very happy."

"I'm glad. Maddy told me you finally talked to her about Daddy. It used to tear her up when you acted like he was away on a trip. She didn't understand that was probably the only way you could keep going. I think she does now, Miss Muchie."

"It can take some of us a long time to understand things, honey."

"I guess you're right, Miss Muchie. And I guess there's all kinds of healing going on for us too."

Tom-Tom kissed my cheek.

"I'm going back upstairs with Maddy. She still has about a million things that she's dying to tell me. Unless you want me to help you fix supper?"

"No, you're probably better off listening to Maddy. I'm trying to hold supper until Ernest gets home, but we can make some sandwiches if you're hungry."

"I like that idea."

Tom-Tom rummaged around in the refrigerator and we quickly assembled a stack of sandwiches worthy of Dagwood Bumstead. I added a couple slices of cake for good measure and Tom-Tom took a quart bottle of milk and two glasses with him upstairs, saluting me with a nod as he left.

"You sure you don't want me to stay?"

"Positive. I need some time by myself because I've got a lot to think about right now, sweetness."

There was nothing for me to do in the kitchen but check on my roast and pat my foot and anticipate Ernest's arrival.

The roast would be ruined if he didn't get home pretty soon. I would probably be no more good either if I had to wait much longer to tell him my news.

I hadn't married him for love, but Ernest had never pressured me. Now I felt free to say words I never thought I'd say to any man other than Teddy.

I loved him. I loved Ernest Winston, no ifs, ands or buts about it, and I could hardly wait to see his face when I told him so.

Suddenly I was filled with joy about my life and the future that stretched ahead of me. I was profoundly aware of God's grace and mercies.

My heart felt lighter than it had in years. That would please Ernest.

I checked the roast again and took it out of the oven to keep it from drying into cinders. Where could Ernest be? Why hadn't he called?

I hated for Ernest to miss dinner with Tom-Tom his first night home. He would be tickled to see the boy, and I knew they'd try to sit up half the night talking.

And Ernest would be delighted to learn of Maddy's recovery. But where was he? I called the funeral home again but no one answered. That was odd, there was always supposed to be someone on phone duty.

Eight o'clock came but no Ernest. I started to worry, pacing the kitchen floor like an expectant father.

Ernest had never been this late without calling. I walked down the driveway time and again, searching the road for his car.

Finally, I put his meal on a plate, set it over a pot of hot water and called Maddy and Tom-Tom to supper.

"Where's Mr. Winston?" Tom-Tom asked.

"He's probably working late, Tom-Tom. They do a lot of that now," Maddy added with a hint of disapproval.

"I called the funeral home earlier and they said he left hours ago. When I called a few minutes ago, no one answered and I'm starting to get a little worried," I said.

"He's fine, Miss Muchie. Maybe he got to talking somewhere and just lost track of the time. Mr. Winston is quite a talker, you know."

"He is that," I agreed.

After they ate, Tom-Tom and Maddy put away the food and washed the dishes.

While sweeping the kitchen floor, Tom-Tom said, "Mr. Winston's dinner looks pretty forlorn, Miss Muchie. You want me to put it in the refrigerator or leave it out until he gets home?"

"Leave it out for him, please. I imagine he'll be hungry when he gets home."

Maddy volunteered to call around and check if any of our friends had seen Ernest, but none of them had.

"Don't worry, Miss Muchie. Mr. Winston will be home soon. He always comes home," Maddy said. I squeezed her hand.

"Get a flashlight, Maddy, and let's go walk out on the jetty," Tom-Tom suggested.

"Come with us, Miss Muchie, it will be fun."

"I think I'll stay here and wait for Ernest. Take a sweater, it can get cool on the water this time of year."

I refused to think the worst. There were all sorts of good reasons for Ernest to be late. None of them had to be life or death reasons. Only I couldn't think of any that weren't.

I clutched to my breast a real eagerness to see Ernest and say, "I love you" for the first time. Like a shield, I held it to protect me from any hint of fear.

It was after 11 o'clock when I finally heard his key in the door. I sneaked a peek in my little mirror hanging over the kitchen sink and smoothed back my hair. When I saw him, my hard-won composure vanished and I threw myself in his arms.

"Ernest, I was so worried. Where have you been? What happened?"

"I'm sorry, Muchie. The car broke down on the Causeway. I walked halfway back to Mobile looking for a service station. They had to tow the car. Then I had to wait for one of the fellows at the funeral home to come bring me home."

"Oh, Ernest. Thank God you're all right."

"Now, now, Muchie," he said, wiping away my tears.

"I have to tell you something, Ernest. For a long time, it seemed like everyone I loved would die. It didn't matter how hard I tried to help."

"Is that what's got into you tonight, Muchie? You thought I was dead?"

"Yes, I did, Ernest, and I couldn't bear it."

"Honey, the dying part can't be helped. You ought to know that working at the funeral home all this time." He smiled.

"But I don't want you to die, Ernest, because I love you. I know I've never told you before, but I love you, Ernest. I do. I love you."

"I know that, Muchie. Everything you do tells me you love me. Words don't really matter that much. It's the way you are when you love someone that counts. You love harder than anybody I know, and the way you feel doesn't die. It keeps on, Muchie. That's why it knocks you down real hard whenever someone dies."

"Ernest, I've been selfish and weak. I've acted like the whole world ought to shake every time my small life got disrupted."

"That's not selfish, Muchie. It's human nature. If your own world is upset, that's earthshaking enough."

Ernest sat me down in a chair and took his supper plate off the heat.

"Nobody can beat you when it comes to being strong. I won't ever let you chide yourself for weakness, Muchie," he said between bites of meat.

"Ernest, I don't deserve you, but I plan to spend the next 50 years making you as happy as you've made me."

"That's quite a pledge, Muchie. Maybe I ought to stay out late more often," he joked.

The tension broken, I threw a potholder at Ernest and narrowly missed his head.

"I have so much to tell you, Ernest. Tom-Tom came home today. And he cured Maddy's headaches and helped me understand healing and love and . . ."

Ernest stopped my babbling by kissing me full on the mouth. His moustache felt soft against my lips and made me giggle, then purr in his arms.

We stayed up half the night.

Like Tom-Tom and Maddy, Ernest and I had a lot of catching up to do.

Reading Group Companion

The Laying on of Hands is a gentle yet powerful story of a southern woman with the gift of healing. Muchie struggles with love and loss as she moves through a life marked by tragedy and triumph. Examining Muchie's life may lead you to a better understanding of your own gifts and how you are called to use them regardless of the pain they can cause.

Reader's Guide

1. Healing and healers have a prominent role in *The Laying on of Hands*. Throughout her life, Muchie struggles to understand and accept the healing gift. How does Muchie really feel about healing? What does she think of healers and of being a healer herself? Is it easy or difficult for her? How does she react to following in the family tradition of being a healer? Discuss your personal experience with healing.

2. Has the world changed for African-American women since Miss Muchie's time? What events have transpired that might alter Muchie's worldview? Discuss how Muchie's life reflects racial and social conditions from her childhood in Mississippi to the rest of her life in Alabama.

3. Is family important to Muchie? Give examples. How does she relate to her father? Her mother? Describe her relationship with her grandmother. What kind of wife and mother does Muchie become?

4. What are the four things that Muchie would say made up her whole world? If you made such a list for your world, what would you include and why? Do you see your world as larger or smaller than Muchie's?

5. Which events in her childhood have the most profound effect on Miss Muchie? How do these events affect her? Do they make her question her faith? Have you ever questioned your faith? If so, why?

6. How is Muchie transformed when she meets Teddy for the first time? Explain Helen's role. Who does Muchie hurt and why? Explain how she reconciles her behavior to her parents' expectations.

7. Who is Reverend Harper and what is his role in Muchie's life? How does that compare with Reverend Hill's role?

8. Describe Muchie's healing experiences and how she responds to them.

9. Love and loss are recurring themes in *The Laying on of Hands*. Who does Muchie love in the novel? Who loves her? How and why does she lose the people she loves? Discuss her relationship with Teddy compared with her relationship to other people she loves.

10. What does Muchie do to get out of difficult situations? For example, how does she escape the sawmill? How does she free herself from her parents' control? How does she relate to Mr. Winston's attentions? Discuss whether her methods tell you anything about her character.

11. Throughout the novel, Muchie builds strong friendships. What new friendships does Miss Muchie form to replace the family she has abandoned? How do friends enrich her life?

12. Food shows up often in the story. Discuss the various events that are celebrated or commemorated with meals in your life compared or contrasted with Muchie's.

13. Is Muchie house proud? How does she feel about where she lives? Describe her emotions concerning where she lives in each part of the novel.

14. Do you think Muchie is a selfish or selfless person? Why do you think so?

15. Would you want Muchie for a friend? For a relative? Why or why not?

16. Talk about how Muchie's personality changes over the course of the novel and what the changes mean.

17. Why do you think Muchie married Ernest Winston? Were his reasons for marrying her similar to hers for marrying him? Did their marriage evolve and grow?

18. How did Tom-Tom help Muchie? What made his relationship with her different from that of his sister? Do you think Muchie loved both her surviving children the same way?

19. If you had to write a sequel to *The Laying on of Hands*, what would Muchie's life be like? How would she and Ernest Winston act? What would her response be to her children and her healing gift?

DISCARD